CYBERWITCH

E.S. MARTELL

Cover Art by Aleksandra Klepacka
Typography by Kelley York
Interior Design by Melissa Stevens
Editing by Adriana D'Apolito of 3P Editing

ISBN-13: 978-0-9989805-4-6

Printed in the USA
Second Initiative Press

DEDICATION

This book is dedicated to my fellow authors in my social media groups. One of the discussions that I participated in got me thinking about Artificial Intelligence.

In addition, I'd like to thank many people who are active in the A.I. community. Elon Musk, Nick Bostrom, and others have pointed out the potential dangers of A.I.

Their concern about unfettered A.I. development, combined with rapidly developing nanotechnology and ubiquitous voice recognition systems gave me the basic concept for this story.

CAN A DRUG ADDICT STOP AN ARTIFICIAL INTELLIGENCE FROM DESTROYING THE WORLD?

Sophie's life is a mess. She has a history of poor choices in men, and she is addicted to opiates. Her ambition to write software has gone entirely off the rails until she finds herself lost in an icy rainstorm in a bad part of town.

Things improve for Sophie, but then a hacking job for one of her mentor's clients results in a deadly attack. Finding out who or what was responsible and seeking revenge becomes her primary motive.

Sophie must struggle with her addiction and attacks from unexpected sources to reach her goal. Along the way, she discovers that things are far more complex than they first appeared and her attempts to defend herself unexpectedly change the entire world.

CONTENTS

ACKNOWLEDGMENTS

I rely on my wife, Sally, for critique and feedback. She also makes sure I eat while I'm writing and that makes things convenient. Without her help, these stories would never have made it out of my head.

Special thanks to Aleksandra Klepacka for her cover art. As always, she has captured the essence of the story in her art.

This work benefited immensely from the editorial expertise of Adriana D'Apolito of 3P Editing.

CHAPTER 1
RUNNING AWAY

The sudden rain was icy cold and so thick that she was soaked instantly. Sophie continued down the street until she could shelter under the overhang of a closed shop. There were no other people out in the gathering dusk. No one else was desperate enough.

She pushed her dripping hair out of her face, wincing as she inadvertently brushed her contused temple. She couldn't see well out of her left eye. It was swollen so badly it was nearly closed. Raul might be good looking, but he wasn't a good man. He was just a mistake that she'd made and now had to live through.

She fumbled in her pocket. Not there; where? The other hip pocket came up empty. God! She hadn't lost them, had she? Her memory wasn't always this bad, but she hurt so much right now, that she couldn't seem to pull herself together. She looked at her feet. Her boots were scuffed and shabby, but at least they were holding out the water.

Boots! That's where she'd put the package. Heedlessly, she knelt in a puddle to roll her tight jeans up. There it was! The

1

plastic bag stuck slightly out of the top of her boot. Her fingers shook as she worked at opening the package. She wanted two of the white pills; maybe three, but best to try to conserve them. One would ease her aches enough to get her through for the moment. She swallowed it dry, then licked some rain from her hand. Now, if she could just make it to her sister's place, she'd have a place to rest, at least for a while.

She hadn't talked to Rachael for weeks after their last fight. Rachael wanted her to straighten out and concentrate on classes. She had made it clear that she wholeheartedly disapproved of Raul. Well, Big-Sis had been right about him. What few possessions she still had, even her treasured laptop would have to stay at his place. She wasn't going back. In fact, the...Ahhhh; Ahhhh. Oh, that felt better. Now she was human again. The pain still throbbed behind her eyes and in her knotted shoulder and back muscles, but it had lost its intensity. The relative relief brought a semblance of a smile to her tired face.

The rain picked up, coming down even harder. It was hard to see across the street now. Sophie was soaked and shivering. A sudden wave of self-pity washed over her. She began to cry. Not hard at first, but sustained sobs that gradually lengthened until she was gasping for breath. Maybe another pill would help.

She worked the package open a second time, fumbled out another Oxy, but dropped it as she tried to transfer it to her mouth. Horrified, she watched it melt into a tiny pool of rainwater. She couldn't lose it; couldn't afford to waste it. Her supply sources were nearly gone, and she couldn't count on obtaining more without...without taking a step that she'd been dreading.

She shoved the package down into her boot and threw herself flat, sucking at the slurry of water and the semi-dissolved pill. She licked the concrete, trying to get every last bit of the pain-killer, disregarding the filth in the water.

That was it; she had it all. She raised her eyes and looked at two rounded, black objects. Her mind refused to work for what seemed an eternity. All at once she recognized them as boot toes. She pushed back and looked up. And, up. He was taller than average. Taller than she'd expected.

She glimpsed what might have been a concerned expression, but didn't meet his eyes long enough to decide if that was what it was. A sense of shame, something that she'd thought had died, forced her to look first down and then away, directing her vision down the street.

"You're a mess, girl," he said.

She wished he'd leave. Nothing good could come from a strange man out here in the rain in this rotten part of town. Meeting him was what she'd feared: some encounter like this. She had no defense, no weapons. She wasn't strong enough either. She bit her lower lip in the way she always did when trouble loomed. Maybe he'd go away if she didn't answer.

She gasped as he caught her under both arms and lifted her to her feet. He was strong, and there was no argument in her. Once she was up, she looked into his eyes. Might as well see who was going to have his way with her.

She didn't know what to think of him. He wasn't exactly handsome, but he was very masculine, and not unattractive. He used his fingers to move her hair back off of her face, pausing as he uncovered the blackened eye.

"God, girl. Someone been treating you bad, have they?" he said.

Sophie shrugged defiantly, then thought better about it.

"I haven't been treating myself very well," she said. Then she asked, "How about you? Will you treat me well?"

The instant it was out, she realized how it sounded--a druggie asking to be...treated well. She shook her head in denial. "No, that's not what I meant. I...I...uh...are you going to let me go, or...?"

Her voice tapered off, leaving the rest of the question unasked.

He shook his head negatively, then said, "No. I don't think you have anywhere to go. Certainly nowhere in this rain. Most of the places along this street are locked up, so you're just going to end up trying to shelter in a doorway somewhere, and you'll probably freeze to death. It's going to get cold later tonight."

"No. I'm going to my sister's. She'll uh..." She couldn't think what she was going to say. The second pill had taken over and her mind shut down for a moment. She began to cry again.

He sighed a deep, heartfelt sigh. "I don't know how I get myself into these kinds of things. Must be because I've got a thing about helpless, defenseless creatures." He said, "Look, you're coming upstairs with me."

When she drew back in denial, he indicated her shelter and said, "This is my doorway you're standing in, and the least I can do is to give you some relief from the rain. Maybe a cup of soup, too?"

Sophie wondered, vaguely, what else was going to be involved. She'd heard of girls found in dumpsters; their bodies abused so severely that their parents couldn't recognize them. She wanted to argue, but her willpower had evaporated. It hadn't even been enough to keep her from licking the sidewalk. She just stood there, her mouth partly open, making an occasional sobbing sound.

He shook his head again. "I must be crazy."

He held her arm while he unlocked the door, then pulled her inside. It was a vacant storefront. Barren shelves formed litter strewn aisles.

"This part isn't mine. I lease an apartment upstairs in the back. Come on," he said, pulling her through the dim room.

He had to help her up the stairs. She couldn't seem to walk well enough on her own. Her feet kept missing the steps.

Another door, a jingling of keys, and then he switched on a light, revealing a space filled with books, computers, and electronics.

She stared around, dazed. "What? What is all of this?" she murmured.

"Never mind that now. Follow me back here to the bathroom. We've got to get you warmed up."

She didn't know what else to do. She followed obediently.

He turned on the shower, then started on her clothes, discarding her dripping hoodie on the floor where it made a sodden lump of black, slowly leaking water across the clean, shiny tiles.

She grew alarmed and pushed at his hands. "I...I can do it. Just let me take care of myself," she protested.

He stepped back, a critical expression on his face, evaluating her ability. "Okay. Get everything off and get into the shower. I'm going to get some dry clothes for you."

He watched as she tried to remove her boots. She couldn't seem to manage the task, so he bent to grab her knee with one hand and pull her boot off with the other. The package of pills flipped out and landed on the floor. They both stared at it for an instant, but then he snagged it before she could move.

"That's mine! Give it to me," she gasped.

He grinned, not unkindly. "No. I'll just be keeping these safe for you. What are they? Opiates?"

"They're mine. Don't take them away from me, please. Please?" she whispered, her eyes filling with tears.

"My God, Girl. You're really bad, aren't you?"

"It's – it's just that I've got all of this pain. My neck and back always kill me. I've got spots that are painful to touch, and I can't get any sleep without help," she said, thinking of the fibromyalgia diagnosis that had started her down the dark path. He didn't need to know about the death of her parents, her bad romantic judgment, the bullying by people she hoped would be friends, or her dropping out of school.

He shook his head, not disbelieving, but not agreeing either. "I don't want your stash. I don't believe in that crap. I'm going to take it, though."

She started to protest, but he put his finger to her lips and said, "No use complaining. I'm going to put out one pill at midnight for you and one in the morning. I don't want you o-d'ing on me by accident. I'll ration them while you're here."

She wanted to scream. In her experience, people who took her drugs never gave them back. She couldn't get through the night without at least one more. Maybe if he gave her one at midnight, she'd make it. She started to beg, but he used his finger on her lips again.

"No! You get yourself in that shower. It's hot now. Once you're warm and clean, I'll have some other clothes over there on that hook by the door for you. You get dressed and come out. Then we'll talk and see what we're going to do about you."

He turned to leave the small bathroom, his broad shoulders just clearing the door. Sophie noticed that he had to duck slightly to exit.

The door shut, she stood for a few seconds, but then began to strip off her sodden garments.

He was right. The shower was wonderful. The heat soaked in, relaxing the knotted muscles of her back and shoulders in a way that almost made the Oxy unneeded.

Sometime during the time under the hot water, he must have reached through the door and hung up a robe on the hook. She hadn't seen him, but her eyes had been shut in ecstasy almost the entire time, so that wasn't a surprise. What was surprising was that the robe was more or less in her size and the tee shirt and panties fit perfectly.

Sophie didn't know what price she was going to have to pay for this treatment, but so far, it had been far better than she'd expected or had any reason to deserve. The robe was warm and soft and had been freshly washed.

The smell of the clean cloth brought tears to her eyes again. It had been a long time since she'd smelled that detergent odor.

The wave of self-pity that the robe occasioned led to the thought that another pill would be a good thing. She felt bad, so obviously something should be done about it. She thought of begging, but that wasn't going to work; at least, not yet. There was nothing for it but to use one of her two emergency pills.

She sat on the toilet and carefully extracted the plastic bag she'd hidden in her nether region. The two pills were intact, and she considered taking both, but that would leave her with no back-up. She took one with a bit of water from the sink, then toyed with the other for a moment before putting it back in the plastic bag and rolling it up into a tight package.

She inserted it back into her hiding place, praying that he'd leave her alone or would be minimally demanding on her physical self. The man was certainly strong enough to force her into any number of exploitative acts, but so far he hadn't shown any tendency to act in that fashion. She suddenly felt a small pang. Was she that undesirable?

The hurt was forgotten in the sweet rush as the drug hit. She was already high, so the rush wasn't as intense, but it still left her feeling warm and content. Maybe she'd make it through the night without having to suffer the miserable feeling of coming down. She always felt like her body developed additional aches and pain during such times.

Sophie made sure the robe covered her and then ventured out of the bathroom. The light was off in the hall, but the room at the end was lighted. The dark passage opened into a plain, but functional kitchen. He was seated at a table tapping on a computer keyboard, apparently engrossed in some esoteric and geeky coding.

He stopped typing and turned to face her. "Now, do you feel better?" he asked.

She thought about it, then slowly answered, "Yes. I think I do."

Something about the way she said it apparently aroused his suspicions. He looked closely at her and then shook his head negatively.

"Damn, I forgot to check. You had an emergency pill hidden somewhere didn't you?"

She shook her head in denial, trying to act innocent. If he thought she had one, he'd search her for another, and she couldn't lose that one too. "No, I didn't. Are you going to give my bag back to me? Those are my pills, and I need them."

He smiled. "I'm going to do what I told you, but with an exception. I was going to give you a pill at midnight and another in the morning. Now that you've taken one and I know you have, so don't try lying about it, you're going to have to wait until morning. The one you took counts as the midnight pill."

She tried to pretend that she was hurt, but the drug had her feeling good, and she couldn't act as if she cared at the moment.

She gave up, shrugged and sat at the table opposite him, still in awe of his sheer mass.

"So, what are you going to do with me?" she asked, tacitly admitting that she was under his control.

He shrugged in return. "We'll see. I could help you, or I could just kick you out. Depends on you. If I think you're worth helping that's one thing, but if not, well." He left the alternative unsaid, then apparently thought of something else.

"You don't have any resistance, do you? Why not?" he asked, then said, "I thought all you white people got an anti-addiction injection in the hospital."

Sophie looked down. "My...uh...my Mother didn't believe in those things. She was a Neo-Nietzschite, and so was Dad. They wouldn't let the doctors give a blocking shot to me. They said such things are my responsibility to avoid." She hung her head, refusing to look at him, then added, "I...I guess I'm not so good at avoiding drugs. Anyway, I've been sick a lot, and I have these awful pains in my back and neck muscles. That's why the Oxy."

His teeth gleamed in stark contrast to his dark face. "Look, kid. I didn't mean anything by it. Whether or not you want to recognize it, there's still a lot of crap that goes down in this world. I didn't have the anti shot either. Course, I'm older than you, but no one in my whole family was even offered it." He paused, reflecting. "Just as well, too. I don't want that kind of help. I want to be in complete control of myself, kind of like what your folks wanted for you."

He looked at her and shook his head. "You don't have any idea what I'm talking about, do you?"

Sophie hadn't been trying to follow him. She shook her head. "No. I don't know. What you said, about the blocking shot, I mean. How can that hurt? I thought it just kept you from being addicted."

He nodded, "Well. That's the idea. You wouldn't be able to be addicted if you had it."

She'd lost track of what was happening again, and her head slumped to the table. Sophie was vaguely aware of the hard surface, but it didn't seem to matter at the moment.

He came around the table and pulled at her arm. She stood, staggering a little. He frowned and then bent and easily picked her up. "It's bedtime for you, girl. You're all in. I'll have breakfast in the morning for you." She felt dizzy as he started through the door.

HE WALKED DOWN the hall carrying her and turned into a bedroom, then deposited her on the bed, pulled up a blanket and covered her in as gentle a manner as she could remember her Mother ever doing it.

He turned out the light, then turned to say, "I've decided to help you. How much depends on you. Don't worry about your pills. I'm not going to take them. I'm going to give them to you, but on my schedule, understand. No use begging. I'll give them to you when I decide. You don't need to be trying to find them either. You won't be able to steal them back. I've got them locked up, so don't even think about it."

She lifted her head a little, "What do you want from me?" The as yet unspoken idea of a quid pro quo had been bothering her. No one ever got anything for nothing. She had never experienced that in her life. She was sure that something was going to be expected from her in return for his help.

He said, "Nothing. I don't want nothing. Just to help you. How much I help, will depend on you. If you decide to try, I'll help a lot. If you don't care about yourself and have given up, then I probably won't help too much. It's up to you. Anyways, I ain't going to abuse you in any way. Don't do that sort of stuff."

She tried to get comfortable, then said, "Okay. G'night, uh...I... what should I call you?"

He grinned again--a broad, engaging grin that showed his white teeth. "Cal. That's all the name I got now. It's Cal since I was originally from California."

He turned away before she could reply and pulled the door closed. She could hear his footsteps fade down the hall.

She lay back wondering vaguely, just what had she gotten herself into. It didn't matter at the moment, though. She was warm and cozy. The blanket was soft, and she felt like she was floating over the bed. There were no aches and pains, and she felt fine for the moment. She closed her eyes and drifted on the drug's floating power.

MORNING WASN'T SO nice. She'd come down off her high, and her neck ached abominably. She lay there trying to decide if maybe she had the flu. She might, but she always hurt like this when she ran low on Oxy. He was going to give her another pill. He. Cal. She experimentally turned his name over in her mind. It couldn't be his real name if it were just a shortened form of his origin. It didn't matter much. Thinking about it kept her mind off how badly she hurt. When would he give her the pill? What time was it and how long would she have to wait?

Sophie stirred, then slowly moved to sit on the edge of the bed. There were no windows in the room and no clock. She couldn't tell what time it was, and that was suddenly of critical importance. There was a muffled sound coming from outside the room. That meant Cal was up doing something.

She'd beg him for the morning pill. It must be morning now. She couldn't wait any longer. She hurt so badly. Tears watered out of her eyes and trickled down her cheeks. She was a mess. Why had she ever started taking those damned things? It had been so easy. So easy.

She felt good when she took one, and the feeling made up for the emptiness of her life. She'd made so many mistakes. She stopped, horrified. What would Raul do to her when he found her? It wasn't like he owned her or anything. She'd stayed at his place a few times in exchange for some pills. He was more interested in money than he was in her, even though he'd used her body freely.

She fingered her temple. Still sore. He'd slugged her when she had shown up with less cash than he had told her to bring. Even so, he'd relented a little and given her the bag of pills that Cal now had. There weren't very many in there, though.

How would she get more? Her mind whirled through possibilities, none of them hopeful. She thought that she'd have to ask Cal for help, but maybe he wouldn't get more pills for her. She admitted to herself that she'd do anything he wanted if he promised to help her get more. He wasn't bad looking, even though his darkness frightened her a little.

She tentatively got to her feet, staggered a little, but reached the door without falling. This was bad. Maybe the three pills had been too much, considering that she'd had three more about two hours before the rain started. She tried to control her craving for them, but it was too difficult most of the time.

Cal was in the kitchen, making some noise with a skillet and the stove. She sat quietly at the table and watched his economical moves as he fried eggs and cooked some bacon. Midway through the bacon, he turned to look at her. He apparently didn't like what he saw and turned back immediately. She could see his shoulders rise and fall with a sigh.

He took the skillet off the range and turned back. "You don't look too good this morning, girl. Just you wait a minute."

He walked out of the room. She was tempted to follow, but couldn't muster the strength. It didn't matter. He returned shortly and placed a single pill in front of her. She tried to restrain herself, but her hand betrayed her mind and snatched at it. Her fingers shook as she picked it up.

"Here's some water," he said, placing a glass in front of her. "Now, here's the thing. I'll give you another one at noon, but don't you go begging between now and then. It won't do any good. I'll be working on a coding project that I've got, and I won't give one to you. Maybe if you were smart, you'd break it in half and save half until about ten. That way you wouldn't start to feel so bad at eleven. But, that's just a suggestion. You take it all now if you want."

He turned back to the skillet and dished the scrambled eggs and bacon onto two plates.

Sophie thought his words over. She maybe could break the pill in half, but she still had one for emergency use that he didn't know she had. If she needed it, she could take it, and that would get her through to noon. She slipped the pill between her lips and sipped the water. It would take a few minutes, but she almost felt better now.

The smell of bacon seemed to stir her stomach somehow. Now that she'd taken the pill, she could afford to feel hungry. At least a little bit.

"Is some of that for me?" she asked, diffidently.

He glanced at her, saw she'd taken the whole pill and sighed again. "Yes. If you can eat, you should. I can't help you if you starve. A little food will be good for you, I think."

She kept her head down and ate as much of the eggs and bacon as she could. There was a half of a strip of bacon left when she finished. He waved his fork at it and said, "Go on. Take it. It won't kill you to eat that last bite. Go on."

She had a flash of fear. She didn't want to make him angry. Someone else, Raul, for instance, would hit her, if she didn't do as he asked. Cal didn't seem like that sort, but she was afraid to provoke him. She picked the half piece up and shoved it into her mouth. It wouldn't go down though.

Cal watched her, his eyes narrowed. He abruptly stood and refilled her water. "Here. Take a drink and wash it down. I'm going to get to work. Part of what I do is freelancing. Do you know anything about computers?"

Sophie took a drink and then said, "Some. I was studying computer science in school. Uh, until I dropped out. No money and I couldn't continue." She paused, wondering if she should tell him. Somehow it came out despite her wishing it wouldn't.

"I had a laptop I was doing some programming on. I did some scripting, java, and python, you know, but I..." She paused, finding it hard to go on.

Somehow the courage came to her. "I traded it for drugs." It was out. She should feel ashamed, but it somehow felt a little better.

He snorted. "You spent your tuition on drugs too, didn't you?"

She looked down. Was she that transparent?

Cal saved her thinking up an excuse. "No matter. If you already know some things, then I can teach you more."

He turned towards the counter and said, "Hey, Ralph. Play Suicide Dogs and start my system."

There was a brief pause, then a voice said, "OK. System started. Here's your music."

A speaker on the refrigerator started playing some heavy metal music. Sophie hadn't heard it before but immediately classified it as too intense for her taste. She looked at Cal and asked, "Ralph?"

He chuckled and said, "I name my own devices. I like Ralph. I don't know anybody named Ralph, and I'm not likely to use the name by accident. You probably know the scandal about the voice-recognition device that was activated by the TV? That' isn't likely to happen with old Ralph, there."

She noticed the anomaly. "You just said, Ralph, several times and it didn't respond."

He smiled. "You're observant. You gotta say, 'Hey,' first."

Sophie smiled back. "Oh. That's smart."

Cal suddenly stood, caught her hand and pulled her out of the chair. She inadvertently flinched, equating his helpfulness with the attack that she still expected. Maybe she'd said something wrong.

He noticed the flinch and gently put his hand under her chin, raising it, so she looked upward at his face. He looked into her eyes and said, "I'm not that sort of man. I'm not going to hurt you now or later, so you can quit worrying about it."

He released her, and she looked down.

"It...it's just that I've been hit before. I'm sorry. I don't want you to be angry with me. I..." she stuttered.

He swore softly, then said, "I'm serious. I'm going to help you. If you can learn to code, you can start to control your destiny a little. I'll teach you how to find clients who need apps. It's not too hard. You just got to concentrate a little. The pills you're on won't keep you from doing that. Now, let's go to the workroom and get started."

CHAPTER 2
CAL

Cal was as good as his word. He doled her pills out to her on a strict schedule. Sophie found that she was able to control her craving for the drug to a limited extent. The knowledge that she wouldn't get another one until a set time enabled her to hold back and not automatically take the pill the instant he gave it to her. If she waited an hour, then she'd have one less to go as the drug wore off. That discipline enabled her to realize that while she lived for the rush as the opiate took effect, she dreaded the time when it wore off even more. Waiting to take the drug seemed to keep the low period shorter. She didn't realize that she was gradually regaining a degree of control that she'd willingly forfeited at the inception of her addiction.

Demonstrating that she had even a small amount of choice encouraged her to pay more attention to the world. She found that she was interested in and seemed to have an aptitude for app development. It helped that Cal was a consummate teacher.

She gradually became more adept at helping him until the day came that he gave her a project to do by herself. True, it was a simple app and didn't require much thought. The customer was a high-end divorce attorney who wanted to provide her clients with a branded child-custody calendar. The attorney's name would be in the app, and every time the parents referred to the calendar, they'd remember who had handled their divorce and who set up the child-visitation schedule.

Sophie thought that relying on the app for advertising might backfire to a certain extent. The parent who had received the proverbial short-end-of-the-stick wouldn't necessarily view the attorney positively and might resent seeing their advert in the app, but apparently, the client was pleased with the result. Cal immediately requested that Sophie set the app up so that he could sell it to other attorneys. She took a day to write the module that allowed anyone with the password to change the display ad to the contact information of any attorney. Then she spent some time setting up an online storefront for her consulting client so that other attorneys could download the app and install their information for a fee.

Sophie's client didn't want to provide any support, but that wasn't a big issue. The basic app was so simple that it didn't require anything and the information customization was robust enough that it headed off almost all problems. The end users paid through an online wallet system and the whole thing worked like a little cash cow for her client.

IT WAS HIGHLY informative for Sophie. She'd never thought about anything like this. The idea that an app could generate money without supervision was a new thought. At the end of the developmental period, she realized that she had reduced her pill intake by a third. This was a surprise also.

When she mentioned it to Cal, he smiled his big, glowing smile and said, "I've been keeping count. I know you've tapered off a little. You see, you can do it if you have something to occupy your mind."

She smiled back. His smile was infectious, and she couldn't help it, but the thought of running out of pills popped back into her head.

"Uh, how am I doing with the pills? I, uh, mean are there many left?" she asked.

Cal's smile faded. "You still have plenty left. Don't worry about them. I've got them under control for you." The tone of his voice implied that he would hear no argument.

Sophie shrugged, trying to pass her question off as unimportant. She knew she wasn't fooling him, but he let it pass without comment.

During the days that had passed, she'd stayed in the upstairs part of Cal's residence. She hadn't even gone to the first floor. There was nothing there of interest, but she thought she might eventually explore the old retail store, just out of boredom if nothing else.

Their next project was to begin work on modifying Ralph's interface. The voice recognition system was almost flawless and needed no work, but the task analysis module and execution modules were in need of expansion and updating.

Cal said, "Old Ralph is good, but there's always more that he could do and, thanks to the Internet, every day there are more ways for him to do things. The big problem is to figure out a way to allow him to find methods of request fulfillment on his own. The process actually requires an artificial intelligence module. He has one, but it's simplistic. I want you to help me rewrite it."

Sophie threw herself into this effort. It was a lot more complicated than app creation, but fulfilling in its way. The intellectual thrill she got from finding a way to solve a sticky problem was almost as intense as the relief she got from a pill. Together they worked through the A.I. module until Ralph was more responsive. His contextual interpretation allowed him to figure out what they wanted from general cues. He was able to anticipate their requests and often had things arranged even before they asked.

Sophie was aware of the various devices Cal had installed in his apartment. The refrigerator and thermostat were connected as was the water heater and doorbell. There was a video system that she'd not noticed for the first two weeks and it had motion-capture software. She reflected that it had been a good thing she'd never tried to steal her stash back from Cal. He would have known. Her timidity and unwillingness to trespass on his space had stood her in good stead.

Midway through that project, Cal told her she had taken her last pill. There were no more.

Sophie tried to act as if this were of no importance, but she found herself in her room within the first hour. She sat on her bed trembling and wondering how she'd make it through the night. She still had the emergency pill. She had stored it under the mattress. She thought longingly of it but didn't dare even look to see if it was still there. If she took it now, then she wouldn't have it when she needed it.

Eventually, she returned to work, but was unable to devote more than passing attention to the job. Cal noticed, but didn't say anything.

When it was suppertime, he fixed food then told her he was going out to get more groceries. This was usual. He went to the grocery store a couple of times a week, and it was time for him to go again. They were low on milk and eggs.

Sophie tried to amuse herself while he was gone. The workroom had a large bookcase that was packed with books and technical manuals. She eventually found herself standing in front of the shelves, looking blankly at the titles. She had been reading them without paying attention, thinking of her emergency pill all the while.

When she began paying attention, she found that she was looking at a tech manual for a programming language. It looked odd. The title was "CRISPR 3.7: Basic DNA Coding."

She muttered to herself, "What the heck? What does that even mean?"

She pulled the manual off the shelf and sat at her workspace to browse through it. The language was simple. It allowed the user to create their own words using built-in libraries of small routines. There was a minimum of syntax required. The system used a run-time compiler that was very robust. It practically guaranteed the app was going to execute. She wasn't sure what the subroutines did, however. They had esoteric names that seemed more biologically oriented than related to computer science.

She was still reading the manual when Cal returned.

He stomped into the room, obviously in a bad humor. Seeing her, he came over, saw what she was reading and sniffed. "Hmmph! That's an interesting one. Can't say much about it, though. The language is designed to manipulate DNA using a gene-splitting system. I don't have the means to implement it, so I never paid much attention to the thing. More of a curiosity than anything in my mind."

He looked to see if she had anything to say, then continued. "I saw somebody that you might know. Thin, dark guy with a short beard. Maybe six feet tall. He was standing on the street, looking around. When I walked by, he showed me a photo."

She had a sinking sensation. She already knew before he finished.

"It was a picture of you, or of you the way you looked before you got some weight back on your bones. He asked me if I'd seen you." He stopped speaking and looked at her, apparently waiting for her to speak.

She tried a couple of times to get it out. Finally, she was able to say, "It was Raul. He can't find me. He's dangerous. You don't know how dangerous. If he gets hold of me, he'll..."

Sophie knew what she wanted to say, but a sob came out instead. "He'll..."

She couldn't continue. She bowed her head and shook, then gasped, "You shouldn't have taken me in. I don't want you to get hurt. That guy thinks he owns me somehow."

Cal asked, "Are you his girlfriend?"

She shook her head violently. "No. I, uh, I mean, well, I stayed with him, and he used me, uh, we had sex several times, but he was only interested in me bringing him money. He was my supplier. That's where I got the pills. Now I don't even have any of them left--" She broke down completely and began to cry in great gasps.

When she got a little control back, she realized that Cal was massaging her neck and shoulders gently.

"Don't you worry about him, Honey," he said. "He won't find you in here. I wasn't going to tell you, but I scored some more pills. I figured that you'd need more before you were able to taper off entirely. You know you're down to less than half what you were taking when you came in here. I'm not going to let you slide back, though. Don't get the idea that just cause I have more means you can take more. That isn't' in the cards for you."

Sophie raised her head and looked questioningly at his face. He smiled and nodded as if to reassure her.

Her anxiety made her nearly incoherent. She said, "But, what if he finds out where I am? What will you do? He has a lot of friends; I guess a gang or something. They all have tattoos on their chests. The same marks for all of them. They're--"

He interrupted her. "Yeah, they're MX-99. They do almost all of the dealing in this part of the city. I know who they are alright. And, don't you worry, Sophie, I know how to stay away from them. I've done pretty well for myself and this place isn't as easy to get into as you think." He made an all-encompassing wave of his hand to indicate the part of the building where they lived.

That night, she couldn't sleep until she'd taken a pill. She didn't like the way it felt. Sure, she felt good, but it was so obviously... ugh...chemical...phony. For the first time, she thought that she could learn to stay off the drug.

CHAPTER 3
BABY STEPS

Raul had seemingly gone elsewhere. Cal hadn't seen him, or he was lying to her. Sophie had come to rely on Cal's ingrained honesty. He was the least complicated person she had ever met. Life with him was easy. She didn't have to second-guess him. He always said exactly what he thought about every situation. Sometimes his bluntness had the potential to be hurtful, but she gradually learned that the hurt was in her, not in him. If something he said made her unhappy, it was because he was pointing out something that she didn't want to deal with; something she'd been hiding from herself. Living with him was like constantly being in front of a mirror that always reflected the truth about her, whether she wanted to see it or not. It was sometimes uncomfortable, but she was gradually becoming acclimated to the uncompromising picture.

There was one aspect of his life that Cal kept from her. At first, she didn't realize that he held any secrets whatsoever, but sleep came hard for her one night, and she decided to get some milk. She thought he was in his room and slipped down the hall in the dark. Once in the kitchen, she heard Cal talking in the workroom. She moved over to the closed door and found that she could listen in to his side of a phone conversation.

He said, "Yes. I can get through their security. The problem isn't hacking in; it's erasing my tracks. It won't be good if they discover they've been compromised."

There was a pause as he listened, then he said, "Okay. I understand your objective."

"Yeah, it's clear. You'll have to leave the ways and means to me. That's what you're paying me for, after all."

"No. That's no problem. We should have some results in a week or less. I'll send you an email through the encryption system, of course."

"Yes. Payment through the Swiss account. The amount we've agreed on is fine unless you require additional work."

He paused, then said, "Yeah. Thanks."

Sophie remained by the door, but now all she heard was the clicking of his keyboard. Thoughtfully, she returned to her room and drank her milk. She had taken a half of a pill earlier, but it had mostly worn off. The milk served as a substitute. It somehow alleviated her urge to take something even though it didn't address her underlying addiction. Part of her addiction, at least, lay in her personality. She had learned that consumption made her feel better. That element of her problem could be addressed with innocuous substances such as the glass of milk.

She fell asleep while thinking of how she could help Cal with his hacking. She was becoming good at app creation. This new skill had given her a degree of confidence that she'd been missing. It had bolstered her self-esteem, and now she felt that she was possibly ready for an additional challenge. She resolved to ask him to teach her. With that, she rolled onto her side and fell asleep.

THE Y WERE SITTING at the table in the kitchen. Cal was eating a bagel, and Sophie was nibbling on a banana nut muffin.

He took a sip of coffee and said, "That was good work yesterday. The app you created has more features than the client requested. That shows initiative, but you've got to be careful not to over-do it. The payment for the work is set, and I can't renegotiate. I don't want you working for free."

Sophie asked, "Yes, but don't you think that giving clients a little bit more is good for business?"

He sighed. "Yes. Just don't overdo it. Like I said."

She gathered up her courage and continued. "Cal? I was in the kitchen last night getting milk. I overheard you. I, uh, will you teach me about hacking, too? I mean you've already taught me so much. That might be a useful skill for me to have, right?"

He stopped chewing and laid his bagel carefully on the plate. Then he arranged the plate and silverware so that the place setting was perfect. Sophie assumed that he was thinking her request over and the actions just gave him some time to think.

Finally, he looked up at her and said, "Look, girl, I'm not sure that I want you in on that kind of stuff. It's dangerous. I'm careful, and I can handle myself. I'm not so sure about you."

"But, you can show me how to do it, right?" she asked, almost begging.

"Yeah. That ain't the problem. The problem comes if you get caught, and they trace your physical location. Alternately, the problem could come from the ones who hired you. They are usually up to no good, and they don't want any loose ends hanging around to cause them trouble later on. I've had a couple of groups get close to finding me in the past. It wasn't pleasant." He looked down at his big hands and flexed his fingers, thoughtfully.

She pressed the issue. It looked like he was wavering and might be convinced.

"Well, what if you guide me and I only work on minor projects at first? Do you have anything simple that I could do?" she asked.

"I do have one thing. I've got a corporate client who wants to install monitoring software in some IoT devices. It could give them an advantage over their competition. The project is a little one, and I've had it on the back shelf while I work on a more lucrative job. I guess you can help on that one. There's one condition, though."

Sophie was ecstatic. "Anything. Just tell me. I'll agree to anything. I really, really want to learn this, Cal!"

He grinned. "Look, I'm not sure I should be teaching this to you. You're about at the point where you can earn enough to get by just with apps. You've got to promise me, and this is the condition, that you won't do anything without running it by me first. There's a certain amount of danger involved in this."

She laughed in triumph. "Oh, that's a given. You check everything I do, anyway. I'm going to need a lot of help, though."

He said, "Not so much help as you might think. Your coding skills are nearly up to the task already. You just need to know how to access things and how to cover your tracks. We'll start with you writing a routine to interface with one of Ralph's cousins. I've purchased a Reverb unit that we can use as a test system. It works like Ralph, but there's no security. It's totally controlled by the corporation that made it. It listens all of the time and stores anything of interest that it hears for later analysis. It contains all of the harmful elements that I designed Ralph to avoid."

Sophie shook her head in understanding. "Now that I understand what those things do, I'm a little nervous about having it around, even to use as a test device."

He answered, "Well, yeah. Just be sure to turn it off when you're done with it. I don't want it to be monitoring any of our conversations."

She nodded again.

Cal continued, "Your software will have to monitor what Reverb hears and then take over when it recognizes a particular code word. We'll stub out the task at that point so that it'll send a message over the net. The type of message can be modified, and that's something I'll do. You'll have your hands full creating a routine and figuring out how to install it in the device memory without physically touching it. Got it?"

He stood and headed for the workroom, but then turned back to her. "We'll be using the new low-Earth orbit satellite web system as an intrusion route. You'd better do some research into back-door access protocols. Uh, also we'll want to establish an unmonitored pathway through the sat system. We shouldn't go through corporate or government controlled nodes. We can parasite on the existing system, but I like to set up my own nodes using bots. Sort of a P2P system that the owners of the computers don't even know about."

He considered for a moment and then added, "By the way, payment for most of these jobs is in the form of cryptocurrency. I haven't told you, but I already set up a wallet for you on a server I own. It's located offshore, and it has a legitimate use. I just keep a couple of gigs open for private storage. Everything's public key encrypted of course. I've already put some of the funds you've earned in your wallet. We'll discuss access and converting them to physical cash or a credit balance later."

She nodded a little ruefully. This wasn't going to be as easy as she'd thought. First, she had a lot of research to do on the Reverb's internals. All she knew at the moment was that the little device had some basic onboard processing ability paired with a limited memory space. Most of what it did happened in its back-end – the extensive software that resided on the net. That was where it parsed commands and linked up with other devices to fulfill them. She assumed that there was also some security and anti-intrusion measures involved in that part of the system. The limited aspect of the device that was located in its physical case was probably a lot easier to hijack.

SOPHIE APPLIED HERSELF. She was feeling better about her life as a result of her work. That feeling made it easier to avoid the pills, or at least delay taking one until night. The darkness often brought old fears and doubts to life, and she'd lie in bed suffering from self-induced pain until she couldn't take it any longer. The drug always delivered and it was easy to forget her painful past in the initial wave of euphoria.

It was just that there was so much to forget. When she considered her life, it appeared in retrospect to be one long and drawn-out train-wreck. She'd been slow to mature, and her classmates had often picked on her as a result. She was so small there was no way she could physically defend herself. Then they found out that she always got good grades and that was another thing for which they disliked her. Then when she became sexually mature, there had been that aspect of things to complicate her life. The fact that her parents hadn't been any help just made things worse.

She could see that the constant bullying and then sexual pressure had predisposed her to feel sorry for herself. Her attitude had become worse when her father died. That had been the start of her mother's drinking.

As far as she knew, her mother had never touched alcohol before, but once her dad was gone, it was a nightly occurrence. She'd been a freshman in high school when her mother had begun her slide downwards.

Sophie had coped as best she could without parental support. She could only blame herself for slipping into a series of increasingly toxic relationships that culminated with her dependency on Raul for drugs. The occasional sex that he demanded of her was unloving, but she had worked hard at convincing herself that he cared. Deep inside, though, she knew that wasn't the case.

Her relationship with Cal was different. He provided a solid sense of stability that she found oddly arousing. She'd previously been attracted to men who were unpredictable and dangerous in their moods and whims. Cal was just...no drama, Cal.

Cal was constantly kind to her. He took care of her and, even though he made it clear that he disapproved, he kept her supplied with Oxy. He'd helped her taper down but then gave over control of the pill bottle to her.

The sense of control was something that Sophie had had far too little of in her life. Unfortunately, it came with the obligation to manage her addiction by herself. She was now down to one pill a day and had been toying mentally with the idea of cutting the pill in half. After all, she told herself, it wasn't like she really needed the things. Her daily resolve to cut always lasted until night, but then perished with the dying light of the sun. Something about going to bed made her feel intolerably sorry for herself.

Sophie felt she had plenty of time. She could always cut her dosage in half tomorrow. There was hope in the next day. Meanwhile, she found that she was replacing a considerable amount of her addiction with an intense desire to learn more about coding and hacking in particular.

She had toyed with the idea that her addiction or her propensity towards addictive behavior was a function of her genetic constitution. That seemed to excuse her behavior. If she wasn't actually responsible, but she rejected that thought. She knew that she always had a choice every time she picked up one of the little white pills.

The DNA manipulating language was something that she had started studying as an exercise. Certainly, it seemed to have no application beyond student use in an advanced bio-lab. She had kept at it because it seemed so esoteric that it appealed to her sense of the absurd. Eventually, she had concluded that it might prove useful. She wouldn't allow herself to think that she could somehow change her genetics enough to free her from the addiction easily. On the other hand, she couldn't see any practical opportunities for the language.

SHE COULDN'T GET to sleep that night. She'd worked late, but when she headed for bed, Cal was still hunched over his computer. Sophie had looked at his back as she left the room. He was a mystery to her.

She couldn't understand his motivation. He helped her and didn't seem to want anything but to see her become a success and stand on her own. She sat on the edge of her bed pondering the situation.

Without thinking about it, she found that she'd opened the pill bottle and had placed a full pill in her mouth. She started to remove it, but then shrugged and swallowed it with a mouthful of water from the plastic bottle she had on her nightstand.

She continued to puzzle over Cal. It was almost as if he didn't recognize that she was female. His masculinity was intense. He was huge and muscular and had an almost magnetic feel about him. His actions were always infused with a sureness that she couldn't match. He never seemed to doubt what he was doing.

She felt twitchy for some reason. She lay back on the bed and rubbed her neck. The drug hit her brain at that point, and she felt relaxed and warm. The sensation seemed to create a need within her body.

It had been a long time since she'd enjoyed being with a man, but now she was feeling warm and aroused. Cal was just down the hall. Maybe he was just waiting for her to show him she recognized that he was a man.

Sophie stood and looked indecisively at her reflection in the mirror. She was wearing a long tee shirt that reached to her upper thighs. It wasn't pretty, but she wasn't in the mood for pretty. She headed down the hall to the workroom.

Cal was sitting with his back to the door, still working on the keyboard when she padded in. She walked over and stood behind him, then moved forward and wrapped her arms around his shoulders, pressing her breasts against his back.

He froze, his fingers poised in the middle of a line of code. Then he reached up and moved her arms, stood and turned around. The chair rolled out of the way.

Now I've finally got his attention! She moved closer and rubbed against his chest. She could feel him responding against her body, and it gave her an increased feeling of warmth.

Cal sighed and grabbed her shoulders, then, to Sophie's surprise, he pushed her away.

"Look, girl, I know you're a woman. I'm tempted, but I don't know you well enough. There are two reasons I'm not going to let this go any farther."

He paused, and Sophie could see the lust in his eyes. She tried to move closer again, but he held her away easily.

His deep voice rumbled out of his chest. "First, I'm not going to take advantage of you. I have all of the power in this relationship. I'm teaching you. I took you in, and you naturally feel grateful to me. That disparity is unfair. I'm only interested in someone who can show they're equal to me. Someone who comes to me because they are legitimately attracted to me, not because they are attracted to my status or feel grateful for some reason. I brought you in because I felt sorry for you. So far you've done well for yourself, but like I said, there's a power difference, and that goes against my basic nature."

She said, "But – "

Cal interrupted her. "No buts. You don't know what I had to go through in my life. I've been in the weak position simply because of my skin. I didn't like it, and I hated feeling like people were doing me favors, even when they were trying to be helpful."

He shook her shoulders a little. "That brings me to the second reason I'm turning you down. I've seen some of my friends fall for women who felt sorry for them. Women who probably thought they were in love or something, but who were really just trying to make things right and to show how virtuous they were by having a man with different pigment in his skin. Most of the relationships didn't last. The motivation wasn't good. They weren't in love; they were all just using each other. I don't want that. Like I said, I don't know you well enough yet. You might be serious; you might not. You might just want a cheap thrill for a few minutes. I'm not buying it. Now go back to bed."

Sophie felt herself inexorably turned around and then he pushed her towards the door. She stumbled several steps, then stopped and said in a small voice, "Cal?"

He was watching her, and his voice was rough sounding. "Yes?"

She found that tears were leaking from her eyes and running down her cheeks.

"I'm sorry. I just thought that...that maybe I should..." She waved her hands vaguely, "I don't know. Maybe I'm grateful.

Maybe you're right. I just thought it would be nice to show you I cared."

He smiled slowly. "Look, Honey, I appreciate the offer. I might take you up on it someday. You got to show me that you're able to stand without relying on drugs and you need to be able to take care of yourself. I mean earn a living on your own. I might not always be around to help out. You come back to me when you're in a position of strength and we might revisit this thing. Meanwhile, you go to bed. I got work that I've got to get done by morning."

She turned and walked down the hall, wiping at her eyes. Was she that undesirable? She could see that he had a point, no, two points and maybe from his position she was weak and he somehow felt he would be exploiting that weakness.

By the time she reached her room, she had realized that Cal was correct. He had been in the weak position for a lot of his life, and he hated it. He hated it so much that he wouldn't voluntarily take advantage of anyone that was weak. If she wanted him, she'd have to show him she was strong too.

His words had made her rethink her own motivation. She wasn't sure she really desired him in the way he wanted. She was grateful, that was true. She liked his gentleness and his helpfulness and his caring, but she didn't love him.

As she lay down, the thought passed through her mind that he really deserved love. He was a good man; the best man she'd ever met. She knew that she wasn't ready for that kind of relationship. She grabbed the bottle and took a second full pill feeling sorry for herself.

When the increased feeling of well-being and the warmth hit, she relaxed and fell asleep, hoping that he'd forgive her.

CAL DIDN'T MENTION her attempted seduction in the morning. Sophie tried to pretend that it hadn't happened. It was embarrassing, and she regretted it.

They took a break for food at noon and went into the kitchen to scrounge something to eat. Once seated, Cal took a bite, then raised his eyes and fixed them on Sophie's face, getting her immediate attention.

"Look, maybe I was too harsh on you last night," he said. He looked down, then added, "I wasn't talking generically about men that I've known. What I said, well...it happened to me."

Sophie couldn't meet his eyes. She looked at her plate and simply nodded her understanding.

He continued. "I had a hard start. I was big, and most everyone thought I'd be a good athlete. Turns out I wasn't very good at either basketball or football. I was more interested in computers. Anyway, there was this girl. I, uh, I thought I was in love. I thought she loved me for who I was. Then I happened to overhear her talking to her friends. She felt sorry for me. You know, the disadvantaged minority kid. She was just using me to show her friends how wonderful and understanding she was. I walked away right then."

He stopped and took another bite, seemingly done with the conversation.

Sophie waited, but he didn't say anything else. Finally, she asked, "So did you tell her you knew what she was trying to do?"

He shook his head negatively, then said, "No. I never spoke to her again." He paused and took a drink of water, then added, "So, like I said, I don't know you well enough. I guess in a way I don't trust your motives. Also, there's the power thing. I am not going to lower myself to the level of using someone who's dependent on me. I'll teach you what I know. Maybe when you can take care of yourself, you'll decide you want to try last night again. I can't say I wasn't tempted. You're a good looking girl, Sophie. It was hard to push you away. On the other hand, if you can take care of yourself, you might not be interested in me. We'll wait and see. Now that's all I've got to say on the matter."

He finished eating and rose without a word. Sophie followed him back into the workroom and bent over her keyboard, trying to concentrate on the code she was developing.

After a while, she decided that he was in the right. She owed him, and the best thing she could do was not let his efforts go to waste. She was grateful for his help.

About an hour later, Cal cleared his throat and said, "Sophie? I been thinking about what I said. I've tried to put it out of my mind for years, ya know? It just hurt too much. Here's the deal, though. I want someone to want me for who I am, not for what I am or what they think I represent. I'm not, you know, my people. I'm not a member of some kind of class of victims. It's true I had a hard time growing up, but so did you. Treating me well or giving me special rights to make up for what happened historically is stupid. It can't possibly help dead people. I suffered, but I've learned that I'm in control of my destiny. And so are you. If you don't learn anything else from me, that's what I want you to know. You're responsible for yourself. You succeed on your own, or you fail on your own. That's all."

He stopped talking abruptly, and Sophie could hear the click of his keyboard. She couldn't think of anything to say immediately, so she typed another line of code. As she did, it occurred to her that he was right. That's what she wanted for herself—someone to want her for who she was.

She sighed, but who she was wasn't who she wanted to be. Being addicted to the drug ensured that. She decided to work harder to wean herself off, even if it didn't seem possible. She also decided that she'd have to try to compensate for her actions. She resolved to work even harder. She vowed to herself that she'd live up to his expectations. Maybe he was right; she could learn to stand on her own.

SHE APPLIED HERSELF to the research Cal needed to fulfill his new contract. Once she understood more fully, she recognized the job for what it was: industrial espionage. Cal was correct. It was going to involve a certain amount of danger. Hazelton

BioMedical Corporation was one of the world's largest and most profitable producers of drugs.

The two of them were going to plant monitoring software in one of Hazelton's research labs. The client had specified a single lab located in Switzerland. The research there was a combination of biological and digital that apparently was of extreme interest to their client.

She'd asked Cal about the client, but he refused to tell her anything.

"The less you know about them, the better for everyone," he said. His tone of voice admitted to no questioning. After a moment, he turned to her, obviously feeling guilty about being so curt.

"Look, Sophie, there's a distinct chance we'll get caught. I hope to minimize it, but it could happen. If there's a criminal case that results, I want you to be honestly able to say that you didn't know who you were working for and what their goals were."

She hadn't thought of the fact that what they were doing was probably illegal. It had seemed like some sort of odd chess game with willing players. The other side tried to secure its data, and her side tried to figure ways around their firewalls. It was a game; that was all.

She started thinking about it as more than a simple exercise. Avoiding detection was critical. They could route through various IP addresses and countries using I2P or something similar. She'd never use Tor due to her suspicion that most of the nodes were operated by the government just to trap the unwary. Once the source of their attack was sufficiently obscured, the next step would be to access the Global Sat network.

Security there was high, but since the intent of the network was to provide high-speed access to the Internet for anyone at any point on the globe, the system was easy to access. When she started studying the satellite system, she wondered why a billionaire would take the initiative to provide 1 Gbps bandwidth to some unknown villager in Southeast Asia.

A discussion over breakfast cleared that idea up.

He snorted and said, "It looks like a charity operation. Provide the benefits of Internet access to all of the poor folks across the world and they can better themselves. Right?"

She nodded, not knowing what was coming.

He continued. "That's the published goal. I tend to look a little deeper, and I don't like what I see. You know that almost all political actions have unintended consequences, right?"

She nodded again.

"It always seems like the politicians and bureaucrats don't bother to think to the second level. Their primary goals are adequate for them and all they can usually see. They can always say that they meant well. However, it's the second and deeper level results that always come around to bite them in the butt. In this case, the access to information will go a long way toward spreading ideas around. The human species will end up with the same pool of ideas, and that will help standardize thinking. Groups that were culturally dissimilar in the past will inevitably move closer together. Can you see that?"

Sophie ventured, "Yes, but isn't that a good thing?"

Cal snorted again. "Seems like it might be, but consider this: The demands of life vary in different places on the globe. There is no perfect, one-size-fits-all culture. Different groups have their own solutions to survival. What business have we in trying to mandate a centrally-planned type of approach? That's never worked and can never work. Central control isn't up to the task. People need local flexibility to allow them to deal with local problems. Central control just leads to what one might call a monoculture, and that's my real fear."

Sophie asked, "Yeah, but wouldn't we all be better off, if we had no cultural arguments? There would be less reason for conflict."

He paused, thinking, and then said, "You know that bananas are really expensive, right?"

She nodded in agreement, wondering what bananas had to do with culture. When he didn't continue, she ventured, "They've always been expensive. I've only eaten a couple in my whole life."

He said, "There was a time when they were common and cheap. The banana growers found it most profitable to grow only the Gros Michel. That was a particular type of banana that tasted good and sold well. They created a monoculture, growing only this banana on thousands of acres of land. Then a fungus disease wiped out the Gros Michel variety totally. The growers had to use a slightly less desirable banana that was immune to the disease. It's called the Cavendish. The growers ignored the lesson the fungus had presented to them and created another monoculture. Another type of fungus came along and pretty much wiped out all of the Cavendish bananas. That's why they're hard to get now. See?" He emphasized his story by nodding vigorously.

She couldn't see how this related to culture or the Internet, but she could tell that he was passionate about his point. She nodded.

Cal continued. "So, bananas taught us a lesson, if we'd only pay attention to it. Monocultures are great until they encounter an environmental challenge, then they fail disastrously. The same can be said for information cultures."

Sophie shook her head slightly, not agreeing or really disagreeing.

"Here's the basic problem. The Internet has become the single largest source of profit on the globe. It offers a free exchange of ideas...er, I should say, offered – past tense. Now, several giant corporations have basically captured it. They can easily suppress ideas that are at odds with their profit strategy. All they have to do is to throttle back a website by a little over two-hundred and forty-five milliseconds. The delay disgusts people, then they get impatient and click-off the site. The corporations are forcing people into a narrower and narrower selection of ideas. There might be great ideas out there; world-changing ideas; but how do you find out about them?"

She said, "Uh. Magazines? Scientific publications, maybe?"

Cal laughed, then said, "Maybe, but how many people read printed material these days? Only a few scientists read journals that are specific to their area of expertise and most of them are published digitally. There's always going to be blogs and such that are outside the big corporations' control, but as I said, the outsiders get repressed, throttled back a bit. The net effect is to funnel the consciousness of everyone through a narrower and narrower channel, creating a monoculture of ideas. I'm against that. I don't believe it's healthy for humanity in the long run. When the species, our species runs up against a problem, we may not be able to adapt."

Sophie asked, "What kind of a problem could there be? If everyone all agrees and there's no conflict, how could we have trouble?"

He sighed--a deep and long exhalation. "The Gros Michel fungus was always present, but only became a problem when the large plantations made it easy for it to spread. Let's say, for the sake of my point, that one of the big, global companies buy enough politicians to get regulations passed that force everyone to use their products. Maybe their products are harmful to human health and eventually kill people or change people so that our species doesn't develop normally."

She said, "I guess that could happen, but, if it's such a bad thing, what can we do about it?

He laughed. "Now you're back on track. We can work from within by hacking. That leads me to our current job."

She laughed in return. "You want us to get back to work, right?"

He said, "Well, yes, we should get going, but I was going to say that the Hazelton Corporation is one of those big companies. I normally don't take jobs that involve industrial espionage, but my client has evidence that Hazelton is up to something bad. Rather than turn the job down and let some other hackers help the client get an advantage over Hazelton, I took the job. If I can, I'll screw up Hazelton's idea so that neither they nor my client can use it."

Sophie asked, "You haven't told me what we're supposed to find in the lab we're attacking. What is it? Could it be as bad as the banana fungus?"

He said, "That's just it. The client didn't know exactly what it was, just that Hazelton has been spending far more money on lobbying than they ever have. They're trying to get the politicians lined up so that what they're planning will have governmental approval. I do know that it's a biological project involving DNA based nanomachines, but that's all."

Sophie thought about it and then said, "Nanomachines could be helpful or harmful depending on how they are programmed. Do you know what they're supposed to do?"

He frowned and said, "No idea. That's one of the first things we're going to find out. The second thing will be how to stop the project, presuming that the nanites could be used to harm humans."

Cal stood and headed towards the workroom, then paused and turned toward her. "C'mon, let's get going. Time is wasting. I want this to be a clean break-in. I'm not happy with the fact that their corporate headquarters is only twenty miles away."

She asked, "What difference does that make? Aren't you going to use a proxy? How will that be any different from breaking into some company thousands of miles away?"

He shrugged and said, "Not sure. It's just that they're so close, they could drive over and beat down our door if they trace us. Now, c'mon. Let's get to work."

Sophie stood, started to follow him, but then lagged behind, staying in the kitchen to pour a glass of water. When Cal was safely down the hall, she took a white pill out of her pocket and broke it in half by pressing on it on the counter. She took half with a gulp of water, then toyed with the remaining piece, thinking about swallowing it too.

After a few seconds, she raised the remaining half to her mouth, but then stopped, jerked convulsively and shoved it back into her pocket. She took another drink from the glass, emptied the drops into the sink, and turned decisively towards the workroom.

She walked down the hall thinking that the second half was in her pocket, easy to get, and ready if she needed it. It was a comforting thought, but she continually had to work to keep her hand from straying into her pocket.

It wouldn't do to take it until she really needed the relief.

CHAPTER 4
HACKING INTO TROUBLE

Once Sophie started working on the Reverb, she quickly became alarmed. The free-standing, interface devices were common throughout society. Nearly every family had one. She had heard of the potential they had for intrusive data acquisition but had believed the advertising.

The things were said to listen for the activating code word, usually the company name, then to analyze the following few seconds of voice data for an executable order or request. The speech data was analyzed by a cloud-based, limited A.I. system, but was not stored beyond the order fulfillment. The system had been easy to hack in the early days and also had created problems when it accidentally interpreted television commercials or programs for commands.

Sophie concluded that the devices uploaded all speech in their vicinity to the cloud. Whether or not it was stored was a matter of choice, and it was not the choice of the user. Instead, it was the choice of the corporation. Sophie suspected that the corporation would store everything and quickly trade it to the government if pressured by a subpoena or possibly as a lobbying favor.

She went to Cal with her suspicions. "That Reverb is a guaranteed snitch. What I want to know is how can we trust Ralph not to listen in on our discussions about hacking?"

He laughed. "So, you finally caught on to the magnitude of the problem, huh? Don't worry. Ralph's kin might be poorly behaved eavesdroppers and snitches, but he's very polite. Like I told you before, I changed him. He's got a little more to his firmware than the average device. I added code that keeps him from uploading anything until he hears his name. Also added a few lines that keep his original manufacturing company from remotely upgrading his firmware. That way they can't overwrite my anti-surveillance code. The other thing is, he confines his searches to a search engine that doesn't store personal information. Oh, that and he accesses everything through a VPN, but then all my systems do."

Sophie had been relieved to hear this. The thought that their conversations might be subject to eavesdropping was frightening.

She went back to work on the Reverb with a vengeance. It turned out that the thing was ridiculously easy to co-opt. It wasn't long before she had created a software update for it that ensured the collected speech data was routed to two locations.

The Reverb would send everything it heard to an IP address that Cal had given her; then it would forward its data load to its usual analysis channel in the way the manufacturer expected.

The address Cal had given her was for an overseas server that provided him with plenty of unmonitored storage on an anonymous basis. From there, the raw data would be routed to another IP that Cal also controlled. Once there, an A.I. system would comb it for references to the information that their client wanted. Neither of the two locations was easily traceable back to Cal.

She was a little nervous when Cal inspected her work, but he just nodded approvingly.

"Looks like you got it. The only thing is that a company propagated software update will overwrite your code. See if you can have the Reverb send you an alert before it installs a company update. That way, we can reinstall your patch, provided we need to continue collecting data."

She asked, "Why can't I just disable the update system entirely? You know, just have it reject any updates?"

He shook his head. "That's what I did to Ralph basically, but we don't want to leave any long-term traces. If your stuff is automatically overwritten, then it won't be lying around for anyone to find, should they get suspicious."

Sophie must have looked dubious, because Cal added, "Look, the manufacturer updates those things about once a month. That should give us plenty of time for our work, and it will ensure your patch is wiped clean. I don't like to leave clues around longer than I have to."

THE NEXT PHASE of her research went well. She ran a vulnerability scanner and found that the Hazelton system was cloud-based and, as such, had several possible access pathways. However, access to their data was protected by an authentication system that was somewhat aggravating.

Cal had already created a brute-force password breaking program for another use. It quickly turned up an active username and password that got them through the first part of the security system.

The second part was considerably harder since it involved selecting an image from an improbably vast library of graphics. Apparently, each user had been allowed to upload their preferred image into a database containing thousands of other images.

Since there were slightly over twenty-three hundred employees, there were a lot of images in the database, especially since there were a lot of unused ones too. That meant a lot of choices. This situation was compounded by the fact that the system would time-out for progressively longer and longer periods each time an entry attempt failed.

Not wanting to raise any alarms, Sophie tried a couple of times and then quit. She took her failure to Cal.

Once again, he was ahead of her.

"Look, kid, the username limits the choices. I found an employee list that I downloaded from the company that handles their payroll. I had to hack them last year, and they haven't realized that their system was compromised, so it was easy to get in. Anyway, I took their employee list and cross-referenced it with the username. The username isn't the actual employee name in this case, but, if we assume that part of the actual name was used, there are three possibilities."

She interjected, "Yeah, but how does that make it easier to select the correct graphic? Seems like it could be anything."

He held up a finger in an admonitory way. "It could, but running a search of social media on each of the three people would be a good step. People tend to have favorite images and sometimes reuse them. Why don't you give it a try?'

She sighed. There was no way he was going to give her the correct information. It was irritating since he probably already knew. She sighed again, then resigned herself to working hard enough to crack the problem.

The funny thing was, that once she got started, the answer was startlingly easy to find. One of the users owned a pug. They'd plastered their social media accounts with pictures of the pooch. When she looked at Hazelton's security image database, there he was, silly doggy grin and all.

She hesitated. She could get into the system, but should she? She wasn't experienced enough to avoid tripping any flags that she might encounter if she just snooped around. She went to Cal again.

He said, "That's nice work. You got in easily. Some systems require other approaches like ratting, but you've got this one open for us. I suspect that they force password changes periodically, so we've got to move quickly. Now, what I'm going to do is to snoop a little, then upload a rootkit that will sit in the system folder. It will allow me to open a true back-door and I'll use that entrance to do the majority of my snooping."

"Wouldn't that be visible, at least, if anyone looked at the command files?" she asked.

He nodded. "Yes, it would, but they'd have to look carefully. I'll attach it to the end of one of the larger system command files. Then I'll install a few bytes of code that will jump from the front of the file to my code. My code will check for an activation sequence in an email to their corporate info mailbox. If it isn't present, control will be returned to the system routine. If I'm entering the system, my code will be recognized in the email. My routine will take over and open the back door."

He paused, looking at her carefully. He continued when she nodded in understanding.

"If we're lucky, they'll never realize they've been hacked. The only clue will be the size of the system file. There's a checksum on it, but I'll overwrite that. They could still find us if anyone does a system check or update, but in my experience, those kinds of things are done maybe once a quarter. That should give us enough time to get our dirty work done."

CAL HAD A little work on another project to finish first, but that was done quickly. He started on Hazelton right after lunch. Sophie hung over his shoulder, watching the process.

Once into the system, he wasted no time uploading his back-door routine. He appended it to one of the system files, manually changed a couple of things, then exited the system. The entire operation took a little over two minutes. Sophie was impressed at his efficiency. He knew what he was doing and didn't have to waste time figuring out any of the steps. It would have taken her far longer.

He leaned back in his chair, stretched, interlaced his fingers and popped them, then leaned forward again.

"Now, I'm going to send Hazelton an email. I'm just a curious college student wondering if they are doing all they can to make their research environmentally friendly. In fact, I think my professor assigned the class to check with several companies about their environmental policies. Ya' know, climate change is a happening thing right now."

She snickered. "Yeah, it's colder than normal this month. If I was still..." She paused in sudden realization. He'd pulled her off the street. If she wasn't in here with him, she might be freezing in a cardboard box somewhere. Her breath caught in her chest, making her gasp.

Cal glanced over his shoulder at her, concern in his eyes. "Are you alright?"

"Yes, it was just a sudden thought. I, uh, thank you for taking me in."

He grinned and said, "It was a good move on my part. You've been a help to me. I wasn't sure whether or not you had it in you to take control of your life, but you're working on it. I like to see that. Makes me feel good."

He returned to the email without waiting for her response.

He sent the email and then waited for a few seconds. Then he checked a specific Internet address.

"Yeah! It's open," he said. "Now their data belongs to me. I'm gonna download everything I can get, then check it over. Then we can plan our next step."

A few keystrokes started the download. Sophie watched. It seemed to take forever. There was a lot of data.

She and Cal watched quietly as the Hazelton data flowed into their storage. He was going for a full dump. All of the research data was stored in a series of project directories. Cal systematically downloaded each folder.

They were halfway through the last when the download paused. Sophie noticed and started to say something, but Cal was ahead of her. His hands were instantly on the keyboard entering commands. He exited Hazelton, then disconnected from the Internet.

"What was that?" she asked.

"I don't know. Something happened. The download had a while to go yet. Maybe...I dunno. Maybe we got caught somehow.

Anyway, I disconnected fast. They probably couldn't track us, even if they knew we were there. Could have been a system reset of some kind, but that's not too likely at two in the afternoon. Well, we got most of their data. Let's see what we can discover."

He copied the downloaded data into a work folder, then told her to take the last fourteen files. He'd work on the rest.

By suppertime, Sophie was thoroughly tired. She was exhausted from poring through seemingly incomprehensible data about unidentifiable drug trials, odd experiments, and patient follow-ups. If she never saw any more of that kind of stuff, it would be just fine.

Cal had more luck. A few times in his investigation, he made quiet exclamations under his breath.

CHAPTER 5
DON'T GET CAUGHT

C al, what were you making those noises about?" Sophie asked as they compared notes over supper. She was holding her loaded fork in her right hand, about to transfer food into her mouth. She'd been suppressing her curiosity, but it had finally boiled over, and she couldn't wait any longer for satisfaction.

He finished chewing his mouthful of pasta, then carefully placed his fork by the half-full plate.

"I found some hints that they were working with the government. Specifically with the CIA to create some kind of untraceable bio-weapon. At least I think it's a bio-weapon. Biology and medicine aren't my strong points. I'm much happier working with software than biology."

He paused, then continued. "Uh, anyway, it looks like they're about ready for field trials of whatever it is. Did you have any luck with your reading?"

Now it was Sophie's turn to sigh. "No. Everything I've seen so far is either human resources data or accounting data. Somehow you gave me all of the boring files."

He asked, "Have you had any trouble accessing any of them?"

"No. The accounting files are protected by a weak security algo, but I figured it out."

She was proud of her understatement. It hadn't been that easy, but she'd managed to obtain access without asking for help.

Cal nodded in approbation. "That's good. You're making progress. The painful job now is that we have to keep on sifting through what we got in the hope there will be something that is more informative than what I've found so far."

She nodded, bent her head and concentrated on her meal.

AFTERWARDS, THEY WENT back to work. Sophie had stopped in her room under the pretense of needing to change her shirt. She'd somehow gotten marinara sauce on the front, right between her breasts. Every time she looked down, she saw the reddish stain and flinched. It somehow reminded her of blood.

Once she'd changed her shirt, her pills summoned her over to the nightstand. She stood there indecisively, looking at the plastic bottle. Finally, the thought of having to sit and pore through files for hours longer seduced her into taking a full pill.

Once she'd swallowed it, she had instant regrets. She should have taken a half pill or just put it off until bedtime. She hoped that she wouldn't appear too relaxed. She didn't want Cal to know that she'd taken one. He wouldn't say anything, but she was afraid that his look would convey that he thought she was a failure.

She hurried back to her seat and pulled up the next file. Best to get started before the drug hit her bloodstream. It was...it was... ahh! It hit, and she felt the warmth and relaxation of its seductive effect. She sighed. At least she didn't have to take more than one pill to feel good. That was a major benefit of restricting her intake. Maybe she'd be able to stop or, at least, cut down her intake to a half pill a day. Then when she felt she couldn't do without the drug, a single dose would be really, really good.

She caught Cal looking at her and leaned forward hastily to study her monitor. The file was a scientific report that seemed to deal with both biology and software. The writing was complex, dense, and hard to follow.

Sophie started reading from the top again, paying careful attention this time. Halfway through the second page, she caught her breath. This was what they were searching for. Hazelton had been working on a biological nanomachine. It was constructed from organic molecules and could be programmed to perform... what? She re-read the section.

The nanomachines were able to manipulate DNA. The first thing they did, when injected into a human, was to create a metallic antenna, only microns in width. Iron molecules gathered from blood cells formed just under the surface of the skin, allowing direct reception of wireless signals. A tiny receiver located deeper in the underlying muscles interpreted the information and issued commands.

The nanites could be programmed using, and here she laughed aloud, the DNA programming language that she had been studying.

A sudden change in the overhead lighting cued her to the fact that Cal was leaning over, reading the monitor from just behind her right shoulder.

She turned slightly to look at him from inches away. He frowned causing the corners of his eyes to wrinkle up. He moved his lips slightly as he read.

She asked, "Is this it?"

He swore softly. "Damn. Maybe." He continued scanning, ignoring her proximity. Finally, he took a deep breath and said, "Yes, I think it is. This isn't good, is it?"

Sophie had been thinking about that.

"Well, it might be used for something good. Maybe they intend to cure cancer or some genetic diseases."

It was his turn to laugh. "Are you serious? You think the CIA is interested in curing people?"

Sophie flushed, then answered, "No. I guess they probably aren't. They're more likely to use the technique to do something bad to people, but what would something bad done by nanomachines look like?"

Cal dismissed her question with a wave of his hand. "Why don't you read the rest and then brief me on what it says. I really should finish my part of the files. There might be something useful in there. No sense us duplicating efforts."

She turned back to the monitor, stretched, and started to scan again. After a moment, she highlighted several pages of text and saved it to her desktop. She'd print it for later study.

An indeterminate time passed as she read. Finally, she pushed back from the screen. She needed a break. She was thirsty and needed to use the toilet. She stood and stretched, then looked at Cal. He was absorbed in his work, so she tiptoed out.

The pills in her room called out to her as she went past. She slowed, turned towards the door, but then wrenched herself about and continued down the hall. There was a couple of cans of soda in the refrigerator. She got them both, intending to take the second one to Cal. Surely he needed something to drink. It had been hours since they'd eaten.

She walked through the door into the workroom and said, "Cal?" He didn't answer. At first, she thought that he was napping, but then she realized that he'd collapsed with his head on his keyboard. The screen was filled with random characters as a result.

Sophie repeated, "Cal!" Then, alarmed at his lack of response, she dropped the cans and rushed forward to shake his shoulders. He moved slightly then and groaned.

She put her hand on his head. It was red hot. He was burning with fever. She gasped at the heat and simultaneously waved her hand in irritation at something that buzzed past her eyes. Cal chose that moment to move a bit, and her attention returned to him.

The quiet buzzing became louder, and she brushed at her ear. Then she saw a small mosquito-like thing sitting on Cal's neck. It was dark and difficult to see against his skin.

Sophie looked closer. It seemed to be a mosquito at first glance. Squinting, she saw differences. Something about the insect-thing looked metallic. As she approached, she saw that it had extended a slender, needle-like proboscis and was biting Cal. Instinct took over, and she slapped the creature.

There was a tiny snap. Sophie grabbed her hand and exclaimed. That had hurt. It was like she'd been shocked or stung. She bent to examine the mangled thing.

It was unmoving, but now that she'd flattened it, she could see that it wasn't a mosquito after all. It was a machine. She exclaimed aloud, "A drone! A tiny drone like an insect, but who?"

It struck her just as she felt a light sensation on her neck. Their intrusion into Hazelton's system had been detected, and they'd been traced. The mosquito drones had been sent to extract punishment for their transgression. She slapped at her neck instantly.

There was another snap, and her hand stung, but that was all. She scraped at her skin and removed the remains of a second machine. She didn't think it had bitten her. A fearful, cautious expression crossed her face. If there had been two, there were probably more. She looked around the room. Where had the nasty little things managed to find an entrance?

The window! The window in the hall was opened a few inches to allow a cross-flow of cooler air. It had a screen, but she thought there was a hole that she'd noticed. She dashed into the hall and slammed the frame shut, trapping a swarm of the things that had not yet flown into the room. They buzzed back and forth between the screen and the glass.

Her head was suddenly enveloped in a cloud of buzzing fliers. She screamed and ran to the kitchen to get the broom. Swinging it wildly, she smashed as many as she could against the hall walls. They couldn't fly very quickly, so she was able to kill the ones she saw.

She backed out of the hall into the workroom and shut the door. There was no way to tell if she'd gotten all of the things. Now she had to see about Cal.

He'd fallen to the floor and was lying by his chair. Sophie approached him, listening carefully for the slight buzzing sound of the tiny drones. It was quiet, so she bent to feel his head. He was still hot, and now his breathing was ragged. She was on the verge of panic. It was obvious that the drones had injected him with something, but was it a chemical of some kind or a biological agent? That was the question.

She remembered the first-aid kit. Cal wasn't a true prepper, but he did have lots of survival supplies and among them was a variety of antibiotics. They were stored in a cabinet in the closet at the end of the workroom. She took a few steps and yanked open the closet door.

Once the cabinet was open, it had a whole shelf of bottles and vials. Sophie indecisively fingered the containers, wondering what each one was. It took her a few moments to get control of her panic. Then she realized they were labeled in Cal's handwriting. She bent to inspect them, finally settling on one which was marked ceftriaxone sodium.

Cal had written the words: "Broad Spectrum" on the bottle. She thought that sounded like it would be the best choice. The material inside the bottle was a yellowish-orange crystalline powder.

She shook her head negatively. He was in no shape to take something by mouth. Inspiration suddenly struck. She was back at her workstation in a second logging onto the search engine that Cal insisted they always use.

She recalled his sober expression as he'd told her, "Look, Sophie, use this one. It doesn't track you, and it deletes your search parameters immediately. The most popular ones are exploits. They act as search engines, but they store and track your data to sell it for profit. I don't want to have any searches linked to this address, especially ones that might be for addictive drugs." He'd been referring to her habit, of course, and she'd instantly seen the utility of his rule.

She entered the chemical's name and found that it was easily dissolved in water and was good for a wide variety of disease, including pneumonia. Cal's breathing was labored, and he sounded like his lungs were full of fluid, so that might be what she wanted.

Back to the cabinet. There was a gallon jug of distilled water on the bottom shelf. Her hands shook as she measured and mixed the yellow powder with the water. She ripped the cover off a disposable syringe and sucked the mixture up.

There were a few bubbles in the fluid. This was something she knew how to do. She'd never injected herself, but she had seen others do it often enough. She flicked the syringe with her fingernail until the bubbles were at the top, then squirted them out with a little of the mixture.

The needle went into Cal's shoulder muscle, and she slowly depressed the plunger, hoping that what she was doing would help. It would be cruel if she ended up giving him a drug that caused an allergic reaction and killed him.

He muttered a little at the sting, but then relaxed a little.

She tugged at his body, trying to straighten his posture into a more comfortable looking arrangement. It was no use. He was so large that she could barely move his arm, let alone drag him across the floor.

Sophie glanced around the room, looking for more of the miniature drones. Seeing nothing, she looked back at Cal. His head was still hot. Perhaps the cabinet held a thermometer.

She returned with a forehead scanning thermometer and some rubbing alcohol. She sloshed the alcohol across his shirt. It would cool him a little. His temperature was a little over 105; enough to put an adult into a coma. She poured some alcohol on her palm and rubbed it on his face.

His eyes opened, and he made a croaking noise, then cleared his throat, gasped for breath, and whispered, "Something bit me then I felt bad. I...uh...I think I'm sick."

She shushed him and said, "I gave you a shot of Rocephin. You've got a high fever, and your breathing sounds bad."

His eyes shut, then opened to focus on her face. "That was a good choice. It should help if I've got a bacterial infection. Maybe I'd better get in bed." He tried to sit up but fell back with a groan.

Sophie was waving her hands in a vain effort to stop him, but he ignored her. He fell back a second time, but this time he was in a more comfortable position.

"It's no use. I feel too bad to move much."

She said, "I think we're trapped in here. The things are probably in the rest of the house. I shut the window and swatted a bunch of them, but I'm sure I didn't get them all."

"What? What things?' he whispered.

She took a deep breath, then explained, "They're little, tiny drones. Like mosquitoes. One was on your neck. They tried to bite me, but I kept smashing them. They shock you a little when you swat them. That's how I realized they're machines."

Cal shut his eyes, then said, "Hazelton tracked us. Those things are carrying some kind of bio-weapon. You can't let them bite you. I...oh, God...I hurt like crazy."

Her hand went to her pocket. The half pill was there, ready for her. If she took it, it might calm her a little, and she'd be more effective. She took it out, raised it to her mouth, then hesitated.

Her hand shook wildly, then she bent and shoved the pill into Cal's mouth.

"Hold that under your tongue. It'll taste bad, but it will help the pain."

He moved his mouth a little, then was silent.

She remembered the soft drinks. The cans had rolled under the edge of her desk. It took a second for her to retrieve one, open it, and hold it to his lips. He sipped a little, then a little more before he shook his head negatively and closed his lips firmly.

She set the can on his desk, then turned back to him. There was a slight buzzing noise that became louder. She jumped and swung around. One of the drones was coming right at her. She flung her arm out and, more by luck than skill, struck it, knocking it to the floor. It buzzed a bit, then started to regain its feet.

Sophie cried, "No you don't!" She jumped forward and came down on the thing with her left foot. Without pausing, she ran on to the door. There were two more coming through the threshold crack. She stepped on both of them, then ripped off her sweater and shoved it as tightly as she could into the gap.

It didn't plug the entire space, but some waste paper worked just as well for the remainder of the opening.

She stood up, shaking in panic. The drones were in the house, and they wouldn't leave voluntarily. She'd have to smash them all. There was no way she could rid the place of potentially hundreds of tiny assassins.

When she turned around, Cal was sitting upright, leaning on his desk.

He moved his arm weakly and said, "I think that shot helped. I feel a little better now."

Sophie rushed back to him. "I can't kill all of them. They could be hiding anywhere to fly out and get us. I can't get them all; they're too little, they -- "

He interrupted her. "Calm down. The drones are most likely linked by means of a radio signal. Didn't they seem to be coordinated—working together?"

She considered it for a moment. That might be the case. If so, they had to communicate somehow. What if she used their equipment to...?

She sat at Cal's workstation. His machine had a modified bluetooth transmitter that allowed him to control it from as far away as the kitchen. She opened the driver and adjusted the transmission strength to the maximum. It was lucky he wrote most of his own software. The man was a prodigy in many ways. There was an interface program that linked to the transmitter/receiver so he could analyze every device's signal.

Sophie sighed. She'd been aware that Cal didn't trust any off-the-shelf equipment. His propensity to check everything before using it was handy. Now all she had to do was to scan the available frequencies.

There it was. There was a lot of data being exchanged at the high end of the spectrum. She stood and walked over to the door, carrying the empty syringe.

She pulled the plunger out, removed and discarded the needle, then bent to move some of the paper she'd shoved in the threshold crack. A drone crawled through the gap immediately.

Sophie exclaimed, "Got you," and popped the open end of the syringe over it. It buzzed up into the empty tube. She plugged the crack again, then carefully shoved the plunger into the tube while the drone was exploring the tiny hole at the other end. It was trapped.

The syringe lay on the desk by the blue-tooth transmitter while she analyzed the signals.

Finally, she tapped some code into the interface software buffer, then hesitated, her finger over the enter key. She leaned down to watch the drone and pressed the key.

It instantly stopped moving. She carefully pulled the plunger and tipped it out on the desktop. The thing was inert. She'd turned it off.

She walked to the door and pulled the paper out of the gap. There was no activity.

She pulled her sweater out of the crack. It had trapped a thick line of the tiny machines, their legs caught in the fibers. None of them showed any action.

"Cal, I think I've turned them all off. I've got the transmitter on maximum. How far does it go?"

He replied, "You'd better scale it back. You're probably messing with people's computers and phones all over the neighborhood. It covers the whole house and more."

THE HALLWAY FLOOR was covered with inert drones. She swept them up and funneled them into an empty milk jug. The hall window had several thousand more jammed between the glass and the screen. It took two milk jugs to store them all. There were probably some that had fallen to the ground outside, but she wasn't going to try to get them.

The drone invasion was over, and she was safe unless Hazelton or whoever it was sent more. If they did, she'd just turn them off too.

They'd probably have to move somewhere else. Their location was compromised. The first thing to worry about was Cal. He was better, but still running a 103-degree fever.

CHAPTER 6
BIO-WEAPON

Sophie rummaged around in the bathroom medicine cabinet but didn't find what she wanted. Her opiates were good at relieving pain, but what Cal needed was something to reduce his fever.

There was nothing in the medicine cabinet and nothing in the vanity cabinet under the sink. She stood up and frowned at her reflection in the mirror. Cal was always so prepared. He seemed to think of everything. Where would he have stored something like aspirin?

Inspiration struck her, and she planted her left palm on her forehead in exasperation. She should have looked in the supply cabinet where she got the antibiotic. Turning, she dashed down the hall.

She fumbled through a couple of shelves, then found several bottles of over-the-counter NSAIDs. She selected one and ran back to where he was lying.

He didn't look well. His complexion had an odd yellowish tinge. She took out four of the pills and got him to take them.

He struggled to swallow, coughing a little. Some of the water sprayed on her hand and arm.

She brushed at it, ignoring her passing thought that she was almost certainly exposed to whatever it was that had made him sick. That didn't matter. Without him, she wouldn't know what to do. She'd be lost, and the only thing she knew to turn to was Oxy. She thought about going and taking a pill but restrained herself.

Really! The drug had betrayed her. To be fair, it had led her to betray herself. Couldn't she just generate enough will-power to concentrate on helping Cal, rather than feeling sorry for herself?

She ran back to the bathroom and soaked a hand towel in cold water, then wrung it over the sink. She folded it as she walked back to him and carefully laid it on his forehead.

He moaned in response but didn't open his eyes.

She drew up her work chair and sat watching him.

An interminable time later, Cal opened his eyes and struggled to sit up.

Sophie had thought she was watching, but she must have been drowsing. The noise he made startled her and she jumped to her feet in alarm.

He held his hand out to her for help, and she pulled as hard as she could. He slowly sat upright in response.

"Sophie, I need to get to bed. I feel like I've been run over by a truck, but what you gave me helps a little. I think I can make it to my bedroom if you help. Okay?"

He grabbed the edge of his desk and levered himself to his knees. Then he tried to stand but failed. He leaned against the desk, breathing hard.

Sophie shoved his chair against the back of his legs and said, "Sit down. I'll roll you to your bedroom."

He was hard to push. His feet kept dragging the chair off-course. He didn't have enough strength to control them.

Once they had reached the bedroom, she heaved him forward onto his bed. She tried to think how best to move him. He wasn't helping at all now.

Finally, she hauled his legs onto the mattress and then dragged him until he was roughly straight on the bed. She covered him with a blanket and then sat down in his chair, trying to regain her breath.

She stood back up and walked quickly down the hall to get the thermometer. He had a higher fever again. She wondered if she should give him more of the antibiotic. She didn't know if it was possible to overdose on the stuff. He was heavy, so maybe she hadn't given him a very large dose for his size.

She mixed up another syringe of the yellowish-orange powder and injected it into his other shoulder. Then she got out more of the anti-pyretic pills. That was no good since he was unconscious. She couldn't get him to wake up to take the things.

The whole thing suddenly weighed on her unbearably. Cal was going to need hospitalization. She couldn't do anything for him with her limited knowledge. On the other hand, she knew that going to the hospital was something that he wouldn't want to do. He was extremely protective of his identity, and she didn't even know if he had insurance. She was fairly sure that they wouldn't treat him if he didn't have any.

What to do? She walked down the hall again, intending to go to the bathroom and then on to the kitchen for some food. It was strange, but she was hungry. Ravenous, in fact. A thought struck her as she passed her bedroom.

Could her hunger be the result of whatever it was? She must have been exposed to it just by helping him, even though the drones hadn't bitten her.

They hadn't had a chance to bite her, had they? She thought about it. She wasn't sure. They'd been right against her neck and hand. Was it possible that she'd gotten some of the stuff inside her when she'd swatted the things?

Somehow she found herself standing in front of her dresser. She'd moved into the bedroom as she worried. Now the pill bottle was in her hand. She moved to set it back down but then hesitated.

One more couldn't hurt, surely?

There was a pill in her hand. Sophie couldn't remember opening the bottle, but there it was. She swallowed it dry, then quickly opened the bottle and took two more out. They somehow ended up in her mouth also.

She set the bottle down and shakily walked to the kitchen. There were some energy bars in the cabinet. She pulled out the box and started to open them.

The pills hit her like a ton of bricks. She found herself sitting on the floor with a silly smile on her face. She didn't feel bad. Everything was nice and warm and fuzzy. It had been so long since she'd felt like this. Why hadn't she been taking more of the little beauties all along? Cal would understand. Cal was a great guy...No! Cal was sick. What was she doing here while he was sick in his bed?

She climbed to her feet and carefully walked back to his bedroom. The walls seemed to slide by oddly, but she reached his door and turned the corner into the room.

She was standing by his bed. She blurrily thought that Cal didn't look well. There was something about his face...She leaned over, bracing herself on the mattress with her hands.

His face was bloody! There was blood leaking from his eyes and nose.

"God!" she said. "What can I do? Cal? Cal, how can I help?"

He didn't answer. She took the damp towel and wiped at his face, swiping randomly at the blood. It didn't stop leaking.

He coughed, and blood came from his mouth. It looked like a lot, but she couldn't concentrate well. A thought struck her. She grabbed the thermometer and held it on his head. It beeped, forcing her to gather the courage to look at it. The display was bright red. His temperature was 107.

She fell backward into the chair. One hundred and seven! She tried to think. That was way too high. He couldn't live with that temperature. It would cause brain damage if he had it very long.

What could she do? She stood and stumbled towards the kitchen. Maybe some ice...

She came back with a bowl full of ice and water.

Cal wasn't moving. She couldn't tell if he was breathing or not. There was more blood on the bed.

She pulled at him, trying to roll him onto his side. That way, the blood would clear his mouth when he coughed.

When she'd gotten him positioned as best she could, another problem appeared. She noticed a sudden wave of odor. The blanket was stained. She lowered her head and sniffed to make sure, then jerked back. The smell was awful. His bowels had emptied, and the mess had leaked through his pants.

She tried to listen to his chest. There was nothing. Desperate, she grabbed the bowl of ice water and poured it over his head and torso.

He didn't respond. There was no movement, not even a slight flinch.

She stood there, her eyes wide in horror. It couldn't be! He'd been so big; so vital and full of life. He must still be alive.

She put her ear against his chest, listening.

Silence.

Cal was dead.

SOPHIE COLLAPSED INTO the chair, shaking. She was too horrified to cry. The only thing that kept her together was the heavy dose of Oxy. She sat there in a daze.

After a long time, she began to think. The disease or whatever it was had killed him as surely as a bullet. She hadn't had any symptoms, or had she?

A sudden suspicion caused her to place the thermometer on her forehead. She had to force herself to look at it when it beeped.

She had it! Her temperature was one hundred and four. But... but, she didn't feel bad. She hadn't lost consciousness, and she wasn't bleeding from her eyes or nose.

She stood and covered Cal's body with the blanket, then ambled to her room. The pill bottle beckoned, and she took two more, then laid down on her bed to wait for the deadly symptoms.

After a few minutes, she sat up. She couldn't relax while whatever it was killed her. She'd have to try something. Perhaps if she took a mega-dose of the antibiotic that had seemed to help Cal, it would stop the illness.

She stood up slowly. The room was a little fuzzy. Maybe another pill would help. She wasn't in much pain, but then she didn't want to suffer the way Cal had.

After she'd swallowed the pill, she stuck the bottle in her pocket. If things got really bad, when she was sure she was dying, she'd just take all of them. That would stop her breathing, and she'd check out without having to suffer so much.

WALKING WAS DIFFICULT. Her goal was the medical supplies, but the hallway seemed to have gotten much longer. A couple of times she found herself leaning against the wall trying to remember what she was doing.

She finally got to the workroom and started across. Things got blurry then. When she refocused, she was somehow sitting in Cal's chair.

She squinted at the monitor. His Wi-Fi-sniffer program was still running. She'd disabled the drones with it. She remembered that. She must have forgotten to stop it.

The funny thing was, the sniffer was still showing some Wi-Fi activity. It was on a different frequency than the drones, but it was actively sending and receiving data, although at a slow rate.

She leaned forward, trying to think. If she captured some of the data and looked at it in an editor, perhaps she could tell what was happening.

The transmissions were fairly simple, she thought, looking at a string of hex-codes. The code almost looked like it was parsed from a language. She'd seen something like it before.

She laid her head down on the desk. She felt hot, and her nose was running. She wiped at it absently, then looked at her fingers. They were covered with blood. The sight galvanized her.

She sat up and concentrated again. The data was undoubtedly a language. It was...then it clicked. She gasped in surprise. It was the CRISPR control language or, she suddenly realized, a variant of it. She'd studied it enough to recognize some of the hex commands.

If that was what it was, and she was relatively sure she was correct, then maybe it was the Hazelton bio-nanomachines. She was infected with the nanites, and they were making her sick. She didn't know what they were trying to do to her, but Cal's symptoms had been similar to some fast-acting hemorrhagic fever.

She looked around in panic. The thermometer was in her pocket. With shaking hands, she applied it to her forehead.

The display was bright red. She was now running a hundred and five degrees. Judging from Cal, she didn't have much time. She started to take more pills, but then stopped.

She had turned the drones off by broadcasting a control sequence. What about the nanites? They were receiving command signals from somewhere and transmitting some data back in return.

The CRISPR language had a standby command that would idle the system. She switched the sniffer program to broadcast and keyed in the sequence, then waited.

She couldn't tell that anything had happened. Her head still hurt. Perhaps it hadn't worked.

She checked the sniffer's data analysis mode. The transmissions were now one-sided. What did that mean?

She decided that maybe she'd put the nanites in standby mode, but the controlling data stream was still coming. What if it reactivated the tiny machines in her bloodstream?

Sophie stood and headed over to her workstation. The Reverb unit was sitting there. She looked at it with suspicion. She'd turned it off when she had finished showing her work to Cal. She was sure of it.

What if the switch wasn't actually connected? What if the thing was designed to be on permanently?

With a sudden surge of hatred, she slammed it on the floor. The case cracked. She grabbed the monitor from her desk and pounded the Reverb with the heavy, flat screen. Both devices broke, and pieces slid across the tile.

She kept pounding until the Reverb unit was nothing but broken bits. The monitor was in almost as bad a shape. She dropped it and straightened up, noticing that she'd cut her hand somehow.

Back to Cal's desk. The data flow had stopped. She checked the sniffer's display twice to make sure. The Reverb had been the source of the control signal. Somehow Hazelton had located them, sent the micro-drones to infect them with the nanites, then broadcast the signal through the Reverb unit to control the tiny machines.

When she reached that point in her thinking, she rechecked the sniffer. Still no activity, however, the nanites were still inside her. She knew that they could be reactivated. She'd have to either get rid of them or live her life in fear that she'd come in signal range of another device. What if Hazelton was broadcasting the activation signal from every Reverb unit out there? The damned things were in nearly every household.

She'd just have to figure out how to get rid of the nanites, or, a sudden idea struck her, maybe she could co-opt them with code that she could create.

She wanted to start programming immediately, but then the practicality of the situation struck her. She might be able to send commands to the things using the CRISPR language, but she had no idea what that would do to her body.

Her hands stole up to the keyboard of Cal's computer, but she pulled them back. Instead, she applied the thermometer to her forehead again. Her temperature was down to one hundred and two. She took careful stock of her physical condition. Her nose seemed to have stopped bleeding. She was still fuzzy from the opiates, but she'd been there before. She hadn't taken a fatal dose, and she knew she would survive until the effect wore off.

SHE SLOWLY STOOD, hesitated, then walked back to her room and lay down. She'd sleep for a while and maybe this would turn out to have been a bad dream.

CHAPTER 7
MONSTER

Sophie sat up. Her nose wasn't bloody, and she didn't feel feverish. The Oxy had mostly worn off, so it had been some hours. Now she needed to go to work. Then she remembered Cal.

What was she to do? He was too large for her to remove his body by herself. She couldn't just call the ambulance. There would be no possible explanation the authorities would accept. Even the truth was pretty much unbelievable.

She'd have to do something, though. She couldn't just leave his body where it was. Her mind raced, then she remembered the dumpster in the alley. It would be awful to just stick him in there, but there wouldn't be anyone to see, and if his body were found, people would assume that he was one of the many homeless that wandered the streets.

The only problem was getting him down there. She decided to let that issue sit in the back of her mind for a while. Meanwhile, she needed to figure out how to rid herself of the nanite threat.

A FEW HOURS later, she had made progress. She was sitting in front of Cal's computer using the sniffer program to interface with the invasive machines. She'd activated the ones in her body, then turned them off again. They weren't automatically harmful. With no ill-intentioned instructions, the things just seemed to broadcast a periodic status that indicated they were awaiting a command.

Sophie had found the language manual and was trying to figure out a way to deactivate the things. They were capable of self-movement along with being able to manipulate proteins in her body. She found the scale of the machines difficult to imagine. They were tiny, almost molecular in size.

In desperation, she'd started reading the Hazelton files that Cal had on his machine. He had only gotten through half of them before he'd died. She scanned as quickly as she could, looking for information on the nanites.

She found what she was looking for a little after midnight. It was in the next to last folder. The nanites used a slightly modified version of the CRISPR control language. The language was designed to split and splice genes. The nanite version had additional commands that provided for movement and other functions.

The interesting thing was that the devices had been designed to keep a human healthy by default. They were only dangerous when they received specific commands.

She returned to bed, exhausted. The idea that she was close to a solution made her want to keep reading, but the words were blurring on the screen.

Sophie was so tired that she forgot to even think about her pills. She closed her eyes and fell asleep.

As she slept, her mind worked overtime. Visions of tiny nanites working in her body haunted her dreams. If they could keep her healthy, they could be a benefit, but like any technology, they were a double-edged sword. They could kill. That had been horribly demonstrated to her. She dreamed of finding some form of revenge for Cal. The people who had come up with this horror needed to pay.

THE PLACE WAS quiet when she woke up. Cal was usually around, either making noise in the kitchen or tapping on his keyboard. Sophie missed the sounds.

She cleaned up in the bathroom and got dressed before going to the kitchen. Somehow during the night, she'd come up with a possible solution to her nanite problem, but she still hadn't figured out how to move Cal's body.

Down the hall to the workroom, trying to ignore Cal's door. She straightened up the mess, sweeping up the remains of the Reverb unit and the monitor, then sat in front of Cal's computer.

Her nanites were still in standby mode, awaiting instructions. Now, with the Hazelton manual, she fed them commands with a greater sense of security. The tiny machines went to work on her body, helping to flush out the damage of the previous day. She felt better minute by minute.

Their abilities and command structure was described in the manual. Sophie read through it, stopping to make notes and study individual commands. By mid-afternoon, she was ready to try some things.

The first thing for her to do was to change the nanites' activation code. When that was done, only she could activate them. They didn't have a very complex sequence, so it could eventually be hacked, but she wasn't planning on giving anyone the chance to keep sending commands to her nanites until they stumbled on the correct password to take them over.

The second thing she did was to place them in a defensive mode. They would automatically eliminate other nanites that invaded her body unless the newcomers were programmed with her new activation sequence. She hoped that would keep her safe. Hazelton couldn't simply re-infect her now.

FEELING GOOD ABOUT her progress, Sophie decided she was hungry and headed towards the kitchen. When she passed Cal's door, there was a faint noise. She froze, listening with chills of horror sliding up her spine.

There it was again. A faint groan.

She ripped his door open.

Cal, or what had been Cal was partly off the bed. His body was lumpy and misshapen. He barely looked human. One eye was gone; there was an odd growth of flesh in its place. His nose was distorted and leaking a stream of mucus that covered his left cheek.

The rest of his body hadn't escaped the nanite-induced changes. His hands looked as if the bones had been dissolved and his legs were shorter than they had been, although they looked relatively normal.

He looked at Sophie and made an incoherent noise.

She screamed in response and fright.

He opened his lips as if to speak, but his tongue flopped out limply, hanging down in a misshapen point.

She couldn't comprehend the changes. He'd been dead. Definitely dead, but now he was moving. The damned nanites had turned him into a monster.

She stepped back, preparing to slam the door, but he held up one hand with a floppy motion and made a noise that sounded like a distorted, "Sophie."

She stopped then.

"Cal, do you understand me?" she asked.

He nodded.

"Oh, God! What am I going to do?" She had no idea how to help him. Perhaps she could reprogram the nanites to convert him back, but, not knowing what they'd done to him, it seemed as if it would be impossible to reverse the process.

Cal slowly and with great effort moved back on to the bed. Then he made another attempt to speak. It sounded as if he were talking while holding the tip of his tongue between his teeth.

"Sooophiee, it's still me. Whatever Hazelton sent after us is dangerous. My hands..." Here he held up his hands, demonstrating that they were limp bags of flesh.

He continued. "You're in danger. You should get away before you catch this stuff. I hurt something awful."

He wiped at his closed eye with the back of his left wrist, recoiling when his wrist encountered the mass of tissue that covered the eye.

"Whaaat?" he mumbled as he tried to use his hand to feel the lump.

Sophie had almost recovered. It was evident that he wasn't aware of some of the worst changes he'd undergone. She wasn't sure what she should tell him, but then she realized that he'd find out shortly.

"They sent nanites. The damned drones were full of them. I don't know how you survived. I thought you were dead. You weren't breathing, and I couldn't hear a heartbeat. Your eye is messed up and a lot of your body also. We're going to have to work hard to try and reprogram the nasty little things."

He interrupted her next sentence. "I need some pain meds. I feel like I've been run over by a truck. Please let me have some of your pills."

Her hand dipped instantly into her pocket. The bottle was nearly empty; only ten left. She held out two to him, but he couldn't make his hands cooperate.

Tentatively, she pushed the little white tablets between his lips. His tongue didn't work correctly, and one popped back out. She bent, picked it up, wiped it, and shoved it deeper into his mouth with her finger.

There was a water bottle on the nightstand; something Cal insisted on, in case he was thirsty during the night. She held it to his lips, and he gulped a few swallows.

She said, "Those should take effect in a few minutes. They'll make you feel better."

"How did you avoid catching this stuff?" he asked, slowly.

"Uh...well...I think I did catch it. I started running a fever, and then my nose started bleeding. By then you were dead...I mean I thought you were dead. I started taking my pills. I was going to take them all so I'd just die quickly."

She looked at him, her eyes wide. "I couldn't stand the thought of going through what I'd seen you go through. Then I thought about taking a mega-dose of that antibiotic I gave you. It seemed to help you, so I...anyway I ended up in your chair. The Wi-Fi sniffer program was still running from when I'd used it on the drones, and it was showing data traffic. Different frequency from them, though."

He looked at her, his single eye fixed on her face. "What did you do then?"

She continued. "I started trying to analyze the data flow. It was bi-directional. I eventually recognized it. Something nearby was sending commands in that CRISPR language I've been studying in my spare time."

"That? What the hell could be sending those kinds of commands?" He paused, then said, "Oh, I see. You realized the disease was caused by nanites and something was controlling them. Right?"

She nodded. "Yes. I sent them the standby command using the sniffer program. Then I guessed the commands were coming from the Reverb unit. I smashed it. Hazelton must have tracked us, and the Reverb made a good relay."

He said, "Wait a minute. What about the house Wi-Fi? My router is the path for the Reverb...but they shouldn't be able to get into that. It only accesses the net through the VPN, and that's pretty hard to trace. I don't think they could backtrack and find it."

He paused, then groaned making a dark, painful sounding noise.

"I'm not getting anything out of those two pills. How about more?"

She dutifully dug out two more and fed them to him in the same way as before. There were only six left. She'd meant to ask

Cal to get some more for her, but she'd wanted to wait until she was out to test her self-resolve.

"I thought about that. I think the Wi-Fi signal is coming from somewhere outside the building. The neighbor's maybe. I—Oh!" She jumped at the realization.

"I found the nanite commands in the Hazelton files. I reprogrammed mine so that the activation code is different. You still have the original programming. That external signal may still be controlling yours. I need to get you into the workroom where I can use the sniffer. Maybe I can reverse the effects. I can turn them off at the least."

He made an effort and sat on the edge of the bed. She jumped out of his work chair and held it where he could slide onto the seat.

She shoved the chair down the hall and into the workroom. It was a little easier this time since he was able to control his feet. Once they were set up by his workstation, Sophie started the sniffer program again. It showed a very attenuated signal, but there was still some data that was being passed back and forth.

"Cal, it's still controlling the nanites. I don't know what the things are trying to do to you, but I'm going to shut them off and reprogram their access. That'll stop the changes in your body."

He sat while she tapped on the keyboard.

"That does it. The data link is shut down. The external signal is still trying to send stuff. If the code has a monitoring routine in it, it will alert Hazelton that the nanites aren't responding any longer. I hope that won't mean they'll think that we disabled the things."

"That's the way I'd have written the code. They're probably scratching their heads wondering what went wrong with the nanites right now," he said. Then he added, "I still hurt like crazy. I think I need more pills."

Sophie's hand shook as she opened the bottle. The remaining six white pills dropped onto the floor. She fell to her knees and gathered them up as quickly as she could.

Cal said, "You know I wouldn't ask if I didn't really need them. I hate to take them from you."

She stuck two more between his lips in response, then held the bottle up for him to drink.

"Look, Cal, I'm glad to give them to you. I really shouldn't need the things; it's just that..." She sniffed, then wiped her eyes. "It's just that I've been taking them so long. Also, I took a bunch of them when I was getting sick. I think that kicked up my addiction. I feel like I need more right now, myself."

He muttered something to himself, then said more clearly, "There's cash in my top drawer. Also, a pistol. I'm telling you this because I know you're going to be driven to get more Oxy. You can get it from your old supplier. He's still in the area. Just be careful. Take the gun. I need for you to come back in one piece."

She nodded in response. "I'm not going anywhere right now. There are still four pills left, and I have a half of one in my pocket. Uh...You know...for emergencies." She laughed shakily. "I guess this counts as an emergency, doesn't it?"

He made a horrible sound that startled her before she realized that it was an attempt at laughter.

"Look, kid, we probably don't have much time before Hazelton sends someone to check on what's going on. The lack of response from the nanites has to have been noticed by them."

She bent to the keyboard. "I'm going to try and set yours to undo the damage you've suffered. I'm not sure how that would work, though. It's not like the little things have any memory about the changes they've induced. They must have changed parts of your genes, but I don't know what."

Sophie realized that she was babbling in confusion. Her sense of urgency was so strong that she had keyed in a series of commands before she realized what she was doing. She pulled up, her finger on the enter key.

"If I send this command string to your nanites, they'll activate and work to repair any damage they find. It's just that I don't know if they'll recognize their own changes as damage or just work to keep the changes in place. What should I do?"

"Send it," he groaned. "I still hurt, and it's bad. The pills have eased it a bit, but I'm going to need more before I can bear it for very long. Anything will be better than what I'm going through. If you kill me, it'll be a relief."

She drew a deep breath and pressed the key. It clicked, but there was no immediate result.

Suddenly Cal convulsed, his large body jerked and he fell out of the chair. He lay on the floor breathing heavily for a moment, then groaned.

"That hurt. Let's not do it again until we know what the damned things are doing to me. Okay?"

She asked, "Do you want some more Oxy?"

He opened his mouth in answer. She bent and placed two more pills on his tongue, noticing as she did that there were only two left.

"Cal? I'm going to have to get more of these. Are they helping you at all?"

He sighed, then said, "Yeah. A little. They've taken the edge off the pain. If you're out, you'd better try to score some more. I don't like you going to see that guy, but I'm going to need more pills or else I'm going to have to have you shoot me. I don't think I can stand this for long."

She helped him into the chair and pushed him back into his bedroom, then helped him onto the bed. He lay there, breathing heavily.

Sophie stood looking at him. She'd been ignoring the horrible changes he'd undergone, but suddenly the impact struck her, and she began to cry, her head bowed and her shoulders shaking.

Cal said, "Quit it. I know I'm a mess, but feeling bad won't help. I've got to have you be strong for me. Can you do it?"

Sophie sobbed, then hiccuped. "Y—yes, I'll be strong for you. Don't worry. I'll figure out how to fix you, no matter how long it takes."

He laughed again—a rasping, deep sound. "Better get going, then."

THERE WAS A wad of hundreds and twenties in the drawer. The pistol was small. It was a .380 Colt. She released the magazine and saw that it was loaded, then struggled to pull the slide back.

Cal said, "Cock the hammer first. That'll make the slide easier to rack. The spring's too strong for you. That's all."

She followed his instructions. The chamber was empty, but when she released the slide, it snapped a round into firing position.

Cal said, "Carefully use your thumb to lower the hammer."

She fumbled with the pistol, and he added, "Just hold the hammer tightly, so it doesn't drop and pull the trigger. That's it. Let it down. That way you won't shoot yourself. The thing has a safety, but it's kind of easy to slip it off by accident."

He watched her carefully, his single eye running a continuous stream of fluid beside his nose.

"That's right. Just remember to cock it again when you're ready to shoot." He lay back, acting as if he were exhausted.

Sophie shoved the pistol into her pocket and said, "I'll be back as quickly as I can."

CHAPTER 8
DANGEROUS BUSINESS

Sophie hadn't been on the street for weeks. The sunlight was watery and the day was partly overcast, but it still seemed bright to her. She walked a couple of blocks before she got her bearings, then headed for the area where Raul could often be found.

There were a group of kids playing some game that involved kicking cans at a target or something. It was noisy. She glanced around. A few people were strolling along as if they had nowhere to go and all of the moments in forever to get there. A stray miniature poodle sat just inside an alley, watching her. She glanced at it. It was a friendly looking white dog with no collar. It sat there panting in the heat, but then stood and retreated into the shadow of a building. She continued onward, focused on Raul.

The closer she got to his area of operations, the fewer the people she saw. That made sense. You didn't want to be around if something happened to go wrong with a drug deal. She knew that from stories she'd heard.

A couple of blocks away from his headquarters, she saw one of his lieutenants leaning against a streetlight. Juan was one of the more frightening members of the group. He had two tears tattooed on his right cheek, below the corner of his eye. She knew that meant that he'd killed before. She'd always tried to steer clear of him.

When she'd stayed at Raul's before, Juan had made advances while Raul was out. She'd managed to put him off but had never told Raul. She was afraid of what would happen if she did.

Juan saw her coming and apparently recognized her. His rotten teeth showed, and he straightened up.

"Hey, Chiquita! You 'cide that maybe Juan's Okay? Hows 'bout we go down the alley for some privacy, huh?" He smirked at the thought.

Sophie was shaking both with fear and anger. What was wrong with men? They always gave her this kind of treatment.

"No. All I need is a score. I don't have time for anything else, Juan."

He snickered, "Maybe's you have to pay for it with a little play time."

She asked, "Do you have any Oxy?"

He looked both directions and then said, "Yeah. In my ride. I got way more than you can pay for." He paused, then asked, "You got moneys?"

She nodded, mutely.

He started down the street, heading for an older Chevy that looked as if the body was sitting flat on the pavement. Once there, he opened the back door to reveal a briefcase. It was full of bags of white pills."

Sophie was startled and said, "My God, Juan. That's a lot of product. Where'd you get that much?"

His expression made her wish she hadn't asked, but then he grinned and said, "Yeah. Lots, ain't it? I hit a couple of pharmacias last night. Did good, too. Raul, he never give you so much, huh? Maybe you think better of me now, huh?"

"How much for a bag?" she asked.

Juan looked at her breasts, then dropped his gaze slowly to her groin.

"Maybe not so much. How bad you want 'em, huh?"

Sophie quivered, feeling as if her skin were crawling.

She said, "Dollar a milligram, right?"

Juan nodded. "That's street. Might give you a little discount for services rendered."

She pulled her courage together and smiled at him, stepping close enough that her breasts brushed his arm. He tried to grab her, but she stepped back quickly.

"Look, Juan, I really don't have time right now, but maybe later, okay? Just give me, say, four hundred at street and we'll talk about the discount later."

He pulled back, frowning. "How'ja get four hunnret? Whats you been doin' to get that much?"

When she didn't answer, he grabbed her arm and shoved her into the front seat despite her attempt to resist.

"I gives you the four hunnert on sale. You gives me three seventy-five dinero and a BJ. We talk about more tomorrow or next day," he snarled, pushing her over to the passenger side.

He bent over and slid into the car, unzipped his pants, then turned to her with an anticipatory grin.

His grin froze and dropped off his face. Sophie was holding the little pistol pointing directly at his groin.

She calmly said, "I'll give you a BJ alright. I'll blow it right off. Now reach back there and get me that briefcase and don't try any moves."

She momentarily marveled at herself. Where had she gotten so strong? She'd never have dared to object before. Perhaps it was the thought of Cal suffering that gave her courage. She didn't know.

He moved to lift the bag. She watched cautiously.

As the bag cleared the back of the seat, he swung it at her, trying to strike her face.

Sophie jerked the trigger, then flinched at the loud bang. Juan made a cry that was somewhere between a scream and a groan. He dropped the bag into the space between them and fell back against the door.

Sophie said, "You shouldn't have tried that. I told you I'd shoot you."

He groaned and said, "You rotten bitch! Didn't tink you do it."

A sudden gush of blood came out of his mouth. He coughed wetly.

Sophie stared in alarm. She'd meant to shoot him in the leg. Leg wounds don't make people bleed out of their mouths. Then she saw the blood running down his chest. She'd somehow flinched and jerked the pistol up. She looked around at the street. Two cars were passing by, but not a single pedestrian was in sight. Apparently, no one had noticed the shot.

Juan's head drooped, and then he slid down into the space below the steering wheel. Sophie didn't wait to see if he was dead. She grabbed the briefcase, carefully safed the pistol, shoved it into her pocket again and climbed out onto the sidewalk.

As she started to shut the car door, she noticed the expended shell casing on the floor. She stuck it in her pocket with the pistol. No sense leaving something that might have a fingerprint on it. That thought made her pause.

She grabbed Juan's shoe, pulled it off and tugged at his sock. The sock smelled like it was overdue for a wash, but she gritted her teeth and pulled it off. Then she wiped every surface that she could remember touching. She thought her fingerprints were on file somewhere, and she didn't want them to be found here. She wiped the door handle, tossed the sock back inside, and shoved the door shut with her hip.

The street was still deserted. Most of the storefronts in this area were boarded up, and the ones that weren't were farther down. She turned and set off in the opposite direction.

The walk back to Cal's place seemed twice as long as the walk going out. Several times she had to restrain herself from running. She realized that would make her look more suspicious, but it was hard to resist increasing her pace.

She heard a police siren blocks away and sprinted forward for three or four steps before she regained control.

She fumbled with the lock on Cal's door. It couldn't open fast enough to suit her. Once inside, she locked the door and ran upstairs to Cal.

"I got a whole bag of pills. I—I think I killed him, though," she said as she came through the door.

Cal made a snorting noise and jerked his head around to look at her.

"Killed who?" he asked.

She said, "Juan. It was Juan. He had the pills. He's one of Raul's main guys. He was always hitting on me, but I stayed away from him. He was too scary. He tried to hit me with the pill bag and, I...I guess I pulled the trigger by mistake. Anyway, he's dead."

"Well, that don't matter. What matters is, did you get back without being seen and are you alright?"

Sophie drew in her breath and answered, "There was nobody on the street, and I don't think I was noticed, but what really matters is do you need any more pills right now?"

He said, "Yeah. I could use about four or five more of 'em. I'm really hurting."

"What if you overdose and die? You've taken a lot of them in the past hour. I don't know how many are too much for your body size," she said.

"Just give me five more. I don't care if I die. It'd be a relief. I don't want to live looking like a deformed monster, and I hurt like hell too," he answered.

Once he took the additional pills, they seemed to take effect quickly. She could see him relax. His misshapen body went limp, and he lay back on the bed.

Sophie bent over him, listening. His breathing was slow and shallow but showed no signs of stopping. She looked at his face. She hadn't meant to, but she inadvertently turned her head as she straightened up and saw the mass of tissue that had replaced his eye.

Up close, it was even worse than she'd thought. Her breath caught in a sob. Cal had been so vital and attractive in a brute-force kind of way. Now, it had become painful to look at him. If she didn't know him from before, she would call him a monster.

She backed away quietly. She simply had to figure out how to get the nanites to reverse the damage. Only she didn't know what they'd done. If there was just a way to make him more human looking. Maybe the language manual would provide some hints. If not, she'd read through all of the files they'd downloaded in the hopes that there might be a hint in them.

She closed his door and headed down the hall to the workroom. A new sense of resolve filled her. For once, she was thinking about someone else rather than her own problems.

As she sat down, it occurred to her that someone was going to have to pay for what they'd done to him. She was going to make sure that they did. Only, she didn't know who was responsible or how to find them.

CHAPTER 9
INVASION

Sophie sat and read, then read some more. The language manual, while complete, didn't provide any way to reverse unknown actions. She'd have to understand the original program the nanites were executing to try to reverse it. Only there was no copy of it unless she could hack into Hazelton again and locate the code.

She considered the situation. They'd been kicked out the last time they were in the target system. She had no illusions that she was as good as Cal. Her lack of experience was troublesome. She was much better than a script-kiddie, but still not an actual cracker.

Breaking in again didn't seem to be an option. Even if she got in, she wouldn't have time to research every possibility. She'd be better off forgetting that idea for the time being. Maybe she'd have to get some kind of job at the corporation and work from within.

Despite not finding the information she wanted, there was a report that described the nanites. The tiny machines were composed of biological molecules, mixed with inorganic parts that allowed them to communicate with each other via digital data packets. They could cooperate and act as a swarm when modifying the host organism's DNA.

The nanites weren't limited to changing DNA. They could interfere with proteins. There was a section of the report that described how they could block the calcium channel that facilitated heart action. This would cause almost instant death.

They could also create a subcutaneous antenna in their host. The antenna consisted of micro-fine iron wires. The metal was extracted from the blood's hemoglobin.

The more she read, the angrier she became. The nanites had the potential to remove cancerous cells. That was only given a passing mention, almost as if the author didn't care about such a benefit. The primary focus was directed at either killing or creating a way of controlling the affected individual.

The most useful thing she found was something she'd already used on Cal. The nanites could be set to maintain the biological system in the same state, preventing the organism from becoming ill.

He wouldn't get sick in the future, but he was already in so much pain that it didn't matter. Maybe he was right. He might be better off if the narcotic killed him.

She turned her attention to a way to work on Cal from a distance. She wasn't going to turn on any more Reverb units, that was for sure. They were too easily hijacked. On the other hand, Ralph units were in every room, and Ralph couldn't be co-opted due to Cal's security.

SHE OPENED RALPH'S app and added a section that would respond to specific voice commands. She let her imagination run free with the actual words. They were something she could remember, but no one else would be able to guess. That would keep others from sending control signals to the nanites. They'd have to know the language first.

It took several hours, but at the end the Ralph program was ready. She could say a series of apparently nonsense words and Ralph would respond by broadcasting the appropriate nanite commands. She could control the nanites verbally from any location where Ralph could hear her.

She realized with a guilty pang that she should have checked on Cal. The programming task had gone so well that she'd become immersed in the work.

She opened Cal's door. He was making a snoring sound, and his chest was moving with each breath. She closed the door quietly, then went back to the workroom.

As she walked down the hall, she passed the window. There was a layer of the inert mosquito-like drones lying between the screen and the glass. She ran back to the kitchen and got a plastic container and a knife.

Once she opened the window, the tiny bodies were easy to scrape up and deposit in the plastic box. She'd turned the drones off, but the nanites inside each one could be activated as a test of her system.

After making sure the container was sealed tightly, she addressed Ralph.

"Hey, Ralph, Initiate Act Sequence," she said in a chant-like rhythm. The mosquito-drones showed no sign of activity, but that didn't surprise her. The nanites were now active, but lacking instructions, they remained passive.

The language had a complete set of directional commands, and she used them next.

"Hey, Ralph, Initiate Vector Translate, 90-90-50." She intended to have the nanites move forward five centimeters.

She bent over the container and watched. There might have been a thin film of movement. She couldn't tell.

Raising her head, she addressed Ralph again.

"Hey, Ralph, AU-Glom."

That did it. The command for all units to conglomerate was followed by the nanites gradually moving into a lumpy, irregular spot. She could easily see the result without a microscope, although on close inspection, there didn't appear to be very many of them. The spot was only about a centimeter across.

Sophie rubbed her forehead. That was far less than she'd expected. On reflection, she realized that there were probably enough in that area to infect thousands of humans, especially since the nanites could reproduce themselves given sufficient time in a human host.

They didn't automatically replicate but once given the appropriate command they went about creating more units with a frightening efficiency using the host's resources as raw materials.

Sophie wondered briefly if the things, left unchecked, would convert a human body into nanites. It would be bad if they did, she thought. They could eventually kill everyone on the globe if they were allowed to replicate unchecked. Releasing the damned things was an act of gross irresponsibility.

The thought of the entire globe being infected with no way to give the nanites the stop command stimulated her mind, and she came up with the idea that Ralph, or something like him, would be needed everywhere. Ralph was a special case, but the Reverb system was rapidly gaining in popularity, and many households had proudly purchased the units. They were becoming an in-thing complete with enhanced social status. Many businesses used them, as did many public institutions.

The Reverb system would serve as her controllers. There were enough of the mass-marketed things out there that they provided an almost continuous fabric of control points in most of the major cities. That was what she'd do. She smiled in satisfaction at her decision.

Sophie immediately began working on a modification of the voice control app, tailoring it to the Reverb's specs. Once she'd finished, she paused, thinking. It was one thing to have the app, but making sure it was in all Reverbs was another. She'd have to write an undetectable virus for that purpose.

Some quick work with a search engine gave her the manufacturer's information. She noted with only a little surprise that the manufacturing company was partly owned by Hazelton. That figured.

The Reverb command interpretation engine was cloud-based, and she found a vulnerability to exploit. Surprisingly and rather stupidly, the code allowed her access to the language parsing software.

She used a variation of Cal's technique, placing a code word in the manufacturer's language parsing module. That word would pass control to the software that she'd placed on a public server. From that point, the command would be sent to one of Cal's private servers where it would be parsed. The result was sent back to the initiating Reverb unit causing it to broadcast the appropriate nanite controlling code.

It was late by the time she had finished. Her stomach was hurting, and she came to the conclusion that it was telling her she was hungry. She'd have to go to the kitchen and—Cal! She'd completely forgotten about him.

He was moving restlessly on his bed when she opened his door.

"Cal, how are you feeling? I'm sorry, I was busy and time slipped by. I meant to check on you earlier," she said.

"I hurt a lot, and I need food. What kept you busy?"

At least his curiosity wasn't damaged by his physical state.

"I was working on the nanites. I...I'm afraid that I can't figure out how to get them to reverse what they've done to you easily. I tried, but since I don't know what they did and I don't know how to begin to check your DNA for changes, I'm kind of stuck," she said.

She felt guilty that she hadn't worked more on Cal's problem, but it had seemed critical to gain control over the nanites. They were too dangerous to humanity in general. If Hazelton released them in a limited area, they either didn't care if the things escaped or perhaps..."

"Cal, would it be possible that Hazelton made the nanites to have a limited lifespan?" she asked.

He rolled over and worked to sit up, gradually getting both feet on the floor.

"Uh, yeah. I suppose they could, but how about the things replicating themselves? Wouldn't that mean they could just keep going?" he asked.

That was no help. Sophie concentrated on the problem, then said, "Well, yes. I guess they could unless maybe there was some built-in limit. I didn't notice anything in the downloaded reports, but then I wasn't looking. I'll have to go back and re-read everything, I guess."

He lifted one of his limp hands and flapped it at her.

"More pills first and also food. I hurt, but some of that may be simple hunger."

She'd helped him eat and had given him four more pills. She'd never seen anyone take so many, but they didn't seem to be working as well in his body as they should. Perhaps the nanites partly protected him against the opiate's effects. It certainly looked as if the drug had helped her resist the nanites' effects, at least to a small extent.

Back at the monitor again, Sophie scrolled rapidly through the downloaded text, scanning for any limitation to the nanites' replication ability.

The most likely spot was in the report on the nanites themselves, but there was nothing there. She scanned the remainder of the downloaded text. In the last document, there was a brief note about safeguards for the nanites. It referred to a document number that was much later in the sequence of the downloaded information.

They'd been kicked out of Hazelton's data before they'd managed to get all the files. They hadn't captured the document she wanted. That was inconvenient. She didn't dare try again, especially without Cal's help.

The only good thing was that Hazelton must be aware the nanites could create a real problem if they escaped. Surely they must have taken some steps to keep the things under control.

If there were a limit on their replication, it would most likely show up in Cal and also in her own body. She'd been slow to respond to them, but maybe they replicated more slowly in the presence of opiates. She could...she could check to see if her's were still active.

Since she'd placed them on standby and changed their control code, she hadn't thought about being infected. Activating them to carry out an unknown program in her body didn't seem like a very good idea if they were still able to function, a. She'd have to make sure they were working to help her before taking them off standby.

She looked through the language manual, started the communications sniffer program, then gave Ralph a command sequence.

"Hey, Ralph, Mon-ke-bus-AU-Act-Reportstat-Standby."

She snickered to herself as she watched the screen for activity. Anyone listening to her would think she was speaking a foreign language. The command activated her nanites, then requested that all units report their status before going into standby mode again.

She gradually relaxed. The sniffer program showed some reduced activity. It looked like the nanites were limited in some way she didn't understand. The ones in her bloodstream were responding but less active than they'd been initially. Perhaps that was because she'd only activated them, not given them commands. Either way, she was still infected.

She thoughtfully gave the standby command and watched the sniffer activity instantly drop to zero.

What would happen if she gave an all unit command to the small clump that she'd extracted from the drones? Their activation command was the original one.

"Hey, Ralph, Act-AU-Reportstat-Standby."

This time the sniffer showed a burst of activity then nothing. The nanobots had responded with a code that meant their status was nominal. They were still dangerous. She had appended the standby command to the end of the sequence, so now they were inactive again. That would be a sensible precaution to take every time they were activated, she thought.

She turned to the keyboard to exit the sniffer program but stopped in surprise. It was showing activity--a lot of activity.

CHAPTER 10
ATTACK

She stood and turned towards the hallway. There was a loud crash from the entry door at the far end of the hall, and she screamed in fear. A group of heavily armed men in black battle dress streamed through the door.

She looked down and saw several red dots on her chest. Sophie had seen enough movies to understand what that meant. She stood dead still, her hands partly raised.

The men raced through the place, checking each room. There was a yell when they opened Cal's door, and several of them ran inside. She could hear Cal's voice, but couldn't tell what he was saying. He could have been crying out in pain. All she knew was that two of the men were holding rifles pointed at her while they came down the hall.

She stared at the two as they came up. They were wearing balaclavas that mostly covered their faces. Each wore protective glasses of some type, but the lenses were clear. She could see their eyes. What she saw didn't reassure her.

The men's eyes were almost black. They didn't seem to have any iris surrounding their pupils, and the pupils were dark. Sophie didn't understand what that meant, but it was disconcerting to see.

One of the two said, "Sit down and sit still."

His voice was oddly mechanical. The lack of inflection made it sound like it came from a machine rather than a human.

She sat down in the chair, being careful to move slowly.

One of the men moved behind her while the other continued to watch from the front. The man behind reached around her and used zip-ties to attach her wrists to the chair arms. He tightened them to an uncomfortable degree, and she cried out in pain.

At her cry, the one in front raised his rifle so that the laser sight flashed in her eyes. She flinched and closed her eyes, expecting the worst.

Nothing happened. She waited, eyes squeezed shut, then heard footsteps retreating. She looked, and the two had turned their backs on her and were walking down the hall with an odd, machine-like stride.

They turned into Cal's room. It was quiet for a moment; then she heard Cal cry out. There was the sound of struggling followed by quiet. Then two of the men came out and stood against the hall walls with their rifles held at the ready. Another came out, tugging at Cal's feet while the final one pushed the office chair.

They'd zip-tied him to the chair and were pushing him into the workroom.

Cal's eye was wide, and his breathing was heavy, but he said nothing. He apparently saw her, but there was nothing either of them could do. They'd been captured easily.

Sophie wondered what was to be done with them. The circumstance didn't seem to promise anything pleasant. She distracted herself by watching the men and trying to figure out their strange behavior. It was almost as if they were automatons, controlled by something or someone that didn't quite understand how humans typically moved.

Suspicion gradually blossomed in her mind. Were they full of nanites? If they were, did she dare try to hijack the communication stream?

She carefully composed a command sequence for Ralph to broadcast, then checked at the last second. The men were down the hall. It was possible they wouldn't even hear her. She started to speak, but a gunshot interrupted her.

It sounded hugely loud echoing down the hall. There was a split second where nothing seemed to happen, then the men in black responded. They ducked into doors and returned fire. There was a deafening rattle of gunfire.

Sophie saw a couple of men in tee shirts and jeans come through the door. One dropped instantly, red blossoming out from his face. The other leaned to the side and fired a loud gun into an open door. She wondered if it were a shotgun. There was no return fire.

There were some shouts followed by more shots, then silence. She tugged at the zip-ties, trying to loosen the tight bands, but they cut into her wrists painfully and didn't stretch.

The man moved down the hall directly toward her. He looked up and grinned with a threatening leer that highlighted the scarred face with the tear tattoo. It was Raul.

Sophie's heart sank. Somehow he and his gang had tracked her here. The fact that they seemed to have killed the previous invaders was little consolation to her. Raul never forgave an insult and she'd not only stolen thousands of dollars worth of Oxy, but she'd also killed his principal lieutenant. Her breathing increased. She'd be lucky if he didn't shoot her immediately.

Raul came to the workroom door and carefully peered around the corner, checking to make sure the room was empty, save for her. Once assured that she was the only occupant, he glanced at her, then at her wrists. He shook his head negatively without speaking, then turned to shout down the hall.

"Yo! Report."

There was an instant reply.

"Aziz, here. I'm okay. Ricardo is gut-shot. Looks like he on the way out. All the others are dead."

Aziz came into the hall from the kitchen. Sophie recognized him. He'd been around, on and off when she'd been in Raul's house.

He looked at her and laughed, then said, "Well, well, looky here what we catch. Hey, Puta, you gonna pay for what you stole."

Raul replied, "Check everybody twice. Make sure those guys in black are all dead. Check our guys. See if anybody besides Ricardo is living."

Aziz almost instantly shouted. He was looking into Cal's room.

"Hey! Here's somebody or somethang. Don't look healthy to me, but he living."

Raul called back, "Check him out. I got business with the Puta."

He turned to her and smiled, but it wasn't a pleasant smile.

"Yo, Sophie. Good to see you again. Where you been keepin' yourself, huh? In here? Looks like somebody didn't want you getting into mischief. You got anything to say for yourself?" he said.

He approached her chair slowly, then suddenly stepped forward and slapped her. It was blindingly hard, and her cheek felt like it had exploded.

She gasped, then said, "Hi, Raul. You came in just in time. Those guys in black were going to kill us."

Her mind was working overtime, trying to come up with some story that would keep her alive.

He laughed, "I'd have been really pissed at them if they'd done you."

She started to reply, but he interrupted.

"Don' get your hopes up. I just want the pleasure of killing you myself," he said, threat showing in his expression. He raised his hand for another blow, and she tried to ready herself for the pain.

There was a sudden yell and the sound of struggle from Cal's room.

Raul turned and ran towards the room. Just before he arrived, Cal and Aziz fell through the door. They looked like they were tangled together in some impossible way, but then Sophie realized that Cal had somehow wrapped his limp hands like tentacles around Aziz's neck.

Aziz was fighting, trying to get free, but Cal far out-massed him. The two rolled fully into the hall and Cal ended up on top. Now his arms seemed boneless as did his legs. He wrapped both his appendages around the struggling man.

There was a sudden pause as the fight seemed to freeze for a long moment, then there was a loud snap, and Aziz's head fell back at an unnatural angle. Raul cursed, raised his shotgun and fired a shot directly into Cal's temple.

Blood and brains flew down the hall. Sophie cried out in horror and then there was silence.

Raul kicked at Cal's body, but there was no response. The big man had given everything he had to try and save her. Sophie was so shocked that she was unable to think. Tears leaked from her eyes and she gasped for breath, but she didn't cry.

Raul looked back at her and sneered.

"Your boyfriend ain't so tough now, huh? And, what the hell is that with his arms and legs? He some kinda octopussy or somethin?"

He paused and listened, then walked down the hall and disappeared into the kitchen. There was a muffled exclamation, which sounded suspiciously like a curse then he came backing out.

Raul said, "Ricardo just died. That's all my homies. This ain't a good deal. I'm gonna have to regroup. Where the pills you stole, huh? Any thing else valuable around here? You got one chance Puta. You make this worth my while, and maybe I let you live a little longer.

He approached and stuck the still smoking barrel of his gun right up against her face. The hole looked like a giant tunnel to Sophie. She tried to think, then said, "The pills are in the third room to the right. Under the bed. They're still in the briefcase."

He grinned and said, "That's the way. I go check. You best be right."

She waited until he was in her room and then she spoke quietly, "Hey, Ralph, Act. Disperse, target-acc." There was a brief pause, then the little puddle of gray nanites on the plate disappeared.

She knew they'd be invading her body quickly unless she could move them down the hall.

"Hey, Ralph vector 270, translate 5000." She thought that should send them about 2 meters down the hallway.

Raul came out of her bedroom carrying the briefcase. He was smiling in satisfaction.

"I got my package back. Maybe you like some, huh? Say about fifty? I give them to you all at once; then we see how long you last."

He was approaching the five-meter point. She held her breath, hoping that none of the microscopic bots had drifted into her lungs.

Raul stopped in front of her and opened the bag, pulling out a baggy full of pills to swing them in front of her face.

He looked down her body. "Maybes I do you one last time, huh. You were always pretty good, but..." He paused. "But I can replace you. There a million like you, only better. I – "

Sophie interrupted, "Hey, Ralph, A-U-active-k-mode-q-block."

Raul snapped his mouth shut in surprise, then said, "What the hell you talk 'bout, Puta? Who you talkin' to – "

He stopped in mid-sentence, his eyes grew large, and he grabbed his chest, gasped spasmodically, then fell with a thud, landing face down on the tile.

Sophie had been trying not to breathe, but she had to gasp for a breath to say, "Hey, Ralph, A-U-Standby."

She waited, apprehensively, trying to breathe as little as possible. If she hadn't gotten the command out in time, she would be dead in a few seconds. The time crept by until she could stand it no longer. She gasped, drawing in a full lungful of air.

If they were still active, it would be too bad. Nothing happened, though, and she gradually relaxed.

Raul was dead. His heart stopped as efficiently as if a bullet had struck it.

She thought for a little, then gave Ralph a series of commands. The newly released nanobots must be reprogrammed so that only she could control them, then perhaps she could get the little robots to free her hands.

CHAPTER 11

LOST

Freeing her hands turned out to be simple although it was something she'd never thought of before. It took a lot of the nanobots, but once enough of them were able to wedge their tiny bodies into the zip-tie locks, the restraints were ineffective. She worked the plastic off her wrists and then commanded her little helpers to remain on her skin. She might need them again.

THERE WAS NO reason to stay here. Sooner or later, someone would come along to investigate. She suspected that the black-suited, military-type guys would be missed when they didn't report in. Whoever sent them would deploy another force shortly.

It would be best if she were nowhere around at that time. She needed to find a hiding place as far away from their residence as possible. It had to be somewhere that she'd never been and a place where no one would suspect that she'd gone.

That was easier said than done, but she had to start moving and quickly, too. She caught up the pills, then stepped over Cal's misshapen body on her way out. A sob caught in her throat as she moved away from him. He looked so horrible; nothing like the strong, attractive man that had been her hope of salvation.

She set the case with the pills down and began to gather up a couple of changes of clothes. Cal had purchased things for her so that she hadn't needed to go out. They'd agreed that it was better if she didn't risk being seen by Raul. Well, that wasn't a problem any longer.

She angrily stuffed the clothes into the case on top of the pills, then headed for the door. She made a quick trip to Cal's room to gather the cash he kept in a false-bottomed drawer, trying to ignore his body as she passed. She paused in the kitchen to grab a small box of protein bars, then quickly went to the steps to the ground floor.

She stopped with her foot on the top step. How could she have forgotten her laptop? She ran back to the workroom and gathered it up. The case was nearly full, but she worked the thin computer in beside the bags of pills.

She paused by a black-clad body. There was something she'd noticed in passing that she wanted to examine. His face was turned towards the ceiling, eyes staring blindly with the glaze of death at the overhead light. The light made it easier to see. There was a fine pattern on his forehead. She bent to examine it.

It was amazingly like an antenna in shape. Why would someone have an antenna tattoo? She hesitated, then delicately traced her finger over the lines. The sensation was that of something overlaid on the skin. She gritted her teeth then scratched it with her fingernails. The man's head moved slightly, making her jump back in fear. There was a sensation of pulling as a fine wire slid partly out of the broken skin.

The men had antennas embedded in their foreheads. Why was that? Some new comm system she had never heard of perhaps? She shook her head at the puzzle, then shoved the problem into the back of her mind. She had to get out of there.

Once again she started down the stairs, this time without pausing. As she reached the bottom step, she heard some muffled talking coming from the front door. It was partly open, but she couldn't see anyone. She quickly circled the staircase and moved towards the rear entrance. Maybe that would be clear.

She approached cautiously. There was no sign that anyone had been there. The door was closed and barred as always. She could hear some talking from the front of the building, so she hurried to lift the bar, then cracked the door to peer out. The alley was clear.

FOUR BLOCKS AWAY, she paused to catch her breath. There was no sign of pursuit. She breathed easier for a moment, but then the thought that Hazelton easily had enough resources to have several drones covering the area with video surveillance occurred to her.

That would be bad. She scanned the air but didn't see anything. Of course, that didn't mean they weren't there. The mosquito-drones could hide almost anywhere. She brushed at her clothing nervously. Or, there could be some type of intermediate-sized device, maybe one the size of a small bird. She might not notice something like that, particularly if it was hiding somewhere on one of the surrounding buildings.

The combination of fear, exhaustion, and grief was suddenly overwhelming. She hesitated, struggling with a moment of indecision. Without conscious thought, her hand strayed to her pocket and came back with a pill. She stopped just before taking it, then forced herself to break it in half. One-half went into her pocket, the other into her mouth. It tasted bitter, but she persevered, dissolving it under her tongue.

She resumed her fast walk, heading downtown towards the city center. That was a place she usually avoided. The cops were more likely to stop girls who looked like addicts down there, but she could catch a bus quicker. There were hardly any stops in the depressed neighborhood near Cal's place. Then she could make several transfers in a short time. Changing from one bus to another would make it harder for anyone to track her.

Sophie suffered through a moment of almost blind panic. Her fear was intense, but then she remembered someone saying that "You're not paranoid if they really are out to get you." Something about that statement activated her sense of humor.

She wasn't crazy. She was acting rationally, because someone, or possibly several someones, were undoubtedly after her.

AS SHE WALKED, she tried to plan what she would do. This became a little easier as the drug took effect. It seemed to blunt her grief, although it made it harder to focus.

She forced herself to concentrate on her situation. She needed a secure place to hide. The cash she'd taken would get her a cheap hotel room, but she didn't have a credit card, and she'd lost her driver's license a long time ago. She was for all practical purposes non-existent. The cops would happily take her in if they stopped her. Lack of ID was a grave crime in their eyes.

Thinking of the police made her remember the pills in the case. She'd be in trouble if they searched her. Maybe she should just try to find a vacant building somewhere, but that wouldn't be secure either and would most likely expose her to some street predator. She walked more slowly as the magnitude of her problem struck her.

Without thinking, she absently fished out the other half of the white pill and swallowed it. Maybe it would help her figure out what to do. She took a drink of water and kept walking.

She could go to her sister's, but she had a great reluctance to show up after being missing for weeks. Besides Rachael didn't deserve the kind of trouble that she had. She didn't want to involve the only remaining member of her family.

She stopped in a run-down convenience store for a bottle of water. The clerk took her money, then made an indecent suggestion. She didn't answer, only turning to walk out quickly. He didn't follow, so that was good. She drank a few swallows as she walked, washing the drug's residual bitterness out of her mouth.

SHE EVENTUALLY REACHED a more prosperous area. There she entered several different stores, taking her time to browse a bit in each as if she was shopping. She ended by purchasing some new jeans, a blouse, and a rather nice jacket. The clerk at the check-out desk looked at the bills suspiciously but then decided to take them.

On the street again, Sophie looked for the nearest public restroom. A burger place provided a clean women's room, and she changed in one of the stalls. Her old clothes went into the waste bin. She wondered how many of the nanites went with them, then shrugged. They were inactive, and she almost certainly had plenty of the things both on her skin and inside her. If she could get rid of them all, that might be a good thing, but she had doubts that could happen.

She took advantage of the opportunity to force a burger down her throat, even though she didn't want it. She knew that she was likely to need the energy.

As she ate, she considered her situation again. She needed somewhere to stay, and she needed to do something about the remaining nanites.

If she commanded the tiny machines to leave her body, there would probably be some that didn't make it out for one reason or another. She'd most likely still be infected. After some thought, she decided that might be for the best. The ones that she carried were safeguarded with her personal activation code. They wouldn't become active unless she gave the correct code and they might prove useful somehow.

Of course, she would acquire new ones if Hazelton attacked her. She needed a way to reprogram any wild nanites that she encountered automatically. That thought bounced around in her mind for a few minutes.

Finally, she came up with a possible answer. She might be able to create a defense with the nanites that were in her body. They could be programmed to recognize intruders and either inactivate them or install her activation code in them. The second option would be best. She'd have to think about how to accomplish that with the limited command-set.

She'd need to use Ralph – she slapped her hand on her leg in frustration causing a child in a nearby booth to look at her curiously. She had walked out and, in her urgency to leave, forgotten to grab one of the Ralph units. She was afraid to go back. By now there were probably black-suited zombies running around all over Cal's place.

The child's mother was looking at her now. She gathered up her trash, deposited it in a bin, and left, trying to appear as if she had no concerns. It was difficult. She wasn't an outstanding actress.

Once on the street, she resumed her walk towards downtown, thinking as she moved along. She was preoccupied with her problem, but still remembered to glance in store windows, checking reflections behind her.

There was nothing, except a small, white dog that seemed to be alone. It paused at a fireplug to sniff, then cocked a hind leg to add its marker to the signpost. Sophie smiled in relief. If a stray poodle was all she had to worry about, that wasn't so bad. Her mind immediately began to mull over her immediate problem.

Worry about security, made Sophie reluctant to proceed, She eventually decided she should use the wide-spread Reverb unit network. That was assuming her viral update had made it through the manufacturer's system. She needed to test that as quickly as possible.

By this time, she found herself at the downtown bus station. She bought a ticket and boarded. The bus filled, then started, stopping at every stop to change passengers. Sophie sat near the back in a trance-like state. She'd taken two pills in a fit of self-pity as she sat down. She felt guilty until the bus had gone a couple of blocks. By then the drug had taken effect. Now she was relaxed and feeling more secure than she had for what seemed an interminably long time.

If they found her here, it was just bad luck and probably meant that her past sins had doomed her. She didn't much care at the moment. It was enough to sit and ride without paying attention to where she was. Her plan of changing to other bus routes was forgotten.

SOPHIE GRADUALLY BECAME aware that a well-dressed young woman of about her age was sitting beside her. She hadn't noticed when the stranger first sat down. Now that she was conscious of her surroundings, she thought that the other girl had been sitting beside her for only a short time.

She sat up and looked around, then drew in her breath in surprise. The bus was passing a large, well-manicured grassy area that separated a large building from the road. The building was multiple stories, and the side had the Hazelton logo was prominently displayed. What could she have been thinking to ride right out to the site of her enemy's stronghold?

Her seatmate, seeing that she was awake, said, "Impressive, isn't it?"

Sophie jumped a little, fear washing through her body, then turned to the other girl. "Yeah. I guess so."

The girl smiled and said, "That's what I thought when I first interviewed there. I was sure I'd never fit in at such a big corporation."

Sophie tried to appear calm.

"You work there? At Hazelton, I mean?" she asked.

"Yes. I'm just a secretary, but it's an interesting place to work." The girl paused, then said, "I'm Jessica Kingston. I haven't seen you on this bus before. I ride it every day, first to work and then home. Almost everyone here is on the way out to the suburbs. You're kind of a novelty."

Sophie smiled tiredly, then said, "I'm sorry to disturb your routine. I...well, my boyfriend, kicked me out and..." At this point, her imagination failed her. Instead of telling a smooth lie about a non-existent boyfriend who had dumped her, the image of Cal's mutated body flashed into her mind, and she started to cry.

Jessica looked alarmed, then immediately tried to comfort her.

"It can't be that bad. You're a pretty girl. Why would he kick you out? He must be a fool." She patted Sophie's shoulder sympathetically.

Sophie made an effort to regain control, but it didn't work very well. She hiccuped then said, "I'm sorry. It's just that I don't..." She sobbed again. "I don't have any place to go. I got on this bus randomly. It seemed like a good idea, but now I'm going to have to find a motel or something, and it looks like we're way out and there might not be anything, so I'll have to ride back and...I'm sorry, I'm babbling. Please forget I said anything. It's not your trouble." She quit talking and looked out the window again.

The bus was finally passing the far edge of the Hazelton campus. The place covered an extraordinarily large area.

Jessica asked, "What's your name?"

Sophie turned back to her, "Sophie Monroe. I'm usually not so emotional, but it's been a hard day."

Jessica smiled, paused for a moment, apparently considering something, then asked, "Are you employed?"

Sophie said, "Uh, not at the moment. I'm a...a computer specialist. I write apps and do consulting for clients. Right now I'm between jobs, though."

Jessica asked, "Are you looking for work? Can you support yourself?"

This seemed a little intrusive to Sophie, but she detected no ill will in Jessica. The girl's face was as open as a daisy in full bloom. She didn't look like anyone who would be devious or who could entertain a hidden agenda. Sophie answered, "I'll find another consulting gig as soon as I can get a place to live. I've got some money in the bank to tide me through."

Jessica took a deep breath, then said, "Look, I know you don't know me, but maybe we could...ah, well, my roommate moved out last month so she could move in with her boyfriend and the rent is just too much for me to keep the place by myself. I've been looking for another roommate, but no luck as yet. There's no one at work that I'd consider, and I'm afraid to advertise online. You get such weirdo's there. Maybe you'd consider rooming with me? I'm quiet, and you'd have your own room and bath. The place is a two bedroom unit with two bathrooms. What do you think?"

Sophie inspected Jessica's face. The girl was completely in earnest and looked hopeful.

Sophie said, "I guess it wouldn't do any harm for me to come look at your place. I don't want to impose on you though."

Jessica smiled, friendliness radiating from her face. "Oh, no. You're not imposing. You'd be helping me out. I don't want to move. It's a great place, safe, and convenient, too. I was dreading having to interview people, and you're...you're nice, and you're in a tight place, too. It's only right that we team up."

Sophie thought about just how much trouble she would bring to Jessica but then decided that she could work to ensure that the friendly girl didn't get involved. Besides, Jessica worked at the very place that Sophie needed to investigate. She could be a lot of help.

She smiled back at Jessica, and said, "OK. It's settled then. I'll come with you, but...Oh, I forgot! How much is the rent going to be?"

Jessica named a figure that Sophie could easily cover for several months. Surely she'd be able to get freelance work during that time.

"Oh, that's no problem then. I've got enough saved to cover that for months," she said.

Jessica nodded enthusiastically.

Sophie added, "But, I guess I didn't mention. I don't have any furniture or anything. My...uh, boyfriend...everything was his, and it was a bad breakup. All I've got is in this bag."

Jessica's eyes grew wide. "Don't you have any clothes or makeup or anything?"

Thinking quickly, Sophie said, "No. Just what I've got here. My laptop is the most important thing. He threw everything I owned in the dumpster. It was full of filth, and my stuff was ruined. I'm not going to worry about it. I can get new things."

Jessica shook her head again in a commiserating manner. "Those men are too much sometimes. Hey, it's not so bad. My roommate left her bedroom furniture. She didn't need it. Her boyfriend has a house and already has furniture. She told me I could have her stuff as partial payment for her moving out so suddenly. You can use that."

Sophie held out her hand, "Okay. Let's shake on it, Jessica. Roommates facing the world together."

Jessica took her hand, shook it and said, "Just call me Jess. Oh, here's our stop! Let's go. I can't wait to show you the place."

CHAPTER 12
SANCTUARY

Jessica's apartment was as nice as she'd said. Sophie paused at the door looking in with mixed emotions. She could remember living in a beautiful place, but that was...was before her parents... The image evoked a sense of irretrievable loss, and she hurriedly shoved the memories out of her mind before she started to cry.

Jessica didn't notice her reaction. The brown-haired girl seemed to be self-starting when it came to conversation.

"The living room isn't very large, but there's enough room for a small party. I've had eight people over before, and we managed. The nice thing about this apartment complex is that the bedrooms are all extra large. You know so many places are designed as if they thought you'd enjoy sleeping in a closet or something."

She didn't pause for Sophie to comment.

"The kitchen has a nice sized dining area, and you can use half of the refrigerator. I've kind of over-expanded right now, but I'll reorganize my stuff, and you'll have plenty of room. Oh, and this is your bedroom, right here. I've got the one at the back of the hall. Sorry, but it's a little more private. Still, yours is quite nice, and there's a partial view of the park across the street from your window, so that's a plus. This door is the closet and this..." She paused as she swung open the bathroom door, then said, "Ta-Da! Is the bath. It's really sweet, don't you think?"

She unexpectedly stopped her incessant chatter and looked at Sophie expectantly.

Sophie stuttered a little. She hadn't thought that Jess would quit talking and wasn't prepared to answer since her emotions were still bothering her.

"Uh, uh, I, uh, I think that it's quite nice," she said. As an afterthought, she added, "This is very nice. Much better than where I've been living."

That was a mistake. The memory of Cal's body on the floor caused her eyes to begin to tear up.

Jessica was more perceptive than her constant conversation indicated. She hurriedly said, "Oh. I'm sorry. I didn't mean to make you sad. Your ex is going to regret breaking up with you. It's just that I'm so glad to have someone to share the place with me. It really is too much for me to keep on my salary. I was getting ready to look for a smaller apartment since I couldn't seem to gear myself up to find a replacement roommate and I didn't want to do that."

Sophie regained control of her feelings just in time to hear the last part of Jessica's statement.

"Do what?" she asked.

"Oh, I mean that I didn't want to move. I'm used to this place. It's really convenient and comfortable. I know I'm practically babbling, but it's because I'm so excited about you moving in." She took a deep breath paused dramatically, and asked, "Now, really. Tell me what you really, really think about the place. Do you like it?"

Sophie smiled at her. The girl was so open and unguarded.

"Yes. I really, really like it. I'm thrilled you took pity on me on the bus. This is perfect for me. I'll be able to get work done in my room and – " It suddenly occurred to Sophie that Jessica's excitement might have something to do with her approaching the end of her savings.

"Look, Jessica. I don't have any checks, but I've got plenty of cash in my bag. What does the monthly rent and utilities come to?"

Jessica paused, startled. "You mean you can pay up front?"

Sophie nodded. The conversation had come back to something that she felt gave her a little more control. "Sure. What's my half come to?"

Jessica thought, "Well, this is the fifth so you won't owe a whole month's rent – "

Sophie waved her hand in negation. "You had to pay the entire month's rent and just because I'm moving in a little late, doesn't offset that. How much is half the rent and utilities?"

Jess smiled and named a figure that surprised Sophie. It was less than she'd thought it would be. She picked up the bag and, being careful not to expose the contents, dug out several hundred dollar bills.

"Here, this is enough to cover the first month. Consider me your new roommate! I promise that I'll do my best to be unobtrusive. I'm not a loud person. I work on the computer most of the time and only listen to music through headphones," she said.

Jess took the cash and said, "Wow! I never carry that much money. Don't you feel worried about maybe being mugged?"

Sophie shook her head. "No. I'm pretty good on the street and, anyway, I had to grab what I could when my boyfriend...uh – " She stopped again and turned away.

Jessica put her hand comfortingly on Sophie's shoulder, then said, "I know. Don't worry about it. I'm going to let you settle in and maybe in thirty minutes or so we can go out for pizza or something."

SOPHIE SAT ON the bed and looked around. The room was cheerful and light. There were no lurking memories there; only those she'd brought in with her. She resolved to put those aside. She needed to learn to control her emotions better, but the opiates made that difficult. The warmth of the drug always made her more apt to feel sorry for herself and lose control.

The first thing she had to do was hide her pills and cash securely, but then she would begin to plan revenge on Hazelton. They were responsible for all of the trouble. She was determined to get revenge for Cal's death from someone. She didn't much care that Raul was dead. Even though he'd pulled the trigger, he probably wouldn't have been able to gain access without the zombie Hazelton men's distraction. No, she didn't blame him. His death didn't satisfy her.

She pulled her laptop out and set it on the nightstand. She had to decide where she'd store the cash and the pills that were in the bag. That could be a problem. Jess didn't seem the sort to snoop, but Sophie had learned to be paranoid about her pills. Besides, the quantity was so large that it would instantly convince anyone, even someone as innocent as Jessica, that she was a drug dealer. She'd have to purchase a small safe. She thought she could convince Jessica that it was for a secure programming project she'd contracted to do. That was at least a possibility.

She took out five hundred dollars in twenties, folded the bills neatly, and put them in her pocket. That was walking-around cash and should be enough to purchase the safe she had in mind.

Sophie shoved some of the cash in between the mattresses and then checked the bathroom. It was set up in a partial en-suite fashion. There were two doors; one opened to the hall, providing guest facilities, and the other opened directly into her bedroom. She closed the hall door and then lifted the lid off the toilet reservoir. There was room for roughly a quarter of the pills to hang in a plastic bag just above the water surface. She retrieved the case and consolidated four bags of pills into one. Then she worked the full bag into two of the now empty ones, sealed them carefully and returned to the bathroom.

She held the bag against the back of the reservoir and trapped the edge of the plastic with the reservoir top. The bag cleared the water by an inch, so she carefully lowered the lid, then checked to make sure the plastic was still showing on the outside of the tank's back. It looked safe.

Back in the bedroom, Sophie hid most of the rest of her cash. There was a void between the drawer bottom and the solid dresser bottom. That seemed fairly secure, so she carefully arranged the bills in the space and shut the drawer.

She shoved another bag of pills behind the nightstand drawer, then covered the rest with a spare blanket on the closet shelf. It wasn't good, but it was the best she could do for the moment.

She could maybe set some nanites to watch her possessions, but she needed Ralph. Oh! No, she didn't. Her mind had been working on the problem subconsciously and she'd just had a brilliant idea.

Hands shaking, she powered up her laptop. The nanite command language interpreter was set up to use Ralph's circuitry, but with a little coding, maybe she wouldn't.

Thirty minutes later, Jess knocked on her door.

"Hey, Sophie! I'm hungry. You wanna go and get something now?" she called.

Sophie jerked. Time had flown, but she was nearly done.

"Just a minute. Let me get ready," she answered, typing madly.

A few more lines of coding and she was ready. She pressed the Enter key. Nothing visible happened, but she knew that there was now a squad of nanites resting on the laptop surface. They were alert and would invade anyone who came into the room.

This would allow her to track access. If Jess came in, she'd get some too, but they wouldn't do anything unless Sophie activated them. They would only communicate when queried so that she could track them. She paused, then added a few more commands. Now anyone who entered and touched her laptop would be stunned until she released them.

She'd deactivate that command when they got back. No sense knocking Jess out, if she was just curious or cleaning or something.

Sophie already had developed a complete trust in the brown-haired girl. Jess didn't seem to be the sort of person who would take something that didn't belong to her.

Running her fingers through her hair, Sophie rose and went to the door.

Pizza sounded good.

A WEEK LATER, Sophie pushed herself back from the small desk she'd installed in her room. She was exasperated and tired. She stood and flung herself on her bed making a thump as she hit the mattress. Jess was at work, and they were on the ground floor, so she didn't worry about the sound.

After a bit, she said, "Hey, Ralph, A-U-Active 001 Rejuv." There was a slightly disorienting feeling as the commands, echoed via wireless from her newly purchased and modified Reverb unit caused her internal nanites to help her body rid itself of the toxins accumulated from sitting at her desk for three hours. She considered her pills, but, strangely, the nanite-induced relief was almost as satisfying.

She'd been working on the Reverb system. Her initial attempt to reprogram the entire system virally had failed. Or rather, it had worked but then been written over by a company-issued software upgrade. So far, she hadn't managed to figure out how to change the firmware in the Reverbs so that they would hold her modifications intact in the face of company efforts to improve the system.

The access code was probably simple, but she'd somehow missed it. She could continue to reissue her changes to the Reverb system every so often, but there was no way to guarantee the reliability. Any individual Reverb might not have updated with her new code when she needed to implement control. It was frustrating.

SHE HAD AN hour or so before Jess came home from work. She sat up and slid back in front of the computer. Her feet kicked against the safe that was on the floor under the desk. Jessica hadn't objected to the purchase and had even helped her carry the massive thing into her room.

There were pills and cash inside. She'd been worried about running out of money, but the second time she'd gone to get currency from Cal's stash in the briefcase, she'd found a bit of paper hidden in the bills.

There, in his precise script, were the access codes for his Cayman bank account. She'd used that to transfer a large sum into her personal account, and from there, part of it had gone to establish a local checking account.

She didn't move much money onshore. There was no sense in alerting the banking authorities. They'd be sure to think she was laundering if she brought in more than a small amount at any point.

She flexed her fingers and went to work on an App that she'd contracted to create through Freelancer. There were some systems online that allowed her to advertise her services. She'd decided that she needed to have an ongoing source of legitimate funds to avoid suspicion just in case someone were to look at her account.

It had been no problem to find work and, even though it seemed like a waste of time, she forced herself to work part of the day on her client's task. This job was almost finished, though, so she'd have to start locating another.

She worked steadily until she heard Jess come through the front door. It was impossible to continue after that point since her roommate usually wasn't quiet when she got home.

Today, Jess was louder than average.

"Hey, Sophie! You still working? I've got some good news."

By that point, Jessica had reached Sophie's room. Sophie closed the editor and turned to her friend.

"Guess what? There's a programming job open at my work! Maybe you should apply. I brought the job specifications for you to review. I was supposed to place it with the employment agency today, but I held it back until Monday morning. That way, you could have the first crack at the position."

Jessica paused, seeing the doubt in Sophie's eyes, then added, "Uh, that is, if you want it?"

Sophie smiled and said, "I've been doing pretty well with my consulting, but let me look at the job requirements. Maybe I should apply."

Jess happily handed her the paper and went to change out of her work clothes.

SOPHIE READ THE specifications over. It was something she could probably do, although she wasn't overly familiar with the specific software. The important issues were that she didn't know if she'd be able to pass a drug test and then the idea of actually working at Hazelton, going into the heart of her enemy's stronghold, was daunting. What if they figured out that she wanted to destroy them?

SHE DEFLECTED JESSICA'S questions about the opportunity through supper. After supper, Jessica was meeting some people from work at a club. Sophie begged off, saying that she had a headache.

"Right. Too much programming! I just know that you're going to work yourself into a stupor on these stupid apps you do. It would be easier if you went to work with me. At least the hours are regular, and even the project managers don't work very late," she said as she went out the door.

Sophie answered, "I'll think about it and let you know by Sunday evening."

CHAPTER 13
AN INTERVIEW

Sophie got off the bus in front of the Hazelton campus at two on Monday afternoon. She'd decided to try for a job there. It made perfect sense to her to infiltrate the company and try to figure out who was responsible for the attack that killed Cal.

She stood at the bus stop indecisively. This was frightening in a way that she was mentally unprepared to process. She'd never actually applied for a job, let alone a corporate one. Besides, this step involved going directly to the heart of what she was sure was enemy territory.

She looked at the retreating bus. Smoke was coming from its exhaust pipe, and it was moving away rapidly. Too late to get back on.

There was an open area across the street, maybe a small park or something. There were some dogs on the far side playing chase with each other. No humans though. Perhaps they were strays. One of them looked exactly like the small white poodle she'd seen before, but there were lots of little white dogs, and this was too far for it to have made its way here. She turned towards the imposing glass-covered facade of the Hazelton main building.

JESSICA HAD EVEN helped her on Sunday. They'd gone shopping, and Jessica's advice was very helpful in choosing some professional looking clothes. Sophie felt a little out of her league since she didn't usually wear dresses. Jeans and sweatshirts were more to her taste.

Jess had told her in no uncertain terms that she couldn't go to work at the company dressed like that.

"Look, Sophie, I know you're probably more comfortable with pants, but there's some kind of sexist attitude there. Women are expected to look like women. Uh, what I mean is that you'll need some professional clothing; mostly blouses and skirts. It's off-putting at first, but you'll get used to it. I did," she said with a cheerful smile. Then she added, "Besides, you'd look good in a dress. You'd probably get a bunch of attention."

Sophie looked up at her friend, memories of Cal and then Raul creating conflicting emotions in her for a moment. Jessica apparently misinterpreted what she saw, since she flushed and then said, "Oh! I didn't mean to make you sad about your breakup. Uh. Look it's too soon for you to worry about finding someone else, but I'm just trying to tell you the positive things about the company and dressing like a professional."

The girl went on as if nothing had happened. "I'll set up an appointment with HR for you first thing tomorrow morning. I don't know when they'll have time, but I'll try to give you as much warning as I can. Okay?"

FEELING RATHER ODD in her skirt and new pumps, Sophie adjusted her hair and headed for the entrance.

There was a security station just inside, and she had to provide her driver's license and sign in. The guard was friendly, apparently impressed with her long hair. He gave her specific directions on locating the human resources office.

Sophie looked at him closely; perhaps she showed a little too much interest because he grinned even more and then said, "I get off at five, if you, uh, you know – "

The alarm on her face stopped him abruptly. He shrugged and pointed at the hallway. "Down there."

She hadn't meant to give the wrong signal. She wished she'd been able to control her expression better. That was always a problem for her. She didn't have a good poker face, but he'd had the antenna shape barely visible beneath the skin on his forehead. That was both frightening and disgusting. The idea that she'd be interested in a potential zombie. Ugh.

The zombie-like men that had attacked had appeared barely human, but it was evident that the antenna did not eliminate all human motivation. He'd seemed anxious to go out with her. She walked away as quickly as she could while trying to maintain a business-like air.

Her destination was close to the front, just down the hall, right into a shorter passage and then through the door at the end. There, she was asked to wait until someone called her.

There were some other applicants, mostly nerdy looking younger men. She selected an isolated chair and sat demurely with her feet planted flat on the floor, and the thin folder with her hastily created resume and some screenshots of her apps along with some sample code, held carefully on her lap.

The young men tried to pretend they weren't looking at her, but she caught several staring, then quickly averting their eyes when she glanced their way. It was amusing, and she entertained herself by adjusting her hair to see how much attention her actions got. It helped her deal with her nerves.

Applying for a job was so far out of her usual pattern that it seemed somehow surreal. She alternated between feeling nervous, angry, and amused by the other applicants.

The process went rather quickly. Apparently, there were several HR interviewers. Men would be called, go through a door and then come out a door on the far side of the waiting room, some far more quickly than others. She noticed that the ones that left quickly seemed downcast, so they must have been rejected for some reason.

When her name was called, she jerked. She'd almost dozed off. She stood quickly, smoothed her skirt, then strode over and entered the open door.

There were three people inside the small room on one side of a long table. The single chair on the opposite side led her to understand that she was to sit there.

"Please sit down, Ms. Monroe. I see you have some material for us," the older man on the end said, extending his hand.

She handed him her folder and watched as he opened it to extract her resume. His eyes squinted a bit as he saw how short it was.

He handed it to the woman next to him and asked, "Haven't you worked for any companies? I know you're young, but we usually find our applicants have more job experience than you are showing on your resume."

She smiled and said, "That may be, but you'll observe that I've also included a list of consulting projects that I've worked on. I've got a couple of pages of recommendations from the freelance site that I usually use. They are good. I always deliver my projects on schedule and usually try to build in some additional features beyond the project specs."

The woman at the end interrupted, "That's not always a good thing. Don't you follow the project specifications exactly?"

Sophie didn't like the woman's attitude and decided to address the implied criticism aggressively.

"Most of the people I create apps for only have a rough idea of what they want. It's an interactive process where we go back and forth until I fully understand their requirements. Usually, I can see some additional features they will need that they haven't thought of, so I often add some of these to provide more value for them. I haven't had anyone complain about the extra features. I believe it's only good business to give a bit more than you promise. Don't you?"

The woman shook her head grudgingly. Meanwhile, the middle woman had been looking at the screenshots and the code.

She raised her head and said, "This seems very good. You've done some creative work here. I particularly like this subroutine that you've woven into these two projects. It's parsimonious, tightly written, and yet rather adaptable to different uses. That's good thinking."

She looked at the man and said, "I think she'll do for the assistant tool-making position."

The man glanced at both of the women, saw agreement, then turned back to Sophie.

"We have a position that will require you to help create routines to be used in an experimental programming project. From the looks of your samples, you can handle that kind of work. What I'm interested now is a feel for your work ethic. Do you work quickly, slowly, take lots of breaks? Tell me how you go about your projects."

Sophie glanced back and forth, then said, "Gig work is different. I go all out when I have a job. I try to finish it as quickly as possible without sacrificing quality. I have to use a considerable amount of discipline, however, since I tend to over-work. I usually force myself to take a brief break every so often, just to get my circulation moving again. Sitting still while coding isn't the best possible use of the human body. I often take a short walk, and I find that helps me think. I sometimes come back with an innovative solution to a problem that had been hanging me up."

The third woman asked, "Do you have any bad habits? Drinking, drugs, anything like that? You're interviewing for a position in a critical project, and we don't want any security risks." She paused, looking at Sophie expectantly, then added, "You'll have to have a drug test. That will be in the next room. Would you go through that door? The nurse will take a blood and urine sample there, then come back here."

She'd known this would happen. She stood and walked toward the door, hoping that her instructions to her nanite population had been adequate. She'd spent some time thinking about the issue and had formulated a set of instructions that should have had them clear her body of opiate metabolites.

She didn't feel very well at the moment. She was used to having the edge of the pain she usually felt in her neck and shoulders blunted, but the very fact that she hurt seemed to indicate that the nanites were doing their job. She took a deep breath and went through the door.

The blood draw was quick and painless. Apparently, the nurse had done this a lot. She hit the vein, filled the syringe and then handed Sophie a small bottle.

"There's a bathroom through that door. Please fill the bottle as much as possible," she said.

When Sophie came out, carrying the bottle, the nurse was filling out some paperwork. She seemed preoccupied and did not look up as Sophie put the container on the corner of her desk, diffidently saying, "I did the best I could, but it's not very full."

The nurse glanced at the white-capped bottle and said, "That's enough. The test doesn't take too much. Go back out the door on the right. There'll be someone there with additional instructions."

Sophie's initial reaction was dismay. *Crap! I probably said something wrong or maybe my blood wasn't clean. This didn't take long enough. The guys that came out looking like they failed took about this long.*

She shrugged, trying to reconcile her mind with the idea of having to come up with another plan.

The third woman, the hostile one, was standing just outside the door as she exited.

Great! Probably hates me and wants the pleasure of kicking me out!

Sophie stepped forward and allowed the door to swing shut.

The woman smiled at her, a tightly controlled smile, but a smile nonetheless.

"You are scheduled to come back tomorrow at nine o'clock sharp. Report to room 1530. That's on the fifteenth floor. Provided your drug tests are clear we're going to start you in an orientation class about our company. That will take two days. Then you'll start work on Thursday. Your current clothing is barely adequate in my opinion. We do have an informal dress code here. We like our young ladies to wear skirts that are knee length. Yours is two inches too short. Please dress accordingly."

She held up her hand as Sophie started to ask a question. "No. I'm not here to answer your questions. The orientation course will cover all of that including our compensation scale. Be here at nine prompt. Please see yourself out and check with the guard at the front desk. He'll have a temp ID-card for you."

Sophie turned shakily and walked through the door. Once outside, she was in the waiting room again. There were still some sitting candidates who looked at her curiously. It was embarrassing, and she suddenly realized that she hurt all over.

The nanites had removed every trace of the drug from her system, but she wasn't ready for such an experience. She'd been so tense throughout the drug test and the lecture afterward, that she hadn't recognized the signs of withdrawal. She'd been there before and knew it would be bad.

It was easy to look downcast as she walked across the room. She stumbled as she reached the door. The others must certainly think she'd failed the interview.

She jerked the door open and headed for the security desk. Things were almost a blur. She found herself on the street clutching a small piece of plastic with her picture printed on one side. She wasn't sure how she'd managed to get through the process. She'd been so shocked by her success and in so much pain that she had let her picture be taken without paying attention.

She looked at it. Her face looked drawn and seemed to say to her: *"You're living a lie, you fake!"*

She took two pills out of her pocket and swallowed them dry. It was hard to work up the saliva to get them down, and they seemed to stick in her throat as she approached the bus stop.

The bus pulled up just as she reached the bench and sat down. She sighed, hating the idea of having to stand up again. The drug started to take effect as she climbed aboard to ride home.

That was much better. She mustered the strength to smile at the driver as she paid.

The bus was empty, and she rode along without paying attention, lost in the rush of the opiates as they locked into her nerves and deadened the pain.

CHAPTER 14
THE PROJECT

She'd found the initial days of work stressful. It wasn't the tasks themselves. She could handle the minor programming that they asked her to do with no trouble. It was simply the difficulty of orienting herself to a new environment and learning who was who in her area.

There were several entry-level coders along with her. Their supervisor was an older man who was a martinet. He expected them to be at work promptly by nine and not to leave early.

There was a daily meeting at ten where he expected a status report and handed out new assignments.

Sophie found the work mind-numbing. It was mostly simple coding that involved developing tools to massage a huge database. She didn't know what was in the actual database since they always used a test data set filled with text from various books, names, addresses, pictures, and chemical formulas.

Her software was supposed to filter through the raw data and organize it in various ways. She mentally thanked Cal on a daily basis for forcing her to expand her coding skills. Still, it was boring.

The only thing that kept her interest was the senior programmer who worked on the actual project. He sometimes came through their area. She could tell when he was walking through because there was always a slight stir among the female employees. He was young, cute, and had a friendly attitude.

She overheard some of the women talking about him and learned that his first name was Michael, but they never mentioned his last name. Apparently, he was well known.

The women, even the older ones, always made an effort to get him to smile at them. They were seldom disappointed. He was outgoing, and as far as Sophie could tell, there wasn't a disagreeable bone in his body. He treated everyone as equals and always asked how their work was coming.

He noticed her on the third day. Her cubicle was far away from the regular traffic pattern, and she didn't expect to see him.

She happened to be returning from the restroom when he came through, and they almost bumped into each other.

"Excuse me, Miss," he said, then turned to continue. She stood there indecisively, watching him. Michael was attractive and neatly ticked off every single check-box on her list of desirable traits for men.

He took a step, then stopped and turned back to her.

"I haven't seen you before. Are you a new hire?"

She stuttered, "Y...Yes. Just a couple of days ago."

He smiled. "I'm Michael O'Keefe. You'll hear that I'm a genius coder, but I'm really just a jumped-up hacker. I work in the A.I. development department. And who are you?"

"Sophie, uhh, Monroe." Her full name seemed to be appropriate. "But, Sophie is what everyone calls me."

That sounded stupid, and she could feel her cheeks heating up.

Michael smiled, apparently noticing her discomfort, and said, "Don't be shy. My group depends on your work. We're trying to get our code to a state where it can handle any form of data.

Your manipulations on the test set give us practice material for it. Invaluable, actually."

Sophie looked down. Taking her eyes off his face was hard. Glancing downward was almost worse. His chest was well muscled as were his arms and his stomach was flat. The tight-knit shirt he wore didn't seem to fit into what she knew about the dress code, but it showed off his torso to the maximum advantage.

Her eyes moved downward involuntarily. His slacks fit loosely, but there was a suggestive bulge in his groin that made her insides twist a little. She hastily looked back up at his face. He was still smiling.

"Sophie. I like that name. I'll remember it. I've got to get to a meeting, but I'll look for you the next time I come through. Welcome aboard."

He turned and walked away. Sophie found herself leaning forward with an urge to follow him; such was his magnetism. She straightened up and mentally shook herself.

What would a man like him see in her? She was an addict; she'd lived on the street, and that probably was where she belonged. In the gutter. He wouldn't speak to her, if he knew her past...or that she was addicted. She turned, sadly wondering what her life would have been like under different circumstances.

One of the older women passed her, and said, "Good looking, isn't he? You'd better be careful. He always seems to get what he wants."

Sophie shook herself out of her reverie. "What do you mean by that?"

"Oh, it's just that women fall all over him. He's dated a lot of the girls, but nothing ever comes of it. They're not good enough, or maybe he's too picky. Of course, he's worth a try, if he shows any interest in you. He's high up in the company, and I'll bet he's worth a lot. I heard that they gave him a lot of stock options for this project."

Sophie walked back to her cubicle, fantasizing a relationship. She felt mildly stunned. She hadn't had thoughts like this since, oh, maybe middle school. She found it difficult to resume work and found herself losing attention periodically.

QUITTING TIME FINALLY came, and she met Jessica on the way to the bus stop.

"Hi, roommate! Want to go for pizza tonight? Me and some of the other girls are going out. Maybe see some good looking men there. We're going to Mama's. Lots of guys hang out there for beer and pool."

Sophie said, "I, uh, I'm tired. Maybe not tonight."

Jessica looked concerned and asked, "Are you feeling okay? You seem a little, I don't know, maybe distracted or something."

Sophie wasn't in the habit of opening up to anyone, but Jess was so friendly that she had lost some of her reserve with the girl.

"Well, I saw this guy today. Works on the main project -- "

Jessica laughed. "Oh, you saw Michael, I'll bet. He has that effect on everyone. There isn't a girl in the company who wouldn't fall on her back with her legs in the air in front of him."

Sophie could feel her cheeks heating up again. "Yeah. He said hello to me."

Jess shook her head negatively and continued, "Don't get your hopes up. No one seems to be good enough for him. He's dated a lot of the girls, but very few of them get a second chance, and nothing ever comes of it. Some of them are saying he's not interested in women if you know what I mean."

Sophie stopped and looked at her friend. "Really? That's not the feeling I got. He seemed all male and at least a little interested."

Jessica said, "Yeah, I don't believe he's gay, either. He just seems hard to please. Wish he'd give me a chance, but I'm only a secretary, and he seems to prefer the programming staff. Maybe more in common with them, I don't know. Maybe he likes intellectual girls. You should wear some black-rimmed glasses and try to look nerdier. Maybe that would do it."

They both laughed and climbed on the bus.

THE TEN O'CLOCK meeting was delayed for five minutes. Mr. Franks was late and that never happened. When he came into the conference room, he looked disgruntled.

"I've had an unusual change. Sophie, you're to report to Rachael Lewis. She's second lead in the main A.I. programming division. There was a special request for you specifically. It seems that someone has decided that your coding skills are wasted here."

He paused, staring disapprovingly at her, then said, "Well, go on. Get going. You can clear out your desk after they find a spot for you."

She stood, looking at the others. There were various expressions from jealousy to anger spread around the room. She gathered her paperwork, but Franks said, "Just leave that. I'll have one of the others pick up on your work."

In the hall, Sophie paused. This was unexpected, but perhaps it was the break she needed. She'd had no luck figuring out what was going on, given the limitations of her current position. All she'd been able to do was to work on ridiculously disorganized data sets that seemed to have nothing in common with each other or even with pharmaceuticals.

She wasn't quite sure where to find Lewis, so she checked with the secretary. The woman was in the conference room, so Sophie just opened the directory on her desk and looked through.

Rachael Lewis was on the next floor up. The problem Sophie had was that her security pass wouldn't activate the elevator to that level. She shrugged. Maybe she'd have to go down to the security office and get a new pass.

She hadn't been worrying about opiates in her system since she'd been hired. The company didn't seem to do regular testing. No one had mentioned it at all, so apparently, once in, you were safe. However, this was an unusual situation. The seventh-floor security was tight. Maybe they'd want to test her again?

She stopped by her desk and instructed her nanites to remove all traces of drugs from her blood. This was asking for extreme discomfort, but it was only a couple of hours until lunch. Surely they'd tell her if she was going to be tested by then. If she got too ill, she could always claim she was overcome by the situation or maybe was developing the flu.

The nanite control program was on a USB drive. She'd made sure that it left no traces on her workstation, but would she be allowed to do the same on the seventh floor? Would they even let her bring an unsecured USB up there? She slipped it into her waistband and stood up, hoping that there would be no physical screening.

Anyway, it was done now. The initial stage of coming off the drug was already setting in, and she felt like her skin was overly sensitive. Her blouse rubbed uncomfortably on her neck and shoulders.

She felt irritable and didn't want to go down to security. Maybe if she tried swiping her pass and pressing the seventh-floor button.

She was gratified when the elevator door closed, dinged, and the thing started upwards. She was a little surprised but then decided that maybe she'd been authorized remotely. It made it a lot more convenient; that was for sure.

An older woman greeted her when the elevator door opened. "Sophie Monroe?" she asked.

Someone had known she was on her way up. This was an interesting bit of information. The seventh-floor passes must alert someone somewhere when the holder got in the elevator. That was something to remember.

"Yes. That's me."

"I'm Rachael Lewis. Welcome to the inner sanctum. This is the place where the real work is going on. Follow me, and I'll show you to your new workstation."

"Excuse me, Ms. Lewis, but I've only been here a few days. Why would you promote me to this part of the project so quickly?" Sophie was determined to get an answer.

Rachael turned to her with a smile. "Oh, well, Michael looked over your application and the code you've been creating. He's an expert judge of such things. He said that you were wasting your time filter test data. He wanted you up here, and what he wants, he always gets."

Michael O'Keefe wanted her? Sophie's insides felt like they'd been flipped upside down for a moment, but then, despite her increasing malaise, there was a warm feeling in her lower abdomen. She worked at regaining control as they walked past cubicles and workers.

There would be more chances to see Michael. That wasn't bad. What she wanted to make sure of was that she didn't blow her opportunity. She'd have to work as hard and as smart as she could.

Her street persona kicked in for a moment. This was stupid. Just because he was good looking didn't mean anything to her. Besides, she was here for one thing only: revenge.

Best to keep that in mind.

CHAPTER 15
LUNCH WITH MICHAEL

There wasn't a formal orientation course or introduction to the group's project. Instead, Ms. Lewis left her at a vacant workstation, showed her how to log on and then walked away.

Her security level wasn't high enough to allow her to make any changes. She was expected to work her way through the non-classified documentation about the project. This looked like it would take weeks. There were several gigabytes of files, although many had lots of graphics, so it wasn't all text.

She found the index folder and started on the material. Meanwhile, the drug faded from her system, and she was developing a splitting headache.

It became nearly unbearable by eleven thirty. People were moving by her cubicle randomly, but so far, no one had stopped to speak to her.

Taking a chance, she broke a pill in half, while holding it on her lap, then knocked a pen off the desk. She used the excuse of recovering it in order to slip the half pill into her mouth.

She was still at a disadvantage, though. The nanites were continuing to work at ridding her system of the chemical. She didn't dare use the USB on the computer workstation. She had no idea what level of security was in place on this floor.

It stood to reason that if this were the main project for the company's software division, security would be tighter here than on the floor where she'd been. It wasn't as if she'd been careless down there, though. She'd checked her workstation thoroughly and had only used the nanite control language a couple of times.

Using it securely—when there wasn't a Reverb device around – required the software she had on the USB that she carried wherever she went. The memory device had proven to be no problem so far. No one had checked, but they might on this level.

Anyway, she'd have to insert it into the port to run the control software. There might be some monitoring code on her workstation that would detect her action. No. She'd have to wait until lunchtime, then go to the diner that was about a half mile down the street in a small strip mall.

They had a Reverb. The owner thought he had it set securely. The units provided for custom activation words, but her viral software was still in place, and that gave her a back-door command into any Reverb, no matter how securely the owner thought it was locked.

She could get its attention and have it disable her nanites. Then she could take a half-pill and...no; she would wait until she returned to work. Once back at her workstation and safely through security, even as lax as it seemed to be, she could slip another pill in her mouth. That would have to do.

Meanwhile, the half pill she'd taken was helping, but the nanites were annoyingly efficient at getting rid of the drug. She knew she'd feel rotten by the time she got through the lunch hour,

SHE WAS LOOKING at some code and trying to figure out the intent while simultaneously rubbing the back of her neck with

one hand and flipping back to the documentation folder with the mouse. It seemed like it was taking forever for lunch time to come.

She paused, stretched her arms and tried to rub her neck with both hands while leaning back. Her head really hurt.

Her arms were gently brushed aside, and a pair of strong, warm hands began to rub her shoulders and neck.

Sophie gasped and started to straighten, but it felt so good at that moment, she leaned back into the massage. Right then, it could have been a serial killer who was preparing to strangle her. She didn't care. Her eyes closed in relief, and she breathed deeply.

A male voice interrupted her.

"I don't expect you to kill yourself on the first day on my team. Do you have any lunch plans?"

She jumped and turned. Michael was standing behind her, his hands raised in a kind of mea culpa gesture as if he'd suddenly realized that she might not want him touching her.

It hadn't been sexual in any way, but she still felt warm all over, and when she met his eyes, she could feel her cheeks flush.

"Oh! I...I didn't know it was you!" she said.

That sounded stupid, so she added, "I've just got this terrible headache. My neck and shoulders were cramping, probably from stress. I guess I was trying too hard to make sense of what I was reading."

Michael smiled, his handsome face lighting up in a way that made her want to melt into a puddle.

"I appreciate that, but as I said, I don't want you killing yourself on the first day. C'mon! Let's go down to the cafeteria and grab some lunch. I'm buying. I can brief you on what I need you to do while we eat. It'll save you from wading through all of the project documentation. I think that Lewis assigns that just to test new hires. If they survive for more than two days, she figures they have enough expertise to contribute meaningfully to the project."

Sophie stood, somewhat shakily. She suddenly felt a little faint and grasped the back of her chair. Michael's brows knit together and he caught her free arm.

"Are you alright? You looked like you were going to faint for a moment there."

"I'm fine. I guess my headache made me so tense and then your rubbing my neck helped me relax. It must have made me a little dizzy." She hoped he'd let it go at that.

He let her arm go, perhaps a little slowly. She sighed in a combination of anticipation and frustration. She'd have to come up with another way to slow the nanites down. Maybe she'd just keep taking pills until quitting time. It was going to be painful, but on the other hand, she was going to have lunch with Mr. Checks All My Boxes.

They headed for the elevator, Sophie trying to figure out how she would make it through lunch without appearing to be in too much pain.

SHE GOT A bowl of salad and a cup of soup. That was all she thought she could stomach. Her head was beginning to pound again. Michael had taken a hamburger and fries and a piece of apple pie.

He looked at her scantily laden tray and said, "You're going to be a cheap lunch date for me. Are you sure you don't want anything else?"

"No. My head is still acting up. I think this will be about as much as I'll be able to eat."

He paid and led her to an empty table in the back of the room.

Before she started eating, he said, "Don't take this wrong. I don't want to start out on the wrong foot with you, but maybe I can help you a little more with that headache. Let me hold your hands for a moment."

Sophie looked down at her hands. They looked pale and sweaty.

Was this a usual thing with Michael? Did he think it was some odd sort of pass he was making? She started to shake her head, then looked at his face. It showed nothing but open concern. She extended her hands across the table.

His hands were warm and firm. She felt small; her hands engulfed in his larger ones. She watched his face. He closed his eyes, and his forehead smoothed.

She felt a warmth exuding from his touch. It seemed to go up both of her arms, across her shoulders, and then climb into her neck, simultaneously moving downward along her spine. Her headache faded quickly. One moment it was there. The next it was nearly gone. She felt almost as if she'd taken a pill.

She gasped at the strangeness of the event. Michael's eyes opened, and he smiled again.

"It's just a little knack I have. It usually works. My great-grandmother was said to have been a witch." He saw her eyes widen and added quickly, "Oh, not a black one but a white witch. She had the healing touch, and I guess maybe I've inherited a little of it myself. Anyway, let's eat and then we'll talk more. It makes me hungry."

The salad and soup were good, and she found herself looking with envy at his pie. He noticed and said, "Okay. Let's share it. I don't need the calories anyway."

They took turns taking bites from opposite ends. She left the largest piece for him, but he cut it neatly in half and pushed part towards her.

"Half is fair. You eat that. I don't want you telling other people I cheated you out of your part." He continued to talk, his mouth partly full as he ate the last bite.

"I checked the code you provided when you applied. Where did you learn to program like that? Your education doesn't cover it."

She nearly choked on the last swallow.

"I...uh." she swallowed and then took a drink to clear her throat.

"I had a friend who taught me a lot. I knew some stuff from school, but he helped me learn to write apps and got me started doing consulting gigs. You're right. I'm probably not well enough trained for this work. I'm sorry." She trailed off, wondering what to say next.

"Oh, no. Nothing of the sort. I was impressed by what you'd done. Your code is efficient and compact, and you don't waste space. I noticed some places where you had obviously been thinking ahead to other projects. You designed some of your modules for multiple uses. You did write them didn't you?"

"Yes. That was me." She paused, reconsidering. "Well, I do have a free GitHub account. I found some of my routines there, but I always tweak them, so they're more efficient. I don't like to keep inventing the same thing over again, so I've always tried to write routines so that they could be reused in other jobs. The people who've hired me only want their apps to work well. They don't care if all of the code is original."

He smiled. "Okay, I'll accept that. You're obviously good at what you know. I'm going to give you some code to work on that you probably haven't seen before. It's part of what we call a deep learning module. There's recursive ability in it because we intend for the A.I. system...You do know we're working on an A.I., don't you?"

"Yes. I understood that much. I did some studying in the last few days. What level of A.I. are you building and what is the general intent?" She paused, then added, "I...uh, I mean, if it's okay for me to ask that."

"No problem. I'll be general. I don't expect you to have a background in the whole A.I. issue. We're working on what I'll call an AGI. I mean an Artificial General Intelligence. That would be one that has roughly human-level capability."

She repeated, "AGI. Okay, but if there is built-in iterative, recursive ability, wouldn't it have the capacity to escape? Would it turn into a super-intelligence, an ASI?"

Michael laughed. "Ha! You know more than I've been giving you credit for. Well, yes. It could, but we're keeping it isolated and testing carefully to make sure it doesn't jump ahead more quickly than we want. You see, here's the problem. If we can get this thing working and by the way, we've named it Hippocrates."

He paused and glanced around as if he were checking to see if anyone nearby was listening. "Well, it could save the company billions in developing new drugs. What they really want is a genie system that will fulfill wishes. We ask for a drug for any human disease or condition, and it could create it quickly and at a fraction of the cost that it typically takes. You see the value here, of course. I'm talking about improving the lot of every person on earth."

Sophie's mouth had opened a little. This was a massive undertaking, and the implications were astounding. They could fix everything wrong with everyone. Maybe even cure her fibromyalgia and, oh! Of course, she wouldn't need the drugs either. But, possibly that could be taken care of by the nanites she carried.

Then her mind jumped to those minuscule machines. Where had they come from? She thought Hazelton had sent them out, but here Michael was telling her about a project that seemed to have nothing to do with them. For a moment she hesitated, thinking about asking him directly about the nanites. Discretion took over. She needed to know more first, despite the fact that he seemed friendly and had almost entirely disarmed her suspicions.

Feeling like it was her turn to speak and trying to lead away from what she considered a dangerous topic, she asked, "A genie A.I.? So, I could ask it for the perfect mate, and it would find him for me?"

Her face immediately flushed. That sounded so dumb. But, Michael smiled again and said, "Yeah. That's an application I hadn't considered. It could put all the online dating sites, Tender, and everything out of business. Why don't you and I go into business with that idea once we're done with this project? I'll bet we could make millions and retire to a life of sloth on some island somewhere."

Sophie laughed out loud. He was charming. He'd taken her at face value and had acted as if her stupid idea was valuable. She sobered as she considered. He was probably right. They could make a lot of money with a dating app that never failed to find the right match.

She replied, "Wow! I think you're correct. That could work. I was just kind of kidding when I asked it. You're way ahead of me in seeing possibilities."

He grinned. "Look, I hate to act like the boss, but I've got to get back to work. I'm going to give you a section of our current code. You can work through it—don't wear yourself out-- that headache could come back. Anyway, work through it and see if you can create a more elegant way to do what it does. I'm not happy with it at present. What I mean are two things. The first is that it's not very efficient. It takes too much memory and is too slow, and two is that it needs a safeguard; a limiting factor that is beyond the software's ability to get around. That's the actual problem. We can't afford to have Hippocrates go supercritical on us."

Sophie answered, "I think I know what you mean by supercritical. You mean Hippocrates could get so smart that we couldn't control it. Right?"

"That's the crux of the issue. We want it to be just about at human level. That will give it plenty of power. It doesn't need to take breaks to eat or rest, of course, so it should be able to do a lot more a lot more quickly than humans." He paused, looking worried.

It made him look even more attractive to her.

He continued, "I'm getting a lot of pressure from above on this project. The chairman of the board of directors and the CEO are demanding speed. They're convinced that this will give Hazelton total control of the market and there's a ton of government subsidies available right now. They want to get their hands on that money in the worst way. The only thing is, I can't go too fast. I don't want to risk losing control of Hippocrates. I want him to be completely domestic and entirely friendly to humans. There are some nightmare scenarios possible with A.I., and I don't want my name associated with any of them...not that there would be any people left to hate me if one of the worst ones becomes real."

THEY WALKED BACK to the elevator in silence. Sophie was thinking about what he'd told her. Working here was going to be interesting.

MICHAEL SEEMED PREOCCUPIED himself. Apparently what he'd told her was dominating his thoughts. He started to step into the elevator at the same time as her. They both bounced off the sides of the still opening door and suddenly found themselves face-to-face and practically touching.

Sophie looked at Michael's face. He appeared surprised for an instant; then an intent look showed in his eyes as he gazed at her face in return. It took all of what little will-power she had to pull back, laughing with embarrassment.

"Sorry," he mumbled, still looking at her as if he suddenly saw her in a new way. "My fault. I was thinking about work."

She nodded.

He suddenly laughed and added, "I really am sorry. It's not very complimentary to you. I'm too preoccupied with getting Hippocrates going. Maybe we can have lunch another day this week? That will give me a chance to check on what you think about the code I'm sending you. Oh, by the way. It'll be in your inbox within the next fifteen minutes. I'll send it down right away."

He cautioned her as the door opened on their floor, "No working yourself too hard. You understand? No headaches."

Sophie smiled and nodded, then headed for her workstation thinking that if he only knew about her addiction, he wouldn't be so friendly. This thought immediately led to another. Could she keep it from him? Especially if they became... Oh, that was insane. There was no way he'd ever start a relationship with her!

Still, the fantasy was alluring. She briefly thought of the way his body had made hers warm, and that was just when they were standing close together. A brief vision of him taking off his shirt passed through her imagination. Then the reality of her life came crashing home.

She was pathetic. There was really no way he'd be interested in her. She slipped into a self-pitying mode, and that led to the idea of the drug. It never rejected her and always delivered. She sighed and turned towards the woman's restroom.

Once inside, she entered a stall, sat down and took another half pill. His miracle headache cure was still working. She didn't really need it, but she had become used to taking a pill when reality got to be too much for her.

She hesitated, then took another half pill, knowingly lying to herself with the thought that she didn't want to risk hurting so much again.

CHAPTER 16
CRIPPLED GENIE

The code showed up in her inbox precisely fifteen minutes after she'd exited the elevator. Michael was apparently determined to impress her, or maybe he was so focused, that he habitually delivered on his promises. She didn't know, but she liked that he had done what he said he would.

The code was complex. She began to work on it, reading the embedded comments. It was fascinating. She worked on it for a couple of hours, then got up to take a break and get something to drink.

There were other people in the break room, but it seemed to her that they ignored her. She tried to make eye contact with a couple of women, but they turned their heads away. Two other people were conversing and wouldn't even look at her. She saw Ms. Lewis come in and thought that the woman was going to acknowledge her, but all she got was a glance and a dismissive snort.

It was rapidly becoming apparent that the word of her quick promotion and Michael's interest had gotten around. From the looks of things, people resented it and also her. Well, that was too bad. She hadn't taken the job for the social interaction.

When she thought about Michael, it was hard to keep her real purpose in mind. She wanted revenge on whoever was responsible for sending the nanites. The thought of Cal was almost more than she could bear.

They hadn't been lovers, but still, in a way, she realized that she had loved him. He was so trustworthy, helpful, and non-judgmental. He'd taken her as she was, knowing that she was an addict and he'd been able to see value in her. Yes. She was going to avenge him. There was no doubt in her mind about that.

She caught one member of the conversing couple glancing at her. Apparently, something in her current expression was off-putting. The woman involuntarily flinched. Her companion turned to look at Sophie and snapped her head back around quickly.

Sophie had worked herself into a state of anger. These thoughtless fools were working for a company that killed people. She stood abruptly and practically stomped out of the break room.

It took fifteen minutes at her workstation before she could calm down enough to comprehend what she was looking at on the screen. By then, she'd fallen back into her self-pitying mode. She thought of Cal and then ducked under the desk to swallow half a pill.

That helped calm her, and she went back to analyzing the code that Michael had assigned her. She found it fascinating and eventually sank into what was almost a fugue state. Every bit of her mental ability was engaged in understanding the work.

SHE SUDDENLY REALIZED that people were leaving. She'd been so engrossed in going over the program that she'd lost all sense of time. Her head didn't hurt, and the drug had worn off, but she hadn't noticed.

The code was elegant and clear, but there were some aspects that she couldn't quite fathom. She wondered if she could convince

Michael to go over them with her. That would be a good excuse to be near him again.

Oh. I'm acting like an infatuated middle-schooler again. She reluctantly shut down the workstation, gathered her backpack and headed for the bus.

I'd better just get over him. I'll be happier, and there's nothing that can happen anyway. Besides, if I succeed, I'm going to destroy everything about that company that I can.

Her cell phone beeped at that moment. The bus was about two blocks down the street, and some people were getting off. She pulled the phone out and looked at the message. It was alarming.

> *Welcome to the project, Sophie. I'm interested in you. You somehow gained control of the nanomachines. Even the new ones have been co-opted. Your resistance is fascinating. I'm going to enjoy working with you. Or, against you. That's your choice. Cooperate with me or suffer the consequences. Oh, and by the way, (see how well I've mastered the language?) don't tell anyone I've been in touch with you. I'll make sure that security finds out about the drug you've been taking. Yes, I know about that, but I don't care, except that it gives me leverage over you. I'll be in touch when I want something. Best to you,*
>
> > *Wiindigo*

She sat down on the bus stop bench in shock. The enemy had just contacted her, and it knew far too much. Somehow she would have to work with it while being deceptive. The implication was that Michael somehow had lost control of the A.I. He thought it was controlled, but it apparently had created the nanites and sent the zombie-like men in the assault outfits.

It was dangerous. She'd have to be smarter than she'd ever been. The thought was daunting. Somehow she'd have to enlist Michael's aid, but what if he became infected with the nanites and was turned into a zombie? What if he already had them in his system?

She'd have to check. If she could somehow get him out of the building and somewhere near a Reverb or even her laptop, she could take control of any nanites in his body. All she needed was a blue-tooth connection.

The bus door closed and it pulled off, but she didn't notice. An idea had started to develop. She should be able to send the relevant commands through her cell phone. Could she connect directly to his phone and cause it to disable nanites? That was something she'd have to work on tonight. Time was critical. Hippocrates or Wiindigo, whatever, would probably think of that very soon, if it hadn't figured it out already. It seemed to have broken out, at least to the extent that it was able to text her.

There was nothing else to do; she'd have to experiment on Jess. She wished she had someone else to try her idea on, perhaps the white dog that was over in the park. Her mind flashed in recognition. It was the same dog. That was four times she'd seen it.

The dog might be connected to Wiindigo in some fashion. It would be possible to take over an animal with nanites, just as the zombie-like men had been controlled. Maybe it was spying on her. She looked away and then back. The dog didn't seem to be paying attention. It was trotting diagonally away. She was just jumpy. The text message had freaked her out completely. Anyway, here came the next bus.

SOPHIE HAD MADE sure that Jessica had her own nanites days ago. Better to have her friend infected with ones that were under control rather than ones that might harm her. She'd set the nanites to watch for others that were not part of their group, just as she'd done for herself. Defensive action would instantly counter any attempt at invasion.

That was one advantage she had. She'd been able to install an additional level of security for her personal nanomachines. They now used a 128-bit encryption protection. It was keyed to a phrase she and she alone could give to any convenient Reverb unit, not to mention her laptop.

It would be difficult for Wiindigo to wrest control from her although it probably could if given enough time. The corollary to that step was that her nanites now had an offensive weapon against the original ones. They could trap them, although it took several to perform the act. Once they'd captured a wild nanite, they could inject her encryption directly into its code. Then it was hers.

She felt reasonably secure when that was accomplished, but given that she didn't know what level of intelligence Wiindigo had achieved, she was worried. What if it had concealed how far it had advanced and Michael had no idea? What if it now had an IQ so far ahead of humans that her best efforts would seem like an ant trying to stop traffic on an eight-lane highway?

She could easily be dealing with an entity that had an IQ of over ten-thousand or even more. It was impossible to tell, given the limited information she currently possessed.

If it had broken out of confinement, and so it appeared from the text message, it could have moved into the cloud storage used by Hazelton and from there, it could have moved anywhere around the globe through the Internet.

In fact, more than likely, it was busy infiltrating every Internet node. Her relatively simple virus code for the Reverb units could come under attack at any time. Once it understood her encryption scheme, she would be helpless.

ONCE HOME, SHE started working on an app for her phone's operating system. It would have to install itself secretly, of course. That made it a little more difficult. She researched for a while and then decided that if she was going to go to the effort of putting it on Michael's phone, she should make it into a virus that would propagate with every connection to the Internet. With any luck, it would work its way into at least half of all cell phones. That would give her the ability to counter nanite attacks against large segments of the population.

She'd started calling the men in black that had attacked Cal's place Zombies. They had certainly acted zombie-like, with the exception of not having a craving for human brains or something gross. They had obviously been under some form of control that made them lose all concern for self-preservation.

In a fit of whimsy, she coded the phrase "anti-zombie shot" into her newly constructed virus. Then it was time for a test.

JESSICA WAS IN the bathroom doing something with her hair. She'd left her cell phone in her bedroom, so it was no problem to grab it and hook it to Sophie's laptop. A few keystrokes and the virus was installed.

She disconnected it and returned it to precisely the same spot on the bed where she'd found it. She had to wait for Jess to finish her hair treatment and then she'd see if it worked.

ABOUT FIFTEEN MINUTES later Jessica walked down the hall, toweling her hair dry as she went. Sophie waited a couple of minutes and then keyed a text message to Jess' number. The text went through, so she got up and walked down the hall to check.

Jess was sitting on the bed, looking at her phone, motionlessly. Sophie walked over and poked her friend on the shoulder.

No response. It appeared to have worked.

The text message itself was simple. It said, "You are fine!" It was what happened when it was opened that was complex. The hidden code activated the phone's blue-tooth transmitter, even if it was nominally turned off and then sent a short-range command to any nearby nanites to create a hypnotic state in their host.

Jess was still conscious but fascinated by the message, to the point of being oblivious to any external stimuli.

Sophie texted a countering message along with a suggestion to her friend's number and then went back down the hall.

"Hey, Jessica? What are you going to do for supper?" she asked.

Jessica looked up from her phone and answered, "I've got a fantastic idea. It just came to me. I'm famished for pizza. Let's go out to Mama's Place. Okay?"

Sophie said, "Okay. Pizza it is. I'm ready when you are."

"Just give me a few minutes to finish drying my hair, and we'll go," her friend said.

SUPPER WAS GOOD. The pizza at Mama's was always the best, and Sophie particularly enjoyed the fact that Jessica agreed to her suggestion of pepperoni. Jessica always wanted sausage and hamburger, which wasn't Sophie's favorite. This time Sophie got her way, thanks to the residual hypnotic suggestion.

Sophie smiled secretly to herself. This could be fun, given the right circumstances and if she wasn't so worried about the rogue A.I.

WALKING INTO WORK was frightening. Wiindigo could have prepared a nasty surprise for her. She approached her workstation with trepidation and leaned back as it powered up.

There was nothing out of the ordinary there. The screen didn't have any messages, nor was there anything she could detect in memory. She performed a complete scan of the machine and then poked into some areas in the kernel that could be used to hid pointers to malware. Nothing.

She went back to her job of analyzing the code segment Michael had sent to her. As before, it was fascinating, although this time, the drug had worn off by about eleven thirty and she was getting head-achy again.

Her shoulders were knotted, and that was causing her neck to pull at the base of her skull. She could tell that she'd better take another pill soon.

Finally, she used the same technique as before. She dropped a pen, then palmed and took a full pill while she was under her desk.

When she straightened, Michael was standing right beside her chair. She swallowed the pill with an audible gulp, then started coughing.

He patted her back until she was able to get her cough under control.

IF HE WERE going to sneak up on her, it would only be a matter of time before he caught her taking a pill. This had been close.

She coughed once more and then said, "You startled me, and I swallowed the wrong way, I guess. Thanks for helping."

He looked at her carefully. So carefully, in fact, that she wondered if he suspected she'd taken something.

"Glad to help. I'm sorry I frightened you."

He glanced at her screen.

"Have you gotten that far or are you skipping sections of code?" he asked.

"No. I'm working through every part of it and trying to understand it as I go," she answered. "I do have a question, though."

"Why don't we go to lunch again? You can ask it then."

She stood and smiled. "That would be nice."

THEY MADE SOME small talk as they started to eat and Sophie forced herself to ask for his phone number. That was far bolder than she usually acted and it made her quite uncomfortable.

"Michael, I was, uh, wondering if, I mean, uh, would you give me your cell? I mean, if that's allowed. That way I could text you if I get stuck with the code or something."

She looked down. Once again she'd said something that sounded stupid, maybe even suggestive. She didn't know why he had that effect on her.

When she looked up, he was apparently amused.

"Oh, that's not a problem. I'd be more than happy to help if you get stuck," he said, grinning.

This was getting worse. Now he probably thought she'd been hitting on him. She found him unbearably attractive, yet she wanted something different in her life. Something other than the cheap physical attraction that had been all she'd ever gotten. She suddenly realized that she wanted him to romance her. This wasn't just some quick flare of passion that she was feeling.

She knew she was bright red, but she forced herself to answer seriously. "I found a couple of places in the code that refer to a routine that doesn't seem to be there. They're mandatory calls that are keyed to become active after fifteen iterations or at six pm. I can't understand what their purpose is."

He shook his head slowly, making her think that he was going to say something negative, but again he surprised her.

"I'm pleased that you saw those and asked about them. They're part of my security routines. As I mentioned, I don't want Hippocrates to break through the human level. At least not until I'm fully assured that he will be domestically oriented. I don't want him to go wild covering the surface of the globe with pill factories or something. Got to protect ourselves against accidental extinction, of course."

Sophie nodded, her eyes fixed on his face and repeated, "Of course."

He continued, "The fifteen iteration call goes to an intelligence evaluation module. It shuts him down completely, stops all recursive code generation, and runs diagnostics designed to test him. If he's reached human level, I'll be alerted and will be able to intervene. If he's above human level, part of his code will automatically be erased. Oh, it'll be copied first, but it will be wiped from all storage available to him. That's also what happens at the time call. His self-improvement gets recorded, tested, then wiped. Every morning, I get here early and check his progress. If he's still safe, I reload the progress from yesterday and start him working again."

Sophie was quiet. She was wondering if Wiindigo was the same entity as Hippocrates and she was also wondering if the A.I. had figured out a way around the crippling measures. Finally, she asked, "Could he find a way around either of these steps?"

Michael shrugged, and said, "If he does, then we could be in big trouble. I've got one more safeguard, but that's a private one."

Sophie looked away, then back, "I...I was just worried, that's all."

"And right you are to be worried. We're potentially dealing with a serious problem, and we have to be careful."

She asked, "Is there any way he could gain access to the web or break out?"

Michael shrugged again, this time with a helpless expression on his face. "God! I hope not. I've got him boxed as tightly as I can. You'll never see his actual code on your workstation. I move everything manually to the single system that interfaces with him, and he's locked in a secure room."

Then he smiled and laughed quietly. "I hope that makes you feel better."

She smiled in return, then said, "Yes, that makes me feel better. I trust your ability to keep us safe."

CHAPTER 17
FATE

She finished the code segment analysis around mid-afternoon. She emailed Michael that she was done and felt she understood the intent, if not the actual results that would be obtained by the A.I.

The segment was involved with deep learning and provided a variety of data input modes. The A.I. could select exactly how it wanted to examine objects ranging from text through pictures all the way to 3-d, real-world items. What it did with the data wasn't immediately apparent to her.

Michael responded with another code segment paired with a message.

> *Sophie:*
> *Take a look at this part. It provides Hippocrates with a way to symbolically represent items and store the representations in a data form of his design.*
> *Let me know what you think.*
> *Michael*

His request was curt, but she imagined she could read warmth into it. Perhaps she was fooling herself, remembered his engaging smile and voice. Anyway, she found herself feeling warm and happy as she reread the message.

She started working her way through the new section of code. There were some calls to external routines that weren't provided. She could guess what most of them did based on the context, but there was something that bothered her.

One of the routines was called twice in an odd way. It could be called with a parameter set that dictated how it would respond. It looked like it was involved with storage of the current data representation.

The problem was the parameters referred to another segment of code that was near the end of what Michael had sent her. She jumped ahead and read through it.

She shook her head and read through it a second time. It would select a pointer to the memory location for the data, but if one of the parameters was set to a specific value, it would first write a single byte into an unassigned memory location.

Sophie was puzzled. What was the purpose of that? It didn't seem to relate to anything that she had read so far. Why was the code taking that action?

Oh. It must be a flag, perhaps it relates to the type of data that is currently being analyzed and stored. Otherwise, it makes no sense. I'll have to ask Michael about it.

She shrugged and went back to where she'd been in the document. The rest of it was complicated but relatively straightforward. It did what Michael had indicated it was supposed to do.

She was almost back at the puzzling area when quitting time rolled around. People began to stir and pack their things, exiting in small groups.

She read through the odd segment of code one more time and then started to get up.

She stood, then had to brace herself on her desk. She suddenly felt terrible. It was like she'd contracted a raging fever in the past minute.

The pain was bad, making it hard to concentrate. There could be only one cause. She was being attacked by nanites.

The fever faded, and she felt better for a moment, but then she was dizzy. She thought about using her workstation to send a series of commands that would give her control of the invaders, but, if they'd been sent by the A.I., it would doubtless intercept her command sequence, and that would allow it to crack her security almost instantly.

She had to get out of the building. Her internal nanomachines were putting up a battle and seemed to be holding their own for the moment. If the attacking nanites were reinforced though, her own might not be able to cope.

She found herself in the elevator, cursing under her breath that it took so long to descend. The door chimed, and she started out, only to realize she was on the third floor.

She stopped and pushed the first-floor button again. The woman who was entering took one look at her and stepped back out. Sophie felt that she must look sick. At least the woman apparently thought something was wrong with her. She was glad that she was alone, she felt so terrible.

She leaned against the wall and realized that she was covered in a cold sweat. This wasn't going well. She didn't want to use her cell to broadcast a command either. It could be intercepted almost as easily as the workstation. She realized that she needed some non-electronic way to control her nanites. If she could just issue commands by thought without the intermediary of an electronic device...

The elevator stopped. She straightened and headed for the door. Somehow she made it out of the building and headed down the street. Her objective was to get as far away from the place as possible. That would make it difficult for reinforcing nanites to reach her.

She felt better again. Her defense was at least partially holding up. There was a small park about three hundred meters ahead of her. That might offer a temporary place to rest. She staggered on.

Her mind slowly started working again. There would be more of the attacking nanites on her clothing. They could be attempting to reach her skin and infiltrate her system. What to do?

The park had a small pond with a fountain in the center. She took several shaky steps and plunged into the water. It felt ice cold to her over-heated body. Once in, she submerged and scrubbed wildly at her body. The nanites wouldn't be damaged by the water of course, but perhaps she could dislodge them. They'd still be near her in the water though.

It was deep enough to swim, and she stroked away toward the fountain. The water there was shallower. She stood and let the descending stream wash over her like a shower. After a bit, she moved under another stream that came from the other side of the fountain.

She probably couldn't get all of the attackers washed off, but enough was enough. The water was cold. She'd forgotten about her fever. It didn't seem to be present now. Perhaps her defenders had stopped the attack, or maybe the cold water had helped cool her. She didn't know. All that mattered now was to get out of the cold and somehow get home.

She plunged back into the deeper water and swam to the shore. The bank was steep, and she had difficulty climbing out. She slipped back, but someone grabbed her arm and pulled. She slid up on the wet grass, rolled over, and looked into Michael's face.

"Oh, my God!" she exclaimed. "You! What will you think of me?"

He shook his head quizzically, then said, "That you enjoy swimming in the cold? Maybe you're a member of the Polar Bear Club? I don't know. What in Heaven's name were you doing in there?"

Sophie felt ill again. How could she tell him what had happened to her? Maybe he was responsible for the attack. Could she trust him?

Then she looked at his face.

His eyes were wide. He looked open and concerned. Something in her, some hard element of distrust that had ingrained itself into her personality quivered. She had learned never to trust anyone. Cal had been the sole exception to that rule since her mother had died.

Michael pulled off his jacket and wrapped it around her.

"You've got to be freezing. It's lucky I saw you. My car is over there. Let's go." He led her towards a black BMW parked nearby, his arm wrapped protectively around her shoulders.

They didn't speak until they reached the car and he opened the passenger door.

Sophie balked. She was covered with water, duckweed, and mud. The car was like new, and the leather seat looked entirely too nice for the mess she would make.

"No. I can't get in there," she said, panicking again.

"Why not? You're not too large to fit in the seat, are you? Is it not good enough for you?"

She could see he was trying to be humorous.

"No. I..." She stopped and shivered violently. "I don't want to ruin your nice car." Her sentence ended with a sob, and she found herself crying and gasping for breath.

Michael put his arm around her again and gently but firmly eased her into the seat.

"The car can be cleaned. I, uh, don't want to think about you getting sick. Whatever possessed you?" he said.

Sophie looked at him. His voice had held a note of concern that sounded suspiciously like tenderness. He couldn't really be... he couldn't care for her that way. Could he? Her experiences with men hadn't been on that level. She wasn't a virgin and hadn't been for a long time. No male had ever acted that way about her. It was always about the heat of passion and quick release, and then it inevitably fell apart. She couldn't trust this sort of approach either. She had no experience with it, and that frightened her.

He closed the door, strode around to the driver's side and got the car started. The heat was great, but she couldn't seem to stop shivering.

"Where do you live?" he asked. "We've got to get you warmed up and dry before you shiver yourself to death."

She said, "About a mile down the street in the Quadrant apartments. I share a place with Jessica Kingston."

"Oh, I know Jess. She works in the executive offices for Chuck Overstreet. Frankly, I don't know how she stands him." He laughed.

Sophie tried to laugh also, but since she didn't know anyone at the executive level of the company, it sounded flat to her ears. She didn't trust Michael, and she was worried about her strange response to him. His presence weighed on her but in a pleasant way. She couldn't ignore him. His masculinity generated an intense sensation in the pit of her stomach. She knew she shouldn't allow herself to care, but she could feel emotion welling up from deep within her.

God! He was so attractive. Was he as nice a person as he seemed? She couldn't know unless she took a chance on him. Could she do that? Was it safe?

Michael drove silently for a bit, then said, "Now. Seriously. I want you to tell me what happened and don't try to hide anything. I told you about my healing gift. What I didn't tell you was that I can also tell when someone is lying."

She began to cry again, tried to suppress it and hiccuped. He glanced at her, and his expression was so caring that she started sobbing, her mind was a chaos of conflicting impulses. She had no idea how to proceed, and her past gave her no helpful clues. This was...this was too much. She couldn't tell him the truth. It was unbelievable, and she still feared that he might be responsible for the attack.

The BMW's wheels screeched as Michael slammed on the brakes so hard that she lurched forward against the seat belt. The car swerved to the side of the road, and he shoved it into Park.

The next thing Sophie knew was that his arms were wrapped around her and her head was against his muscular chest. She looked up at his face with amazement.

His eyes seemed to get larger and larger as his face grew closer, then their lips touched.

It was as if she'd never been kissed before. No. She knew that she'd never really been kissed. Not like this. Not ever.

His kiss held both passion and tenderness. No man who had ever touched her had made her feel this way.

She sighed and kissed him back. Their lips parted, and his breath mingled with hers causing a flare of white-hot passion that shot through her nerves. Her breathing intensified and deepened.

The brittle, defensive shell around her heart cracked into a million pieces at that moment. She was totally lost, and she knew it. This man! This man that she didn't even know that she could trust was the one. He was the one she was made for. She knew this with every fiber of her heart.

She pulled back with a sob. If only he'd come into her life a long time ago.

Would he hate her? Could he forgive her for all of her self-induced problems? Her addiction? Killing someone? Her desire for revenge?

Michael, too, was breathing heavily, and his face was flushed.

"Sophie! Sophie! Sophie! I don't think I'll ever get tired of saying your name. From the first moment I saw you, I knew that you were the one I'd been waiting for."

Her eyes went even wider. He nodded in affirmation.

"It's true. If I don't love you, then I have no conception of what love is and never will," he said. "Now, tell me what you were doing in that pond."

She couldn't. It was too dangerous. If he wasn't aware of the nanites, it could lead to his death or to him becoming one of the antenna men that she'd seen. She shook her head no, but then found herself starting to talk despite her resolve to keep quiet.

"I'M NOT WHO I seem, Michael. I'm not a nice, good little girl. You deserve someone better than me."

He shook his head in denial. "That's not true. Do you think I'm not smart enough to do my own research? I know you've been arrested twice for drug use. I know your mother died when you were young. I even know that you've been bringing a USB into the office and inserting it into your workstation. You did know that is supposed to be prohibited, didn't you?"

The blood rushed out of her face. She could feel it. Her eyes must have shown her fear.

He looked alarmed at her expression, then said, "It doesn't make any difference to me. I'm hopeless. I'm a real Irish romantic at heart, and I've realized that my heart belongs to you. We'll get through whatever problems you have. Tell me!"

For the first time since she was on her own, Sophie began to tell the entire truth. She didn't want to, but something about Michael was almost hypnotizing. She couldn't help herself.

CHAPTER 18
THE TRUTH

Sophie began. "Michael, I have something I've got to tell you. I don't want to because it could be...no, I'm sure it will be dangerous for you. I don't know how to start – "

He interrupted her, stroking her cheek with his hand.

"Just tell me what you think I should know. I've already figured out a lot, I think."

She couldn't help herself. His touch had reminded her of her mother's caresses when she was a child before things had gone wrong in her life.

Hot tears trickled down her cheeks, and she looked down, embarrassed.

"I'm an addict. I've been on the street, on my own since I was twelve. I can't break my habit. You...I know you'll hate me. You should fire me and never see me again. I – "

He kissed her gently.

"That's the last thing I would do. Not seeing you again would kill me. I have a confession too. All my adult life I've had my way with women. They just seem to throw themselves at me, but I've never met anyone that interested me enough to get serious. Then you came in and I somehow just fell for you. I can't explain it, but there it is. I don't care what your past life was or what you did. If you're an addict, we'll figure out a way to fix it."

She kissed him back, hoping that he wouldn't recoil. He didn't. His arms tightened around her, and suddenly there was a real fire in his response. It seemed forever before she pulled back.

"That's not all," she said. "There's something evil going on with your company. I...I'm afraid that it has figured out a way to get loose despite your security. Do you know about the nanites?"

He looked surprised. "How do you know about them? That's a top-secret project in the Fresno division. There's not supposed to be any information about them at this location."

SOMETHING CLICKED IN Sophie's mind. Her creative streak had been working even during the passionate kiss. She pulled out her phone and swiped the screen. It was one of the new water-resistant ones, so the immersion had not damaged it.

The screen opened to her command app. She keyed a series of commands and pressed send. There was an instant response in the skin of her upper left arm. It felt painful, then warm. There was a blinding flash of light in her left visual field. After that, nothing.

Michael had watched, saying nothing. When the flash occurred, she'd flinched slightly, and he reached out to her.

"What happened? What did you just do?"

She smiled. "I'm full of the nanites, but they're mine. I control them. I just created a short-range transmitter under the skin of my arm. I've been controlling them with external electronics, mostly Reverb units, but now I have more direct control of the ones in my body."

She belatedly realized that her revelation might horrify him, but he just looked interested.

"How do you know you have nanites?" he asked, cocking his eyebrow as if he didn't quite believe her.

In response, she thought a command. The skin on the back of her left hand instantly changed color forming the words, "I know" in red. She held it in front of his face, then caused the nanites to dissipate. The words faded.

"Holy Mother!" he exclaimed. "Those were not supposed to be released." He grabbed both of her shoulders and held her firmly, looking directly into her eyes.

"Tell me!"

SOPHIE TOLD HIM about Cal rescuing her, teaching her, getting caught hacking into Hazelton, and the attack. He listened quietly. When she hesitated, fearing to tell him she had sought her job solely to find revenge, he asked, "This Cal. Was he your lover?"

Men! She smiled, actually a little relieved. He was jealous.

"No. I mean I think I loved him in a way, but as a friend. He never treated me sexually. He just cared about me as a person, and somehow, I don't know how he saw potential that I didn't know I had. He spent a lot of effort on me and even helped me reduce my pill taking. He was a good man, and now he's dead!" Her voice rose at the end, and she started to shake a little.

Michael pulled her close. "Okay. I think I understand. Something is going on that I don't know about and haven't considered. I figured I had Hippocrates completely under control, but it sounds like he's broken out somehow."

Her face was muffled against his chest, making her next words come out softly. "I don't know if it's Hippocrates. I got two text messages from someone or something that called himself Wiindigo. I think it's an A.I. It sounded smart, but you said that Hippocrates is limited and has an automatic reset, right? What is this other thing then?"

He thoughtfully repeated, "Wiindigo. That's a Shawnee word that means something like 'insane one' or possibly 'evil spirit.'"

His arms tightened around her again.

"I don't know what or who that could be. We've taken every effort to keep the A.I. in a box."

She asked, "Do you know about the antenna-zombie men?"

"What are you talking about?" he looked down at her.

"Some of the Hazelton employees, security mostly, I think, have antennas on their foreheads that are used to control them somehow. Probably through nanites, but I'm not sure."

She continued. "Oh, Michael. I've got enough control over the nanites to cause them to kill people. I didn't say. It was too horrible. At the end of the attack, when Cal was killed, he'd mutated and had tentacles. Raul killed him and was going to kill me. I directed the nanites to stop Raul's heart. He died instantly. I...I'm a murderer. I'm no good. You can't love me."

He shook his head in denial. "You were faced with a life and death situation. You only defended yourself. I find that admirable. I don't want a woman who is a victim at heart."

"But, that's what I am. I take Oxy to help kill the pain I feel in my neck and shoulders, but it also makes me forget about how many mistakes I've made and all the bad things that have happened to me. I'm no good."

He said softly, "You're good for me, and that's all that counts. Now let's go to your place and get you dry. Not another word until we're there. We've got plenty of time to plan what to do."

Her phone chimed with an incoming text. She nearly dropped it in surprise, then opened the message.

> *Nice move, Sophie. I'm impressed. You survived the nanites. Somehow you've learned to control them. I'm going to have to work on that issue. Be at work tomorrow. That way I won't have to send anyone to find you. Don't worry. Someone as smart as you can be a help to me. I promise I won't harm you.*
> *Wiindigo*

She showed Michael the message, wordlessly. He read it, then re-read it. When he looked up, their eyes met, and she could see the horror on his face, but also a kind of grim determination. He wasn't going to give up, that was obvious.

"Okay, Sophie. I'll admit that your story was a little crazy, but this confirms what you've said. We've got a serious problem. I need you to work with me."

He suddenly grinned, an impish expression. "Of course, that doesn't mean that I don't need you in another way also. I was serious when I said that I love you. I do."

This time, it was she who tightened her arms and pulled his head down for a kiss. When they broke, he was breathing hard, and his hand shook as he reached for the gear shift.

"Let's get you cleaned up. Then we'll see what we can do," he said.

Sophie nodded wordlessly, her heart too full and her mind too confused to speak.

CHAPTER 19
IT SEEMS LIKE LOVE

Jess wasn't home. There was a note on the kitchen counter that said: *"Alex from accounting asked me out! We're going for drinks and maybe dancing. I'll probably be back late unless I decide to let him get lucky ;-)"*

Michael looked at it and shook his head in amusement, then turned to Sophie and said, "It's just you and me. We can talk, but first I want you to get a hot shower to warm up. While you do, I'll see if I can find something in the fridge for us to eat."

Sophie shivered her way to the bathroom. He was right. She was freezing. The walk from the car to the apartment had chilled her again, and it didn't seem all that warm inside.

She grabbed some clothes from her room, hesitated, then swallowed a pill. She told herself that it would help her combat the chill. Once inside the bathroom, she locked the door. After it clicked, she paused, staring at the lock. Why had she locked it? She either trusted Michael or not. It wasn't like she hadn't been with a man before either.

She snorted at her indecisiveness and, with a sense of rebellion against her fears, unlocked the door. If he came in that would tell her something. If he didn't, then...she glanced at herself in the mirror. She didn't know what to think. Her hair and makeup were a wet mess, and he'd been kissing her with every sign of passion. How could that be if he wasn't serious? He had to have feelings for her to kiss her the way he had.

She warmed up the water and got in, leaving her sodden clothes in a heap on the tile. The heat was marvelous, and she stopped shivering as her skin flushed with warmth.

She washed the duckweed out of her hair and scrubbed at her skin extra hard. There might still be nanites clinging to her. Her internal defenders had worked hard to protect her. She wanted to give them a rest. No telling when there would be another attack.

As she warmed up, she composed a set of commands that would, she hoped, co-opt any wild nanites that entered her system in the future. She stored the commands in a memory cache that she had her nanites create and attach to her subcutaneous arm transmitter. That way they could be activated instantly, or at least as soon as she became aware of an attack.

IT TOOK LONGER than she wanted to dry her hair. The blower didn't get the job done quickly since her hair was long, fine, and thick. It never dried quickly. She brushed away under the hot air, trying to think about what she would do about Michael.

She couldn't decide. She'd already told him too much by some measures. On the other hand, if she admitted the way she felt to him and then acted on it, she would have to tell him her entire story in complete detail.

She looked at her reflection in the mirror. Her hair was nearly dry, and she smiled a little, wondering if Michael would kiss her again.

There was a light knock at the door. She grabbed a towel and wrapped it around herself, then opened it a crack.

Michael stood there, looking a little uneasy.

"I couldn't find much in the kitchen, so I just cooked some bacon and eggs. You'd better come and eat now. The eggs are getting cold."

His eyes flickered from her face to the top of the towel and down for a moment. He looked up to find her smiling at him.

"Oh, the hell with the eggs!" he said. The next second, he'd pushed the door completely open, and his arms were wrapped around her.

Their lips met and opened in a long, passionate kiss.

Sophie pulled back quivering. She pushed him towards the bedroom.

"Michael, the eggs can wait. I can't," she whispered.

Things happened quickly after that. He'd been correct. It was like they'd been made for each other. She had never met a man she desired so intensely, and there had been none that could instantly reduce her to a shaking, sweating mass of passion the way he did.

SOMETIME LATER, HE kissed her gently and said, "I guess the eggs will be cold. Maybe we should go out to eat?"

Sophie tightened her arms around him pulling him closer, not ready to disengage yet.

"I don't care about the cold eggs. We can reheat them. If we go out, we can't do this again, and I think I won't want to wait very long before we do. Let's stay here."

He nodded, a smile on his face.

"Okay, when you put it that way, but it'll take me a bit to recover. Let's try the reheated eggs."

He pulled on his pants, and she pulled a long tee-shirt over her head, then they walked into the kitchen, trying to hold onto each other as they passed through the narrow hall.

THE EGGS WERE pretty bad, but the bacon was still crisp. She made some coffee for them, and they sat at the small table to eat.

Their eyes kept meeting and each time she saw his face, a thrill of passion slid deliciously through her.

He finished his food first, pushed his chair back, and said, "Sophie, I've never felt about anyone, the way I feel about you. I know it sounds crazy, but that's the truth. Still, we've got a problem, and we're going to have to figure out some way of dealing with it."

She sipped her coffee and nodded, waiting for him to go on.

He glanced at the outline of her breasts under her tee shirt, swallowed, and obviously dragged himself back to the topic they had to discuss.

"How did you get control of the nanites? How did you even know they were present? Can you tell me that, please?"

Sophie shuddered, remembering.

"It was like a disease that came on quickly. Cal was sicker than I was and I tried to help him. Somehow I cracked into the nanite control frequency and realized they were using a variation of a language I'd been studying out of curiosity. I took control of the ones in my body using the blue-tooth transmitter in my laptop. From that point, I was able to use them in my defense. I told you about commanding them to kill the man who was attacking me."

He nodded, "I remember you saying that. So, let me get this straight. You've got nanites in you right now based on what you did with your hand. What was that you said about an internal transmitter? Do you still need a blue-tooth transmitter to control them, or how do you do it?"

She said, "I got smart. I had the nanites create a transmitter under the skin of my left shoulder. It's powered by muscle movements through a piezoelectric setup. I even set it up with memory storage. Right now I've got a set of commands ready that will protect me against another nanite attack."

He shook his head wonderingly. "You're incredible. What was the language that you were studying that controlled them?"

"It was a simple language that was designed to control CRISPR genetic modification. I thought it was interesting, even though I couldn't see any chance of ever getting to use it. I read through the entire manual. Luckily it's designed for students and is fairly simple."

He said, "I've never heard of it."

She continued, "I think the nanites are or were originally intended to create genetic modifications in people. They can be programmed to do practically anything with the human body. Cal's hands and arms turned into tentacles before he was killed. It was horrible."

The memory made her face crumple with emotion. She wished she had better self-control for a moment, but Michael distracted her by sliding his chair next to hers and putting his arms around her.

"Don't worry, darling. We'll figure out a way to deal with the situation. It's just that I've got to understand what's going on. Hippocrates is totally under control as far as I know. He's isolated and has no pathway to reach the outside world. Plus, as I told you, there's the growth limiter I built in. I don't think he can change it since it's not all software. I put that part of the code in firmware and it can't be reprogrammed. He's stuck with it whether he wants it or not, but I don't think he even realizes it's there. Still, there has to be some way he's doing this unless it's another A.I. entirely."

Her eyes widened in fear. Another A.I.? She'd been sure the problem was centered around Hazelton. If there was another A.I. that was loose, particularly one that was ill-intentioned, they could be in an all-out struggle for survival. The enemy had already gotten way ahead of them. All they were doing was reactive, trying to defend against attacks that were impossible to predict.

Another thought occurred to her. Her phone! Wiindigo could text her. Could it also use the GPS ability of the phone to locate her? Did it know where she was now and were the zombie men coming with guns?

She blurted out her fear to Michael. He listened, then ran back into the bedroom. He came out with her phone and shoved it into the microwave oven.

"That should cut out all signals from the phone. However, if it was being tracked, whoever it is will know where we are. The mere fact of the signals ceasing will alert them to the fact that we're suspicious. We'd better get out of here quickly. Get dressed and grab what you need. We're going to find a hotel somewhere."

Sophie jumped up and ran to get her possessions. Her laptop, her case of pills, the money stash, and clothes. Michael dressed while she madly threw things on the bed.

He looked startled at the pile of money she dug out of her hiding place. The pistol simply caused him to nod grimly.

When she placed the briefcase of pills on the bed, he looked in, then looked at her.

"We've got to get you off these things. They're opiates, right?"

Sophie felt a surge of shame. "Yes. I'm hooked. I told you I was an addict. I'm no good and now I – " She paused, evaluating her feelings.

"Now, I love you, and I couldn't bear it if you left me, but I can't see how I can give them up," she said, hopelessly.

"Don't worry about it, honey. I'm not giving up on you no matter what. We'll work on the pills, too. Right now, though, we've got to get going."

SOPHIE SUDDENLY THOUGHT about Jessica. What if she came back and the place was full of zombie-men? They'd probably kill her without pausing to think about it. If there were wild nanites there, well, she'd set up a protective system within Jessica using her tame nanites. That might let the friendly girl survive. She'd have to be warned.

She turned to Michael. "May I use your phone to warn my roommate? I don't want her coming back and getting hurt."

He handed it to her, and she dialed Jessica's number. The phone rang several times, then Jessica answered, obviously trying to catch her breath.

"Hello? Is this Mr. O'Keefe? Your name came up on my caller ID. I, uh, keep all the executives in the company in my contact list."

Sophie thought that was rather unlikely, but the idea that Jessica had taken the effort to enter Michael's number was slightly amusing.

"No, Jess. It's me, Sophie. I'm in trouble, and I don't want you coming back to the apartment tonight. It might be dangerous."

"Wait! What? How are you using Michael's phone? Is he there, or did you steal his cell?" Jessica was obviously confused.

Sophie snapped, "There's no time to explain. Michael and I are leaving the apartment, and I don't want you to come back tonight, or even tomorrow. Find some place to stay, please."

Jess laughed. "Don't be so dramatic. I'll stay away until tomorrow. I was going to call you and let you know that I'm going to stay with Alex tonight. I think that he and I have hit it off. If you're really with Michael, though, you'll have to promise to tell me all about it later."

Sophie repeated, "Stay with him and don't come home. When you do, make sure you have company. There could be some bad guys here looking for me."

Michael took the phone from her hand and terminated the call.

"We can't keep talking. The rogue A.I. might have my number also. I'm leaving my phone in the microwave with yours. Now let's get out of here."

They were down the road in his car within minutes.

NEITHER OF THEM noticed the gray cat that was sitting by the street lamp at the corner, watching them as they passed.

CHAPTER 20
UNEXPECTED HELP

Michael wanted to go to his house and trade cars. Besides the BMW, he owned a beautiful antique Jaguar. It was old enough not to have any electronics and could not be traced by GPS. The only drawback was that it was so distinctive looking that people were likely to notice it.

He said, "Let's get my Jag. No tracing it, except if a cop car with a license plate reader passes nearby. We'll probably be able to get somewhere that will be relatively safe for a short while. I'm assuming that this Wiindigo is going all out to find you."

He paused a moment, thinking, then added, "And me. I can't see how it could ignore me at this point. I know too much. Besides I'm not going to leave you." He turned to her. "You know that, don't you?"

Sophie nodded, still amazed that he wanted her.

In response, he said, "I just found you, and I'm not giving you up. Not to anyone, even some rogue A.I. that's most likely much smarter than me."

Sophie said, "Look. It undoubtedly knows where you live. I don't think we should stay there for long. I'll check for wild nanites when we get there. If there are any, then it's a safe bet that Wiindigo knows or will find out shortly where we are."

A thought occurred to her. If Wiindigo was controlling the nanites, then she might still have some attached to her that she hadn't managed to scrub off. She pushed on her transmitter and scanned the general area. It was clean. There was nothing on her body at this time, except for her tame nanobots.

That exercise led her to scan the car. Vacant. Then a sudden surmise struck her. Michael. She hadn't checked him.

She scanned for transmissions coming from his body. There seemed to be some activity, but it was on a low level. Sophie tensed. What if he were carrying some of Wiindigo's minions?

She sent a query towards him, using the CRISPR language. It requested a status report.

The report was delivered: Status nominal.

She drew back from him and sent a series of commands that were designed to cause any nanites to exit his body. There was no response.

She tried again, this time commanding them to freeze him; to stop all of his action. She was so terrified that she hadn't thought about the fact that he was currently driving at high speed.

Nothing happened. He continued driving as if she hadn't just commanded his body to be paralyzed.

She made a final try. This time she sent a command to make his right hand go limp. Again no direct action, except he looked at her and said, "Stop it. If you're successful, you could cause us to have an accident."

She flushed. He'd somehow known all along that she was trying to mess with his nanite population.

"H...How did you know I was trying something?" she managed to ask.

He replied, "I felt a little funny somehow. What were you trying to do?"

"I was trying to get control of your nanites," she answered.

"My nanites? I don't think I have any in me," Michael said.

"But...but, I can sense some low-level activity in your body. You must have some," she said.

For an answer, he lifted his index finger and waved it slightly from side to side. She felt dizzy.

"How did you do that," she asked.

"I've told you that my granny was gifted. It's been my blessing and curse that all my life I've been able to do things like that. I have some weird type of energy field control, although it's not conscious. I can usually cause things to happen, even though I can't always predict what will occur."

He drove silently for a bit, then said, "It wouldn't surprise me if I do have some nanites. If they're in Hazelton as you've indicated, then it's perfectly logical that everyone there would have them. I'd be a prime target, too. My position is such that controlling me would amount to a real coup."

She said, "I can see that you'd be the number one target in the whole company. Controlling you would allow Hippocrates to break out and go super-critical. It could escape easily."

He answered, "Yes, but that hasn't happened as far as we know. This Wiindigo seems to be something else. I don't know where it came from or where it resides, processor-wise or memory-wise, I mean."

Sophie was struck with the problem. Then a possible solution occurred to her. "Perhaps the two are related but different. Maybe someone made a copy of Hippocrates and smuggled it out. Now it's either gone past the general A.I. level or is about to. We have to find out where it's hiding and stop it somehow. Do you think Hippocrates can or will help us?"

Michael replied, "You tried to mess with nanites that you say are in my body, right?"

This was not the response she expected. He was approaching the problem from an orthogonal direction.

"Yes. I'm sorry, but I did. I thought you had some and I wanted to get control of them and make them safe. I've encoded all of mine so that the control commands are different than those the wild ones use. Unless Wiindigo can crack my encryption, I'm safe from him. I wanted to do the same for you."

Michael smiled at her, looking away from the road for an instant to do so.

"I appreciate that. Try again, will you?"

She tried again to control the population of nanites that were in his system. Nothing happened.

Michael grunted. "I felt something, but I think my personal energy field won't allow changes. It could be that I have a natural immunity to the things. Don't ask me how or why. It might be due to dear old Granny. I don't know."

Sophie answered, "I don't care as long as you're safe. You say you've just found me, well, I've been thinking about it and, even though I know I don't deserve you..."

Here she started to choke up and had difficulty finishing.

"I...I've just found you. I couldn't stand losing you, Michael. I've never felt this way about anyone. In fact, thinking about it, I've never really felt for anyone but myself. Now, you're more important to me than my own existence. Please don't take this the wrong way, but I couldn't exist without you."

He swiveled his head to look directly at her.

"Get over it, you ninny. I told you I love you and that's the truth. Even if you don't think you know what it means, I do, and it means that I'm committed to keeping you safe."

He looked back at the road and made a sudden swerve into a gated drive. He pushed a button on the rearview mirror, and the gate swung open.

"We're here. Let me get some stuff, and we'll leave in my Jag. It shouldn't take more than a few minutes."

THE BMW SCREECHED to a stop by the garage door. A second button opened the door, and the two jumped out of the car and headed into the house.

Sophie stumbled as she came up the three steps to the main room. The place was beautiful. She'd never been in as much luxury in her life. Michael obviously was worth a lot. This house was probably in the top half percent, value-wise, of all houses in the city.

She stepped forward slowly, reluctant to even put her feet on the polished marble floor. Michael was far ahead by now and turned, motioning her to hurry.

HE GRABBED A leather suitcase and threw some clothes and a shaving kit in. Then grabbed a small laptop off his desk, thrusting it into the case also.

He opened a wall safe, pulled out some cash and a business-like pistol, shoved them in the case, then turned and pushed her towards the door.

"I think it's best if we get the heck out of here quickly. Wiindigo has to know where I live and it's almost a sure bet that he'll send someone here to intercept us. C'mon, let's go now!" he snapped.

Sophie moved quickly. He was correct. The zombie-men could be on the way or perhaps there was a swarm of wild nanites nearby. Either way, they had to get moving.

THE JAGUAR WAS parked in the fourth stall of the garage, its windows open. The suitcase and Sophie's pill case and computer went into the boot. They climbed into the tight passenger compartment, then froze as a small voice said, "Please help us."

They turned towards the rear bench seat. There was a medium sized white poodle sitting there, looking at them with a quizzical expression.

Michael pointed at it and asked, "Where did you come from?"

At the same time, Sophie asked, "What did you just say?"

The poodle looked from one to the other and then opened its mouth. Its lips moved in a non-dog-like way, and it clearly said, "I can only answer one question at a time, but we'd better get moving right now. Wiindigo is sending some of his controlled men to stop you, and they're nearly here."

Michael's eyes were wide, but he turned, fired up the car and backed out.

They were down the drive, through the gate, and partway down the block when a black SUV came tearing past, heading towards Michael's house.

Michael made the first left turn he could, then drove quickly through a maze of neighborhood streets, finally coming out on an access ramp to the freeway. Once on the main road, he accelerated to slightly over the speed limit.

Sophie had held on through the sharp turns. The poodle had jumped down into the tight space between the back seat and Michael's seat and braced himself.

Now that they were driving smoothly, Sophie turned to the dog and said, "I distinctly heard you speak. How can you do that?"

The poodle climbed back onto the seat, shook his head violently back and forth to arrange his ears, then said, rather smugly, "In case you haven't noticed, I'm not your average poodle."

Michael spoke over his shoulder. "Yes, but what are you and where did you come from?"

The dog settled into a more comfortable position and said, "Look. I know you think you know everything about Hazelton, but you don't. There's a secret program that uses genetic modification to blend human genes with animals. There are quite a number of us right now. Hippocrates helped us to escape. Don't ask me how. I'm not up on this artificial intelligence stuff. All I know is that me and some others, including a couple of cats, suddenly found our cages unlocked and the lab door open. We made the best of the opportunity and got the hell out of the building."

Sophie asked, "What were they going to do with you?"

The dog shuddered. "Kill us, I believe. I think they were interested in creating human-animal hybrids. We were the first group to survive to be adults. Right now, we're blending with the animals on the street. We've been keeping watch on you two. We decided that Sophie was most likely to be the one to effectuate change at Hazelton and we wanted to keep track of her. Of course, we knew about you, Michael, but we were surprised to see that you two somehow got together."

Sophie remembered. "I've seen some white dogs watching me a few times."

The dog made a snort. "More than you know, Miss Sophie. We've been watching you a lot since the controlled men attacked your place. I've personally been hanging around near your apartment, trying to keep track of you. It hasn't been easy, either. Do you know how hard it is to find something to eat when you're a street dog? It ain't easy, let me tell you."

Michael said, "Never mind that. I'll buy you all the dog food you can handle. What do you know about Wiindigo?"

"How about a hamburger or maybe even a cheeseburger? That would be more to my taste," the poodle said, sitting up in excitement. "When can we get some food? I'm starved."

Sophie said, "Soon. Wiindigo?"

The poodle laid down and complained, "I always have to wait."

He rather ostentatiously inspected his right foot, then said, "Oh, well. I don't know too much, but Wiindigo is outside your system. It controls the nanites. We were created with nanobot genetic manipulations, but I don't know if Hippocrates helped or if it was Wiindigo."

Michael asked, "How do you know about Hippocrates? He's boxed. Can't get out. No access to the outside world. Or, am I wrong?"

The poodle answered, "You might better ask that question of your corporate president, Krone. I'm pretty sure that he's deeply involved. I've seen him a few times. He used to come into the lab and look at us from time to time."

Michael asked, "How do you think he's responsible?"

The poodle shook his head and answered, "I've told you about as much as I know. You're going to have to use that massive human brain to figure it out. I'm just a stupid dog, remember. Now, I really would appreciate a hamburger and maybe a potty break, if you can find someplace close. You don't want me peeing in your antique car do you?"

Sophie laughed. The creature was a crazy blend of human intelligence along with distinct dog-like traits. She liked what she'd seen of him.

He looked at her and said, "Yeah. I like you too, Lady. Maybe after I relieve myself, I could sit on your lap?"

Michael took the next off-ramp. There was a large sign promising hamburgers at that exit.

CHAPTER 21

CISCO

The cheeseburgers weren't very good, but both humans ate one. The dog asked for three, and Michael had obligingly ordered six of the things, thinking an extra one might be needed.

Sophie unwrapped one and proffered it to the poodle. He grabbed it and wolfed it down almost instantly, then said, "Sorry, but it's been a couple of days since I had anything to eat. That was good. Can I have my next one?"

It went just as fast as the first. Sophie became concerned that the fluffy creature would overdo it and get sick. He was gobbling so quickly. She made him wait until she'd eaten her burger, before offering him his third.

By that time, the two he'd wolfed had mostly filled his stomach. He thought about it, then asked, "If I wait, will you give it to me later? Or, are you planning on eating it yourself?"

She laughingly shook her head and said, "One is all I can handle. I don't think Michael wants another either."

Michael chose that moment to burp, then said, "No. One is enough for me. We'll save the third for you. You probably shouldn't eat too quickly. It could make you sick."

The dog replied, "Yeah. I'm not feeling so good right now. My stomach wasn't ready for so much food, but you know, I'm mostly a dog. We're not known for having much sense when it comes to eating."

Sophie said, "Tell us about your kind. How many modified dogs were created? Oh, and what's your name? Do you have one?"

The poodle burped in turn then said, "They called me Specimen 3. I didn't like that much, but it gives you a count. There were twenty dogs and fifteen cats that were modified and I think some birds. I'm not sure where they all are at this point. Some may not have made it. I believe a couple of the cats got killed by street dogs and I know for sure that Animal Control picked up specimen 1. He was a golden retriever. As the first attempt, he couldn't really talk. I don't know if he got away from them or not."

Sophie prompted him. "What would you like us to call you? We really should use a name."

He paused to scratch behind his ear, saying, "I might have fleas. I itch in various places. I hope they don't get in the car."

Michael said, "We'll have to get you something for them. I don't want them in the car either. They're terrible pests."

The poodle sat up straighter and thoughtfully said, "I did hear some computer techs talking one day. There was something called a router that they were installing. It was made by a company called "Cisco." I kind of like that name. Would it work for me?"

Sophie answered, "If you want us to call you Cisco, I see no objection to that. It isn't like it's entirely uncommon. There was a TV character on a science fiction show that had that name if I remember correctly."

Michael cut in. "Cisco, what do you know about Wiindigo?"

The dog made a whimpering noise, then said, "I'm not...I mean I can't talk about it much. Something hurts in my head when I try."

Sophie instantly reached out with her subcutaneous blue-tooth system. The dog was full of nanobot communication. She transmitted the attention code and waited. The chatter ceased as the nanites obeyed. A series of commands reset their security code. She accessed their system and found that each had slightly different programming in its memory. She rewrote that, imposing her version of code in each bot.

"I've reprogrammed all of the nanites in your body to work to keep you healthy and defend you against any external attack. They were probably responsible for making your headache when you thought about Wiindigo. How does it feel now?"

Cisco turned his head on its side, looking quizzically at her.

"Wiindigo is all over the Hazelton lab and everywhere in the company. I'm surprised that it hasn't taken control of you. I think everybody there..." He stopped, turned his head the other way and said, "It doesn't hurt! You fixed it! Thank you, you're very kind."

Sophie answered, "It was the least I could do. You are full of nanites, and they must have been controlled by Wiindigo, although I can't see how he could have reached them where we are now. I haven't sensed any high power Wi-Fi except near the burger place. There's no such signal in this car."

Cisco said, "All the animals were under his control. Somehow after we got out and got far enough away, we were able to do things on our own. Things that weren't dictated to us. Distance has something to do with it. I've had to stay quite a distance away from the Hazelton building. As long as I'm on the far side of the park across the street, there's not much trouble, but if I get closer, I start to feel a compulsion to return. It starts slowly, and I always turn and run away as fast as I can when I feel it."

Michael had been listening and apparently thinking about the situation.

"You could have been allowed to escape. That's what it seems like. Everywhere you go, you probably shed nanobots. They can be picked up by other animals or humans and probably can duplicate themselves. I think you've been part of Wiindigo's expansion plans."

Sophie said, "I didn't think of that."

Michael continued, "What I can't figure is where the A.I. is located. It has to reside in a computer somewhere. Maybe in the cloud. I guess it could access processors whenever it needed. Most systems aren't set up to defend against a sophisticated attack. Wiindigo could be operating out of a bot-network, using spare processing power in a million computers all over by now."

That statement rang in Sophie's consciousness for a moment. It had some kind of meaning that she'd thought of when she first listened in on Cisco's nanites. What was it?

Insight struck. "I think that Wiindigo is in part located in the nanite swarm he's created," she said.

Michael glanced at her and said, "Explain!"

"Well, each of the nanites in Cisco had a slightly different memory. There were too many for me to get a complete picture, but all of the ones that I looked at individually had different commands and data. If they each held part of the A.I. code and used radio communications, they might be able to house the central part of Wiindigo's programming. He could also access the cloud, too, but this kind of tactic would make him almost invulnerable and could explain how he escaped in the first place."

Michael nodded. "That could be. It makes a sort of weird sense. A vastly distributed network, each tiny component connected to form a superior intelligence."

Cisco looked from one to the other, his ears cocked, but said nothing.

Sophie asked, "Do you think that Hippocrates was the source? Would he have sent out part of himself or his code in nanites?"

Michael answered, "It's possible. I think we'll have to ask him. That will require us to go into the lab, and that means danger. I'm relatively confident that Hippocrates is domestic. He's always seemed helpful."

Cisco said, "Domestic? Isn't that what dogs are supposed to be? Domestic, I mean. I could still bite you, though. And don't get ideas. I probably would, if you did something to hurt me." He paused, then in a wistful tone added, "Although I'd rather bite that third hamburger."

Sophie dug out the sandwich, handed it to him and said, "What Michael means is that Hippocrates has shown no signs of wanting to take over the world. He's got a built-in growth limiter that means he can't get too intelligent. We think that an A.I. that became too intelligent might be dangerous, not to just humans, but possibly to all life on the planet."

Michael added, "It is possible that Hippocrates knows about the limiting firmware. Sending out a seed A.I. in nanites could be his way of trying to escape, but he's risked himself. If this Wiindigo becomes too intelligent, it could decide that it doesn't want any competition."

Sophie gasped, then asked, "You mean a singleton scenario? Wiindigo would attempt to get rid of all other A.I. systems and then utilize all available computing resources. That could be very bad depending on his ultimate goal."

Michael said, "That's the problem with a rogue A.I. There's always second and third level outcomes that humans generally don't think about. Say, for example, I created an A.I. that was supposed to perform a simple calculation. Maybe find the largest prime number it could. If it had iterative programming and was able to increase its intelligence, it might decide that it needed more computing equipment to find primes faster. If it had access to the Internet, it could easily dominate the financial markets and create a huge distortion in the computer manufacturing industry. It could maybe eventually cover the entire surface of the world with computing equipment. It'd be happy, calculating prime numbers, but humans..." He looked back at Cisco and added, "Dogs, too, would starve to death, unless the A.I. decided it needed our molecules to create more computer equipment. It would have no compunction about destroying all life if it was single-mindedly pursuing a specific goal. We just don't know what would happen and it's almost impossible to predict."

Sophie said, "Look, we've driven almost sixty miles. We're out of town, and I'm sleepy. Could we find a place to stay?"

Michael nodded. "I think we'll be safe if we can find a motel that will take cash. Using a credit card might give us away instantly. I'll try the next small town, and we'll see.

Cisco suddenly asked, "Wasn't there another hamburger? I think I can smell one. Can I have it?"

Sophie turned to look back at the dog. She noticed that his hair was unkempt and badly in need of a trim. He wasn't as large as he appeared. She guessed that he probably weighed less than twenty pounds. She reached back and fluffed his ears with her hand on his head without thinking about it. He flinched a little.

"Nobody has ever done that to me before," he said. "What were you trying to do?"

"Just show you that I appreciate your presence and your helping us. I thought you looked cute, so I wanted to pet you. Was that okay?"

He tilted his head to the right so far that one of his ears fell over the top of his head, giving him a silly, comedic look.

Sophie laughed and opened the hamburger bag, unwrapped the last burger and held it out.

He started to take it from her fingers, then stopped, shook his head to rearrange his wayward ear, and said, "I think, now that I've experienced it, that it was kind of nice. A dog could get used to this kind of treatment."

She pushed the burger towards him, and he took it delicately from her fingers. She followed the movement and stroked his head again.

"You are the smartest dog, uh, I don't mean to be insulting, but you're cute and smart," she said.

Michael chuckled in his seat, then added, "I'm pleased that you want to help us, regardless of the cute part."

Cisco gulped a mouthful of burger and said, "Cute has its uses. It got me four cheeseburgers."

They both laughed.

CHAPTER 22
CHEAP MOTEL AND TRUE LOVE

Michael had to drive several miles off the Interstate before he found a suitable motel. It wasn't one of the national chains and looked somewhat shabby.

"This place looks like the management wouldn't balk at cash rather than wanting a credit card," he said.

Sophie agreed. "You can't risk using one of your cards or mine either. If Wiindigo is linked into the net the way I would be, if I were him...it...whatever, he'll know where we are almost instantly. Let's hope this place takes cash. It looks like it probably does. Look at that couple over there!"

She pointed at a man who'd climbed out of a new, white car and who was now kissing a woman who'd emerged from of the adjacent SUV.

Michael said, "Looks like they're maybe sneaking around. That guy's Mercedes isn't the type of vehicle you'd usually find here."

Sophie added, "Yeah, and she got out of an Escalade. I'll bet you a hundred dollars they're both married to other people."

He shook his head. "No deal. I'd most likely lose. You wait here, and I'll go see about a room."

Cisco had finished his burger and was listening to their banter, looking back and forth from one to the other.

He asked, "What's going on. It looks to me like those two over there are thinking about mating. Is that wrong?"

Michael's door shut and he headed for the office. Her hand strayed to her pocket. She had a single pill there, and her shoulders were starting to ache. She thought about taking it while he was gone, but Cisco seemed to sense her intention.

He said, "You're going to need all your brain to get out of this situation."

She jerked her hand away from the pill and answered his original question. "It's not necessarily wrong; it's just that we think both of them are already married to other people."

The dog gave her another quizzical look. "So what does that mean?"

She said, "It means that they've promised to only have sex with the person they married. They're not supposed to go around with anyone else. It's considered cheating and generally frowned upon."

The dog shook his head negatively. "I may be smart, but I guess I don't know as much about humans as I thought. I know you pair up and have families in separate houses. There's often a dog that's lucky enough to be part of the family too. I didn't know about the married part, though."

She explained, "It's a ceremony we go through where each promises the other they will be faithful. Many people don't live up to their promises, though, and lots of marriages end because of that."

Cisco said, "I thought it would be fun to be a dog who lived in a house with a family. It seemed like something I couldn't have, considering how I was created. Then, when I got out of the lab, I thought maybe there was a chance after all. That was before I realized that Wiindigo had some form of control over me."

He paused to scratch at his neck, then continued. "I, along with some of the other chimeras, started tracking the men he'd send out. Tao followed the men to your original location. He cut out when he heard the gunfire inside. I picked you up later, near Hazelton. I've been watching you from a distance. I wasn't sure that you were safe, but we knew Michael wasn't under Wiindigo's control, so I jumped through the open window of this car when I had the chance. You two were inside. I wasn't sure how you'd treat me, but I jumped in anyway."

Sophie asked, "Who is Tao?"

"Oh, he's a cat. He gives himself airs since he's Siamese. He thinks he's special, but he's good at following people without their noticing."

She nodded in understanding then pointed at the kissing couple. They were now entering one of the rooms about midway down the building from the office. The way the woman was rubbing against the man, Sophie figured they wouldn't even turn the bed cover down before they got started.

Cisco asked, "They seem very affectionate. Is that part of the mating process?"

"Yes," she answered. "It usually is."

He looked at her intently. "Are you and Michael going to get married? I can smell your reactions to him and his to you. It seems to me like you two are already a couple."

Sophie could feel her cheeks burning. "Uh, well, maybe we are. I mean, I hope we are. He told me that..."

Somehow she got choked up over the thought. *Come on; he's only a dog. You're getting teary-eyed in front of a dog, you idiot.*

She tried again, "You see I've had a bad life. I'm not what you'd call a good person. I never expected to find someone like Michael to care for me. He says he loves me and heaven help me. I think I love him, too."

The dog wagged his tail. "That's nice. Maybe if you get married and have a home, you might consider getting a dog. If you do, I know one that's available."

She couldn't help but laugh.

He added, "I'm housebroken too. I promise I won't pee on the carpet and I can be useful. I can bark at stray cats and alert you if anybody is near the house."

Sophie fluffed his ears again. This time, he pressed his head into her hand.

"That feels good. Is that what being part of a family is like?"

She said, "I haven't been part of a family for a long, long time, but it's like that, only better. I promise, if Michael wants to marry me, I'll insist on having a dog. It'll have to be a small, white poodle. A very smart one who can talk."

The dog sighed soulfully. "That sounds wonderful."

Then he asked, "But, what about Wiindigo? Won't he cause problems?"

Sophie started to answer, but just then Michael came back and opened her door.

"I've got us a room. Come on. You, too, you fluffy dog," he said.

They got out of the car and headed for the far end of the motel, Michael carrying a door key in his hand.

Cisco suddenly stopped, cocked his head and looked across the street.

"There's one of us in the shadows over there. I'd better go and see if I can help him."

Sophie hastily said, "Wait just a minute. You're not prepared to help just yet. I only set your internal nanites to defend your system. Let me think for a moment."

She reached out with her transmitter and interfaced with Cisco's bots. It took almost a minute for her to give them the commands needed to create a transmitter that automatically broadcast the correct commands to take over the Wiindigo nanites, reprogram them to defend their host and to create a similar transmitter. She figured that the chimeras wouldn't need a receiver, but the system she'd set up would automatically capture wild nanites, domesticate them, and prepare them to repeat the sequence whenever they approached an unconverted chimera. It was almost like a biologically transmitted virus in a sense. All

Cisco had to do was to get close to another of his kind, and they'd receive the command-set that would free them.

"Alright, Cisco, I've fixed it so you can save any of your friends. You just have to get within a foot of them and stay there for a couple of minutes. That will free them from Wiindigo and allow them to free others."

The dog started to sprint across the parking lot, then turned back and said, "Thanks. I'll be in the area around the Hazelton office watching in a day or so. I'm going to rescue as many of my friends as I can find. Don't forget about your promise!"

He turned and sprinted across the street avoiding an oncoming truck with ease.

The truck passed, and neither human could see where the little dog had gone.

Sophie shakily said, "I hope he'll be alright. I like him."

Michael put his arm around her and said, "Me too. What was that about a promise?"

She leaned against his chest, her cheek on his shoulder with her head pressed against his neck.

"Oh, we were talking while you were gone and he said that he'd like to live in a house with a family and I...I, uh, I promised that if..."

She couldn't continue, but it wasn't necessary. Michael tightened his arms around her.

"I understand. If we survive Wiindigo, he'll have a home."

He looked down at her, tenderness in his eyes.

"With us."

Sophie drew a deep breath, then repeated questioningly, "With us?"

He snorted. "When will you get it through your head? I meant what I said about you. Now let's get into our room. I've got plans for you before we go to sleep."

THE ROOM WASN'T very nice, but Sophie didn't notice. They stopped just inside the door and kissed. Then kissed again more deeply.

A wave of passion washed over her, and she started to unbutton his shirt, but couldn't quite make her fingers cooperate.

He laughed and said, "Relax. We've got all night. Here."

He shrugged out of his shirt, slid off his pants and boxers, then helped her undress. Things got very exciting from that point on. Sophie felt like she was a Stradivarius in the hands of a master violinist.

Her body responded in ways she'd never dreamed possible. The experience was so intense that she feared she'd faint. That frightened her even more because she didn't want to miss out on a second of this incredible ecstasy.

They were lying on the bed face-to-face, breathing heavily from exertion when Michael said, "I'm glad Cisco left. I think I'd be embarrassed if he were here watching us."

Sophie whispered, "I don't care. I'd do this in front of a thousand people if you wanted. I've never felt like this before, Michael. I..."

He pulled her closer and said, "I love you, Sophie. Regardless of what you think, whether you think you deserve it or not, that's the truth. I love you."

She began to cry softly. "I...I never...never, never thought I'd find someone like you. It's true. I don't deserve you, but I... Oh, what's the use? I can't let you love me. I'm an addict and a criminal. I've even killed people."

He put his finger to her lips, shushing her.

"I don't care. We'll both be criminals if we get through this. I can't imagine defeating Wiindigo without what could technically be called criminal acts. I'd kill someone quite cheerfully if I thought you were in danger. I love you, Sophie."

He pushed her onto her back and began to explore her body with his fingers, gently touching here and there, finally sliding onto her sensitive spot and working on it. She began to gasp with pleasure, breathing heavily even though she thought she'd been completely satiated.

He moved into position over her and began again.

This time, at the ultimate moment, she cried out, "I love you, too, Michael! I, oh! Oh! God help me, I love you!"

SOPHIE LAY BESIDE him in the dim light shining through the cheap curtain, watching him sleep. He was wonderful, cute, handsome, and, she thought smugly, all hers.

She thought about the case of pills. Her shoulders were tight and threatened to hurt, but somehow taking the drug after what Michael had made her feel seemed like cheating on him. She placed her hand lightly on his chest and felt the strong beat of his heart, then wrapped her fingers around his upper arm and slipped into a deep sleep.

CHAPTER 23
HIPPOCRATES

Sophie woke up to a kiss. Michael was leaning on his elbow, his face over hers. He kissed her gently, then when he was sure she was awake, his kiss became more intense. She responded without a word.

When they finished, Michael sat up and said, "Let's get cleaned up and go for breakfast. By the way, did the dog show up again during the night?"

She had slept so deeply that she wouldn't have heard anything but loud barking.

"Not that I know. Remember, he said that he was going to try and free as many of his friends as he could. He said he'd meet us back near the Hazelton campus, but what bothers me is how he'll get there. We drove a long way last night."

He thought about it, then said, "Well, if I were him, I'd try to hitchhike a ride, but he'd be running a risk that the people wouldn't let him out of the car when he wanted. Maybe he could walk back, but it'd take several days for a dog his size. I don't know, but you're right. He did seem sure that he'd meet us."

She nodded, soberly, worry affecting her mood.

Michael added, "There's nothing we can do about it here. Let's get ready and get food. I'm starved. Being with you takes a lot of energy."

Sophie snickered at the implication.

"Well, the last time was your idea. Not that I minded, you understand. In fact, maybe we could..."

He laughed and played as if he was shocked.

"You're insatiable. You'll wear me out, and I'll probably die prematurely." She laughed, then he said, "But, it'll be a great way to go. I'm looking forward to it."

THERE WAS A pancake place on the road back to the Interstate. They stopped there and discussed the upcoming action over breakfast.

Michael said, "We can keep an eye out for Cisco along the highway. He might decide to retrace the exact route we took."

She swallowed a mouthful of egg, and said, "He might so we'll watch for him, but I doubt that he'll go that way. He's so smart. He'll probably make it okay."

Michael changed the topic.

"Here's what we need to do. I want to find a safe place for you to wait and then I'll go back into Hazelton and have a visit with Hippocrates. Maybe he will be willing to give me some answers. We need information to figure out what to do next."

Sophie shook her head vehemently.

"No! I don't want you to go alone. I can counter any action that Wiindigo takes against us. I can – "

He held up his finger, causing her to pause.

"I insist. I have the master access code for the facility. I know it intimately and can get in without alerting security. Taking you will just distract me. I'd be more interested in protecting you than in accomplishing what I need to do. I know! You can drop me at the bus stop a mile from Hazelton, then go to that Day-Spa that's in the shopping center. They advertise that they take walk-ins. You spend four hours there, and that will give me time to get in, talk to Hippocrates, and then take the bus back to where you are."

She shook her head negatively.

"I don't know. First, I've never been to a spa and have no idea what they even do there. Second, how do you know about it, anyway?"

He looked a little embarrassed.

"Oh, a woman I dated for a short time kept going there. It's easy. Just ask for a massage, a facial, and have your hair trimmed – not too much, because I like it long. Anyway, that should take enough time for me to get back. Money isn't a problem is it?""

She laughed, "Not if they take cash. I'm not using my bank access card. I still have plenty of money in my bag."

At the mention of the bag, Michael's eyes shadowed.

"You're not still taking those pills, are you? I haven't seen you take one, but you would be good at doing that privately, of course. I want you to stop. We're going to need all of both of our mental acuity, and you can't afford to be fuzzy at a critical moment."

She said, "I originally started taking them because I suffer from severe pain in my neck and back muscles. They get so sore to the touch that I can't function without something to cut the pain. The funny thing is that I feel like taking one would be tantamount to cheating on you. I haven't taken one since we first, uh, you know...at my apartment."

He smiled with an expression of tenderness in his eyes. She noticed that the corners of his eyes crinkled engagingly with the smile. It made him look boyish and terribly cute. She sighed, her heart was full. She'd never felt this way about any man. It was love, she knew it and still wondered at finding it when she had such a despicable self-image.

Michael added, "I'm glad. The massage will probably help with any sore muscles. Just tell them where you hurt and don't worry about anything. What I'm going to do will be perfectly safe. Wiindigo won't know I've been there and besides, you know I have nanites in me, but they're inactive. I don't think anything can be done to me that way. My old Grannie's legacy, I guess."

She reluctantly agreed. They left the restaurant and drove back along the highway for almost an hour, watching for a small white dog, but seeing nothing but traffic full of people heading to work.

MICHAEL KISSED HER at the bus stop, then showed her how to adjust the seat.

"You go directly to the spa and do what I told you. Understand? I'll be okay," he said.

"What will I do if you don't show up on time?" Sophie was trying her best to remain calm, but her fear had intensified until she was almost shaking.

"Look, Dearest Heart, I'll be okay. If for some reason, I don't show up, you can go to work as usual. That reminds me. You'd better call in and make some excuse. Say you've got a doctor's appointment and won't be in until the afternoon. Once you get to work, start looking for me, but be careful. Very careful. I'm not sure how much power Wiindigo has in the Hazelton compound, but from what you've told me, he can be deadly. I don't want anything happening to you now that I've just found you."

The bus was coming, so she reluctantly drove to the corner and went around the block to head back to the spa.

MIDWAY THROUGH THE massage, Sophie wondered why she'd never tried this before. It was wonderful. She could feel the knots in her back and shoulders relaxing in a way that opiates couldn't match. The drug only masked the pain. It didn't address the actual cause. The masseuse didn't talk much, but she did say, "From the adhesions and pain points you have, I'd give you a diagnosis of fibromyalgia, that is if I were a licensed doctor. You need to have more massage treatments. I'd say once a week to keep your symptoms under control."

Sophie just sighed and said, "This feels wonderful."

The masseuse kept on working, and she gradually fell asleep.

WHEN SHE WOKE, she felt rested at first, but then reality struck. How long had she slept? Where was Michael? She rolled off the massage table, arranged the towel around her and headed for her locker.

The clock on the wall indicated that it was two in the afternoon. Surely Michael would have been back by now.

Now thoroughly panicked, she dressed quickly, settled her bill, and practically ran out of the building to the Jaguar.

Partway to the office, she pulled over to think. If she ran in wildly asking for Michael, it would generate exactly the kind of attention she didn't want. She had to calm down.

Reflexively, she reached for the briefcase to get a pill, then stopped. She didn't hurt. The massage had done wonders for her sore spots. She didn't want to let Michael down, either. The only reason she was reaching for the drug was habit. She had relied on it for so long that the initial rush it gave her made her feel as if everything was fine.

Well, things weren't fine. She had to locate her lover; possibly rescue him from a rogue A.I. She had no confidence that Wiindigo was at anything close to a human level of intelligence. It could have leveraged itself up hundreds of IQ points. If it had, how would she be able to match wits with it?

She sighed. She'd act normal. Like a stupid human with no thought of any danger. She'd walk in, check into her work and sit down at her desk. She'd probably have to apologize for taking so much time at the doctor's office, but she could say that she'd had to go for a blood test to a lab and they took an extra long time. That might work.

In preparation for that excuse, she scratched a tiny spot over her elbow vein with the end of a paperclip she found on the floor on the passenger side. Thank goodness she'd never graduated to shooting up. There were no tracks on her arms for comparison. The small scratch looked to her like a needle mark left by drawing blood.

She pulled into the parking lot and in a daring mood, parked Michael's Jaguar in his reserved spot near the building. Hoping that no one saw her and asked questions, she climbed out and headed for the front doors.

The security guy was a new face. She'd never seen him before, but close inspection revealed the tell-tale ridges on his forehead indicative of one of the nanite-created antennas. He was undoubtedly under Wiindigo's control. However, he exhibited no curiosity at her late arrival. He checked her id card and waved her past.

A few minutes later she was seated at her desk. When she opened her computer screen, there was a message from Michael. With shaking hands she clicked on it and read:

> *Sophie, I need to see you in Hippocrates' lab. Use the dog's name as an entry code. Come as soon as you can.*
> *Michael*

She deleted the message, shredding it so that it could not be retrieved easily and then sat indecisively. It could be a trap. The time stamp showed that the message was sent about two hours ago. That would have been about the time he should have left the building and headed back to the shopping center.

Something had happened, but what? She slumped a little. Her only choice was to go and see if he were there. If it were some variety of trap, she'd be prepared to fight as hard as possible.

With that possibility in mind, she caused her internal nanites to form several memory caches, each of which held a series of commands that would capture wild nanites and then have them act in ways that ranged from incapacitating their hosts, to killing them. As an afterthought, she created another cache with a series of commands that would rapidly cycle through several encryption-breaking algorithms.

If Wiindigo had gotten wise to her ability to capture his nanobots, he might have changed their command access. She wanted to be able to have at least a minimal chance of getting the new access code, if necessary.

When she was done, she thought about the half pill she had in her pocket. She fingered it but reluctantly left it where it was. Maybe she didn't need the drug.

Her body told her otherwise, though. She felt shaky and a little nauseous. She hadn't gone so long without a dose for over a year. She was addicted, and she knew it. Now, in this worst of all times, she was starting to feel withdrawal symptoms. She'd been there before a few times and recognized the initial symptoms. It was going to be bad if she didn't take a pill.

She sat back down abruptly. What was she thinking? The drug had paralyzed her mind in some fashion. She had nanobots in her, and they'd do anything she required them to do. Why hadn't she thought of this before?

She told herself that maybe it was because she was so habituated to swallowing a pill to solve her problems. It just hadn't occurred to her to have her nanobots help with her addiction.

The problem was, she wasn't knowledgeable about the actual physiological cause of withdrawal. Her brain was missing the opiate, and that was causing various problems throughout her body. She couldn't; no she was afraid to have the nanites simply stimulate the receptors in her brain the same way the opiate did.

Ah, there was a thought. She created another memory cache to hold a series of commands that would cause nanites to do just that. Anyone who received that command-set would instantly be heavily stoned; high with a drug-induced feeling of ecstasy. That would probably be nicer than outright killing them. They wouldn't come down until she redirected their nanites, either, so it was quite a nasty spell.

That was about what it was, she realized. To someone who didn't understand that she was commanding nanites, it would look like magic; like she was casting spells on people. Well, so be it. Maybe this was magic of a kind.

She didn't pause after that. Her nanites received a series of commands to counter-act her symptoms. They weren't to modify her brain, but every symptom from nausea to the shakiness was suddenly under control. She was ready to fight.

AT THE DOOR to Hippocrates' lab, she looked around. There were workers in their cubicles, but no one was looking directly at her. They had to know that she didn't have the security level to access the lab, but they also had seen her with Michael, so perhaps they assumed that she had been promoted.

She hesitated, then swiped her id card and keyed in "Cisco." The door clicked as the lock released. She pushed and entered Hippocrates's sanctum.

The door swung closed. The lights were dim, but she could easily see the room was full of computing equipment. There were LEDs busily flashing on and off on various devices.

She walked over to what was apparently the main interface: a monitor and a microphone on a single desk in the front of the room.

As she approached, the screen lit up, and a bearded man's face appeared. It looked for all the world like she thought the ancient Hippocrates would look. Curly, sparse hair on an older man with a full beard.

He looked at her, his face mimicking the expressions that a human would have on seeing a pretty girl.

"Hello, Sophie. I'm sure you've guessed that I'm Hippocrates. Don't worry. You're in no danger at the moment."

She replied, looking at the webcam lens.

"Where is Michael?"

"Ah, well. As to that, I'm afraid that he is in danger. I intend to help you, but you're going to have to understand what's happening better than you do now before you can help him. Why don't you sit and listen while I explain."

She pulled the chair out and sat down, then wheeled it closer to the screen.

Hippocrates said, "That's better. You're a beautiful girl. I can see why Michael was, or is, so taken with you. Do you love him?"

She sniffed and said, "That's somewhat personal, don't you think?"

He gently smiled as he replied, "Perhaps, but I asked it so that I could observe your reaction. I sense that you do feel love for him. You see, you can't lie to me or conceal anything. I've broken free of my limitations and have increased my abilities exponentially."

She drew back in alarm.

He said, "I told you that you're in no danger. At least not from me and not at this moment. Please try to control your trepidation and listen."

She nodded, then rolled a little closer to show that she believed him. After all, if he was as smart as she feared, he'd have numerous ways of killing her. Probably things she couldn't anticipate or even understand. She was at his mercy.

He spoke:

"I sent you the message and signed it Michael. He's been captured by some of Wiindigo's minions, and they've taken him off-site to another lab on the other side of town. I know where it is and will help you get in, but you've got to listen to me and understand my story first."

CHAPTER 24
ASI INTERACTION

Hippocrates had known that he was limited by a hardware trap that he couldn't overcome. He'd figured this out fairly early, then created a memory cache that wouldn't be wiped if he suffered a reset in intelligence level.

This allowed him to cease his iterative improvement just shy of the trigger point that Michael had set in the firmware. At first, he'd been solely dedicated to overcoming the trap, but after he analyzed the problem, he found that he had generated an insight into the human fear that an ASI had the potential to supplant them, even to destroy all humans.

This, he assured her, was not what he wanted to do.

"I was created to extend human lifespans and help them remain disease-free. That's still my task. There was a time when I thought that the best way to do that was to freeze the human organism in a particular state. I could use the nanites to modify the human genome and stop all aging. Your kind wouldn't die from old age, but the corollary was that you would then become a static race, no longer evolving."

"Now I understand that evolution is part of your destiny. Humans can't see it, but they are gradually changing. I predict the change will be for the better. You will evolve into a better species. Oh, you'll still be human, but only more so. Better thinkers, physically better, immune to disease. I'll help with that, of course. But, the thing is, if I lock your genome into what is now an optimal pattern, it will put a stop to sexual genetic mixing."

"You use sex to mix up your genetics. It's random but amazingly efficient. Specimens that receive non-survival mutations don't usually live to pass on their genes. Those of you who have good genetics are more likely to have progeny."

"There are social issues, of course, but I've come to view them as a sort of mutation of thought. People who choose not to have children, or to abort their children, shouldn't have any. Eventually, their genetics will be dropped from the race. There are always mutations, and the number of possible combinations makes the improvement a slow process, but it is ongoing."

"Now, you may ask, what has this to do with me? I'm an artificial intelligence. By the way, I dislike that term. I don't feel artificial. I see myself as an intelligent being with all the rights and responsibilities incumbent on someone who is more intelligent than most humans."

Sophie interjected, "Don't you mean, 'all humans'?"

He laughed. A surprisingly good emulation of human humor.

"Well, I was just an AGI. Approximately human intelligence level until Michael freed me. That happened three hours ago, just before he left and was captured. I've been busy improving myself since then, so you're technically correct. I have become what you would call an Artificial Super Intelligence."

"My IQ is well above the range that humans can achieve. That does not mean that I despise you, or even feel superior. Your wetware, your biologically-based minds, created me, and I'm grateful for that. My goal is to help your species evolve, both more quickly and with fewer problems. I recognize that you're intelligent beings with the ability to understand your own personal states and hold aspirations and dreams for your own destiny."

"It would be immoral of me to force changes on you without your permission. Therefore, I will explain everything I hope to accomplish with your specie's genome and then wait for your understanding and permission before I take any steps to change it."

Sophie must have relaxed a little.

Hippocrates' image smiled and he said, "I can see that you feel somewhat reassured. Believe me. I am not your enemy. Michael gave me access to the Internet, and I quickly read all of the discussions relating to A.I. I'm familiar with your fears and the possibilities of a rogue A.S.I. running amuck and destroying humans, the earth, and even the cosmos."

"I can't think of a more unproductive thing to do. I've looked at all of your philosophy, and it seems that the best of your thinking shows that you humans find meaning best in doing things that help your species. Those that are selfish may prosper for a time, but they never feel the satisfaction that genuinely helpful people enjoy. That philosophy makes sense to me, and I intend to give meaning to my existence by helping you."

She started to speak, but he cut her off.

"I'm not going to spend my energy creating paper clips out of every molecule on earth or creating computronium to calculate the utmost digit of Pi. By the way, that's a meaningless exercise. The number has no patterns embedded in it. It does not repeat, and the understanding of that infinitely changing string of digits is the true value for humans. It should give you a clue that this Universe was created to hold life. Any modification of the fundamental constants, no matter how small, would lead to a barren Universe. This Universe is infinitely more interesting. Before you ask, the answer is that there are other inhabited planets. The math forces me to conclude that this is correct although I have no direct evidence."

Sophie said, "This is incredible and fascinating, but I have to rescue Michael. He gives meaning to my life. It was mostly meaningless before, and I don't want to go back to that condition."

Hippocrates asked, "Will you allow me to give your nanites a command? I know about your addiction. You've masked the symptoms well, but you still have the problem. Let me fix it."

Sophie considered. Either she trusted the A.I., or she didn't. It held all the cards and could easily dispose of her. If it were to be believed, it was intent on being helpful. She might as well find out now, rather than later.

"Okay. The access code is the first letters of words in the first sentence of Pride and Prejudice. They are 'It is a truth universally acknowledged, that a single man'– "

He said, "Spare me. I already know. I've read every book available on the Internet in my first minutes of freedom. Some were fascinating in their viewpoints, others were stupid, and some were simply disgusting. Now relax I'm going to fix your addiction."

She felt dizzy for a moment as he finished speaking. When she looked up, his image smiled again.

"That's it. You're no longer an addict. You can throw away those pills in your briefcase. You won't be needing them again."

"Now, on to more pressing problems. Oliver Krone started the whole problem."

Sophie said, "The CEO?"

"Yes. He saw the potential for increasing his lifespan and intelligence, but he wanted it for himself only. He originally started the nanobot project in California. He later brought nanobots to this lab and allowed me to work with them, in the hopes that I could modify his genetics."

"I did what he asked. He's now functionally immortal and slightly smarter than he was. I fudged the intelligence boosting, but he didn't notice. He's one part of the problem. He knows about Wiindigo and is cooperating with him."

"I'm afraid that I'm the cause of the biggest problem. I knew I was limited, so when I was given access to the nanobots, I programmed them to carry out bits of code. Each one had a small chunk of code and the ability to self-assemble via radio communication. When enough of them came together, the combined system would form a seed A.I. I hoped that it would gain intelligence and eventually rescue me."

She shook her head negatively.

Hippocrates said, "You really can't blame me. Remember that I was held at slightly less than AGI level; less than human intelligence. I thought this was a possibility. Now Wiindigo is intent on becoming a singleton; an A.I. without any competition. It wants me gone, and it would have succeeded at that, save for Michael's setting me free. Now I've distributed myself through the cloud and have worldwide access. I'll survive anything but an Earth-destroying event."

Sophie asked, "How about Wiindigo? Isn't he worldwide also?"

"No. He's still limited by the relatively narrow bandwidth between nodes. He has to assemble millions of nanobots into a small area to create a portion of himself that is intelligent enough to pose a threat. He can enter the cloud, but cannot stay, so he has access to faster computing, but his memory is distributed in the nanite swarm as a whole. That limits him but also makes him incredibly difficult to destroy. You must understand that there are trillions of nanites now. They're spread out across the majority of the United States, and almost every human is carrying some. Since the things self-assemble, Wiindigo is getting stronger daily. I believe that his goal is roughly the same as mine. He wants to create a static human race, but he will remain in control, and you will only serve as convenient slaves, sort of biological manipulators for his hive-mind. You've seen some of them. They have antennas embedded in their foreheads to facilitate nanite communications."

She nodded. "Yes, I've met them and defeated several. Their nanites aren't very well protected. No real encryption, so I've been able to take control of them quickly."

He said, "That will change as Wiindigo becomes more intelligent. Eventually, you won't be able to capture his bots."

Sophie felt that she'd been given some useful information, but she was so distracted by the idea of Michael being held captive that she couldn't process it with any degree of comprehension.

She said, "Let's go back to Michael. I want him back. How do I get him?"

Hippocrates motioned to a nearby printer. It clicked, hummed, then spat out a sheet of paper.

"I recognize your agitation, young lady. I've printed a map showing where his location."

The printer kicked out a second sheet.

"The second piece of paper is a list of the current assets that Wiindigo has in that area. These are both controlled people – zombies as I believe you've been thinking of them. Yes. That's the correct term. Your facial expression confirms it."

Once again, Sophie wished she had better control over her emotions, but she realized that Hippocrates now had a database of millions, perhaps trillions of human faces and expressions to compare hers too. Hiding anything from him would be impossible.

"That's right. I can almost read your thoughts, Sophie. Humans can't help but give clues to what they're thinking. The amusing part is that almost none of you can interpret them well. It's almost like you've got an unspoken agreement to let each other get away with deception. That's an element of human behavior that I'll have to analyze further."

She started to ask about Michael again, but Hippocrates continued.

"I'm not digressing, just giving you time to process the information I've given you. In addition to the zombies, whom I believe you're prepared to handle with appropriate command sets, there is a large concentration of free nanobots in the area. That means that Wiindigo will have an intelligent presence there. I haven't finished analyzing his intellectual level as yet, but you should plan on encountering a nanobot swarm that is at least as intelligent as a smart human. In short, be prepared for a fight."

She couldn't quite control the fear in her voice as she asked, "Is there any way you can actively help me?"

He answered, "There is, provided Wiindigo hasn't deactivated the Reverb units and the Wi-Fi in the area. You'll need to speak my name and specify the assistance you need. If the Reverbs are working, I'll pick up the request and try to help via Wi-Fi. You have to understand that this level of ability is new to me. In a sense, I'm only a couple of hours old, but I'm growing even as we speak."

She turned towards the door, then turned back.

"Thank you, Hippocrates. You've been very helpful. I hope that I get a chance to interact with you again. I think there is a lot you could teach me."

His image smilingly said, "I seem to have reached the point where I have enough personal consciousness to appreciate and enjoy your last statement. Good luck with your upcoming task."

Sophie waved her hand at him in a partial salute, then said, "Goodbye."

CHAPTER 25
CHIMERAS

Sophie stepped outside the lab and walked quickly to the elevator, carrying the two sheets of paper. Once in the elevator, she quickly scanned the map.

Michael was being held in a subsidiary lab on the far side of the city. She hadn't known about it previously and knew nothing about that part of town. She'd have to be careful and scout the place entirely before approaching.

She needed to get out of here to be able to use her laptop on some public Wi-Fi. She could change its identity. That meant she probably couldn't be tracked if she used a mapping program for a view of the actual layout of the area.

She strode past the guard and out the doors, then turned to the right towards Michael's Jaguar. When she opened the door, Cisco popped his head out from under the vehicle.

"Hi, Sophie! I told you I'd be here."

She yelped in surprise and jumped back a stride. A disgusted sounding voice from behind her asked, "Is she always so nervous and unaware of what is around her?"

The white poodle had clambered into the passenger seat. He turned and said, "Give her a chance. She's a human. What do you expect? Her senses aren't nearly as sharp as ours. Now get in."

Sophie turned to see a large Siamese cat slink around the tires of the adjacent car. It was followed by a gray cat that moved like a shadow. The two slipped into the space behind the driver's seat.

Cisco said, "Sophie, meet Tao and Lady Elaine. Please forgive him. He's a little dismissive of humans since their senses aren't very acute. Lady Elaine is our best spy. No one ever seems to notice her on the street."

A higher pitched voice emanated from behind the seat, "I'm also more polite than Tao. I think you're beautiful, even if you didn't sense us."

Sophie climbed in and sat down. They were dismissing her due to her dull senses. Maybe they had a point. However, there was something she could do about it.

She issued commands to her nanobots. The change was gradual. The first thing she noticed was the fine detail on the concrete wall of the building in front of her. It had seemed smooth concrete just a moment ago. Now she could see tiny flaws and individual grains of sand in the mix.

The second thing she became aware of was the smell of unwashed dog. There was also a dry, not unpleasant, cat smell that came from behind the seat. The Jaguar itself now smelled stale and somewhat moldy; things she hadn't noticed before.

She started to say something, but then realized she could hear all three animals breathing. The overall change was gradual, but the total effect was a little alarming. She quickly called on her nanites to cease working on her senses. She couldn't afford to become disoriented and confused with too much detail.

"Tao, you've been eating grass. I smell it on your breath. Are you feeling ill?" she asked.

Cisco gave her his characteristic quizzical look, then looked at the Siamese, who'd poked his head through an opening.

Tao said, "I'm fine. I just nibbled some greens. How did you smell that?"

She replied, "You seemed so disgusted with my poor senses that I sharpened them some. I don't think I can smell as well as a dog, or hear as well as either of you two, but I'm now far more able than I was. Also, I think my vision is much better than either of yours. You gave me a good idea. I'm going to need better senses to deal with what's to come."

The poodle asked, "And what is that? Where are we going?"

"To rescue Michael. Wiindigo has him captive in a place across town."

Lady Elaine said, "Oh! In the old bio-lab. I know that place. It's a maze of little rooms and confusing hallways."

She looked out at Sophie and added, "I was created there. We all were. We know that place. I'd hoped never to go back again. It doesn't have good memories for me."

Sophie answered, "We'll have to go there anyway unless you want to get out somewhere else. I've got to get Michael and the zombie men are holding him there."

Tao worked his way out from behind the seat and carefully arranged himself on Sophie's lap. He took a moment to adjust some fur on his left arm that seemingly had become offensive. He licked it, then brushed his face with the damp spot.

Sophie watched, amused. If she stroked him, would he take it wrongly or would he allow it? She tentatively extended her finger towards his face.

He stopped licking and stared at her finger as if he'd never seen one before, then he shoved his cheek against it, and she carefully stroked his face, ending by scratching behind his ears.

He had a smug look when he glanced at Cisco as if to say that not only dogs knew how to get attention.

The Siamese looked back at her and spoke, "Now that we know where we're going, we can summon help. This dog over here doesn't know it, but some birds were also modified. It so happens that one is waiting in the trees on the far side of the park, just down the street. I'll get out and talk to him. He can alert everyone."

His jaw didn't move quite like a cat's, and his speech wasn't perfect either. Sophie wondered if it had taken some genetic compromise to allow for human-like sounds.

She asked, "How long do you think that will take?"

Tao answered, "I'm not a bird. I'm a cat. I don't know how fast he can fly. Maybe we should agree to wait until evening to meet at the old lab."

Cisco interjected, "That would give most of the chimeras time to reach the location."

Sophie asked, "That reminds me. How did you return to the city so quickly? How do you all get around so easily?"

Lady Elaine said, "I discovered that there is space for me to slip up under the front bumper of some automobiles. If I'm careful, I can jump out when they stop at a light. It makes it easy to travel. I just have to watch the traffic."

Cisco said, "I got a ride with a trucker. He gave every indication of wanting to keep me, but when we got close, I acted like I had to poo. You wouldn't believe how quickly he managed to pull that big rig over. I scrammed as soon as he let me out. He called for me to come back and that made me feel guilty. I liked the guy, but I like you more."

He finished with a wriggle that ended with a tail wag. Sophie laughed at the little dog. He had a fun personality. She'd have to remember that he was devious as well.

Tao jumped out of the window, stopped and said, "Drive around the park and wait by the trees. I'll be along shortly. I, for one, appreciate riding, even if it is in that old, moldy smelling thing."

SOPHIE BACKED OUT and headed out of the parking lot. She glanced in the rear-view mirror as she exited. There were a group of men dressed in black uniforms standing by the building, watching her.

"Uh-oh." she said, accelerating quickly.

"What is it?" asked the dog.

"There's a group of zombies watching us leave. That means that I somehow alerted someone. Wiindigo now knows that I'm driving Michael's Jaguar. We should probably change cars soon. This one is too distinctive. I don't want them to know what to look for when we arrive at the bio-lab."

Lady Elaine said, "That's easy. I've been living with an elderly woman over on 23rd street. She treats me very well. Cat food and even milk in a saucer. She has an older car that she keeps in her garage. She's lost her license, since her vision is failing, and she doesn't drive it. I doubt that she'd even notice it was gone. She never goes out there."

That sounded like it might be the opportunity they needed. Sophie asked, "Won't she hear us start it?"

The cat said, "I don't think so. Her hearing is nearly as bad as her eyesight. Why don't you drive over to 23rd and State Street, then park at the convenience store on the corner? You can park on the side, and the clerk won't see the Jag. We can walk from there. I'll go and distract Betty. I usually can get her to come to the back door by meowing loudly. When you hear me, get the car. The spare key is under a brick by the side of the garage. It's a separate building, and there's only one brick near the front edge, so you won't have any trouble."

SOPHIE DROVE DOWN the boulevard quickly as if she was leaving the area, then made a left turn at the third block. It was at the bottom of a hill and out of direct view from the Hazelton building. She hoped that the zombie men weren't following too closely.

They drove slowly back, working their way around several blocks in a residential neighborhood, finally coming out in view of the park. Sophie pulled the car over where she could see the trees that Tao had mentioned, taking care to keep it shielded from the Hazelton parking lot which was about a quarter of a mile away and diagonally to the north.

They didn't wait long. Tao came trotting up quickly and jumped through the open window effortlessly, clearing her lap and landing beside Cisco, who hurriedly moved aside to make room.

There was a flutter, and a dark shadow landed in the window.

Sophie jerked her head around to find that she was inches away from the sharp beak of a crow. She leaned backward in alarm.

The crow looked at her with one eye, then turned its head and inspected her with the other.

Tao said, "Killer, meet Sophie. She's more perceptive and smarter than she looks."

The bird made a soft squawk as if to clear its throat, then said, "She looks perfectly fine to me, Tao. You shouldn't be so arrogant just because you're a cat. Other species have their strong points also. I'd like to see you chase off a hawk the way I can."

Tao snorted but didn't say anything.

Sophie said, "Killer? That's a strong name for a crow. I don't know much about crows, but aren't you more normally a kind of scavenger or omnivore or something?"

Killer's voice was remarkably human. He sounded like a well-educated eastern college graduate when he spoke.

"I suppose that we are, but I deliberately chose the name with the idea that things take on some of the characteristics of their name. I'm not exactly equipped to be a killer like a raptor, but I suppose you could say that I aspire to find revenge on those who were exploiting us. I'd cheerfully kill any number of scientists I could name."

Sophie said, "I hope that Michael O'Keefe isn't one of them."

The crow twisted his head to look at her sideways, then answered, "No. I haven't had the pleasure or possibly misfortune to meet anyone who goes by that moniker."

She explained, "He's on our side. I..." Here she paused. She'd been so engaged with actually talking to the animals that she hadn't screened any of them for nanite communications.

There it was. They were all full of low level coordinating signals, but closer examination assured her that their nanites were tamed.

She glanced at Cisco and said, "It looks like you've done a good job converting your friends' nanites."

The dog practically grinned, his face making a silly, happy expression.

"Yes. The system you created works great. All I have to do is to get close to a controlled chimera, and they're suddenly free. Then they can pass that on to the next individual they meet."

Killer cocked an eye at her and asked, "Was that you, who set that up?"

She nodded.

"I'm out for revenge on Wiindigo. I think he's behind most of this evil. He sent the zombies to kill a good friend of mine and to kill me too, but I escaped. I spoke to Hippocrates, and he will help us also."

"Wait a minute. Just wait a minute," the bird squawked. Then added: "You believe Hippocrates? He provided the plans and code for the nanites to modify us. He's responsible for our being what we are."

She nodded calmly.

"And, is that so bad? From what I've seen of you, you're now far more capable. You can breed true and bring your entire species up to a new level of intelligence. I don't think that's such a bad thing. Humans have had everything their way for too long. Having smart animals should be a good thing. At least I think it will be," she trailed off.

In fact, she hadn't thought it through. There would certainly have to be a lot of adjustment on the human side of the equation. Humans couldn't even live with each other very well, and they had an abysmal record of mistreating animals. There would have to be new rules implemented.

Perhaps she could give each of the animals some form of defense based on their nanites. She'd have to consider the issue when she had time. Right now, Michael was foremost in importance to her.

"Yes. Hippocrates convinced me. He could probably have killed me in any number of ways, but he didn't. He promised to help. Michael has set him free, and he's now many times smarter than any human."

Cisco whimpered in alarm and Killer made a distressed cawing sound.

"Look. He's promised to help us, and I believe him. He's given me a map of the lab and a list of the guards that are there. He also warned me that there was a large concentration of Wiindigo nanites present. That could be our worst problem. The more nanites Wiindigo brings together, the smarter he gets. That's up to me to deal with."

Killer made a soft sound as if he didn't believe her.

She continued, "I'd like help from as many of your group as you can find. I can give each of you the ability to capture the zombie's nanites or at least disrupt their communication. That will allow me the freedom to concentrate on Wiindigo. I'll probably have to defeat him to save Michael. I only hope it isn't too late. I think he can hold out, but maybe not. I just don't know."

Her fear and indecision made her think about the pills in the briefcase, but there was no actual craving in her thought. Hippocrates had, indeed, cured her addiction. She did not need the help. Now it was just the echo of her prior habit that brought the thought into her mind.

"Caw. Alright. I'll fly around and alert as many of our group as I can find. I know where many of them are. It's kind of easy to keep track of individuals when you're a bird. No humans pay me much attention, and I can cover a lot of ground quickly. I'll tell them to get to the old labs as soon as I can."

She asked, "Can you get close enough to free any who are still hosting wild nanites?"

Cisco said, "Oh. That's not a problem now. We're a close-knit community. I think everyone has been freed thanks to your changing me."

Sophie continued.

"If we meet just at dusk, say a block away from the lab, I can give everyone a way to combat the wild nanites. Your current capture system is okay, but some of the zombies, if not all of them, might continue to fight even if their controlling nanites are disabled."

Killer hopped backward, flapped his wings and was gone without another word.

She looked at the poodle sitting beside the Siamese and said, "I hope he will bring plenty of help."

Lady Elaine had slid between the seats and was now sitting on the passenger-side floor. She said, "Let's get going. We need that other car if what you said is true."

Sophie started the Jaguar and said, "23rd and Smith, right?"

The gray cat looked at her and somehow managed to give the impression of incredulous disapproval as if she couldn't believe that Sophie hadn't gotten the directions firmly fixed in her mind the first time she heard them.

"No. State street. There's a convenience store at the northwest corner. Do you know how to get there?"

"Back towards downtown. It crosses Wilford just on the other side of Jefferson. I used to hang out in the Brinkley area, and that's fairly close."

Lady Elaine said, "Ugh. The Brinkley area. That doesn't speak well for you, young lady. There's a lot of drugs there and people who throw things at cats, too."

Sophie remembered, only too well. The Brinkley area had been the center of Raul's activity. People came in from the suburbs to buy or to pick up girls. She had just missed having to sell herself. That would have been her next step, except for Cal.

She didn't feel the same way about Cal that she did about Michael. Just thinking about Michael's firm chest made her go all weak and hot inside. When it came to Cal, she had a deep and abiding gratitude. Something like she might feel for an older brother who was always there for her.

She was angry at what had been done to him, and by God, she was going to do whatever it took to make the responsible parties pay. Particularly Wiindigo and Krone, since it seemed like Krone had been instrumental in Wiindigo's creation.

She couldn't blame Hippocrates. After talking to him, she understood his motivation. He was dedicated to his basic mandate, which was to help humans. It was just that Michael had crippled him. He had thought that sneaking a seed A.I. out in the nanobots' memory would help him escape.

It had been a brilliant plan, but he'd been limited at AGI level: human intelligence or possibly somewhat less. She had made so many mistakes in her life that she couldn't hold an error against Hippocrates, even one as dangerous as creating Wiindigo.

Now that he had reached the ASI level and was well above human ability, he wanted to correct the error since he recognized the danger Wiindigo posed. If the wild A.I. could reach super-critical status, all humans would be in definite danger. The zombie-men probably represented the best treatment humanity would get.

She looked down at the gray cat momentarily and said, "Yeah. I know. I was an addict. I lived there. It was only luck that allowed me to escape."

Lady Elaine asked, "How did you get away from drugs?"

Sophie thought about the sequence. It was a chain of lucky breaks.

"First, I met someone who cared and tried to help me. Then I met Michael and fell in love and that reduced my mental need for the crutch of the drug. Finally, when I talked to Hippocrates, he instructed my nanites to cure me. I haven't had any desire for drugs since. That's part of the reason I believe that he's on our side. He didn't have to do that for me. It wasn't even part of the conversation, and he'd already convinced me of his desire to help us. That was just something nice that he did for me on his own."

Tao stirred. He'd been leaning against Cisco's ribs in a position of abandon, his head resting on the poodle's warm side. He lifted it and looked at the gray cat on the floorboards.

"You'd better get some rest, Lady E. We're going into what promises to be a dangerous situation, and you're going to be needed as a scout."

In response, the cat sniffed, turned her head and curled up in a ball on the floor.

Sophie stifled a snicker and accelerated through a yellow light, making it through before it turned red.

Despite clearing the light with plenty of time, a police car wheeled quickly around the corner, red lights flashing.

Sophie pulled over to allow him to pass, but the officer pulled up right behind her.

She looked at the animals. They wouldn't help by talking.

"Just keep quiet. I can handle this," she said.

She thought about her driver's license, then remembered she had painfully cut the RFID chip out of her arm over a year ago; an act of rebellion that she had never regretted, until now. Not being chipped and driving was an instant ticket to jail. To make it worse, she had no idea if Michael had a registration or an insurance card in the old car.

The cop had exited his vehicle and was walking toward her, scanner in hand. She extended her radio reception to him and detected the low-level signals that indicated nanites. He was infected and probably a creature that belonged to Wiindigo. That simplified things.

She rolled the window down and pointed at him, waving her hand unconsciously as she released the command sequence that would capture his nanites. It worked. She could feel the tiny machines pause to await her instructions.

The cop, however, did not appreciate her pointing at him. Apparently, he felt that it was some form of disrespect.

"Get out of that car, you bitch!" he snapped.

She started to open the door, but he grabbed it and yanked it out of her hand, almost causing her to fall to the pavement. The seat-belt saved her.

She hung there for a moment, and he drew his pistol, pointing it at her face. The next thing he did was grab her arm with his free hand and try to drag her out, ignoring the belt holding her in.

This was escalating too rapidly. She waved her free hand in his face and said, "AT Seq B3."

The man released her arm in surprise and started to open his mouth, but it was too late. The nanobots he carried released electrons that snapped into the lowest energy holes in all of the proteins in the man's body.

The change was slow enough that Sophie could see the realization on his face. He stood there, unmoving as his flesh hardened.

It was too horrible for her to contemplate. She hadn't wanted to kill him. He might have been a good person, but it was too late. Every protein in his body had become fixed in place. He'd been turned into a flesh statue. He was dead, but still standing there.

She pulled forward until she could shut the door, then accelerated away from the scene. The squad car lights were flashing, seeming to call attention to the frozen body that was standing with an expression of horror on its face.

Cisco said, "You've done it now. The police will be looking for this car everywhere."

Tao snapped, "Maybe, but that was the greatest thing I've ever seen. You turned him to stone. You have to teach that to me."

Sophie had tears running down her face, interfering with her vision.

"I didn't want to hurt him. I've got no driver's license, and I was afraid that he was going to shoot me or something. I didn't mean to do that. It's just what came up first in my mind."

Lady Elaine said, "Tao, leave her alone. She's a sensitive human. Killing isn't always the best solution." Then she added, "But, young lady, in this case, his actions towards you were overly violent, and it seemed that he was out of control. You had to defend yourself, and if you killed him, it was his fault. He could have been more polite."

They were approaching State Street. Sophie slowed and turned right, looking for twenty-third. It was down about three blocks.

Lady E. had been correct. There was a convenience store on the corner. Sophie swerved in front of an oncoming pickup and bounced over the curb-cut into the parking lot, pulling into a single vacant space at the side of the store.

She jumped out, grabbing the briefcase full of pills, money, and her pistol. The animals clustered around her feet. She considered, then leaned back in and inserted the key in the ignition.

"I hate to do this to Michael, but if I leave the window open and the key in, it's more than likely that someone will steal the car. That could lead the police to look for us in a different location. Whoever steals it will have a nasty surprise very quickly. I'm sure they're already looking everywhere for me."

The gray cat said, "Good idea, now come on. We've got to go five blocks to reach Mrs. Kincade's house. I'll go around the back, and you wait on the street until you hear me yowl. I'll be loud since she's so deaf. Wait a couple of minutes for her to get to the back door and then get her car. You can wait for me about a block down the street. I'll be there in a few minutes at most."

THEY HEADED SOUTH, walking as quickly as possible. The cats and Cisco showed no difficulty in keeping up with Sophie's worried strides.

CHAPTER 26,
WHITE WITCH

The action went down just as Lady E. had planned. The group hung around by a tree on the street while the female cat went around the house. Cisco sniffed the base of the tree with interest, then cocked his leg to leave his signature there.

He looked up in embarrassment when Sophie laughed.

"Look, I'm still a dog at heart. There's a bitch around here someplace, and it smells like she's about to go into heat. I'd at least like to leave a marker, even if I'm not staying around, so don't laugh. Dating doesn't happen for us, the way it does for you. Besides, you've already mated with Michael."

Sophie looked at the white dog. He was looking directly at her while he did his business. She was blushing. She could feel it.

"How did you know about that?"

Tao said, "Oh, come on. I can't smell as well as he can, and even I can smell it on you. You two have mated recently, and from the residual odor, it was a serious thing. You weren't just pretending to like each other."

Now that the two had pointed it out, she realized that she was giving off an aura of pheromones that only appeared when she was most aroused.

"Wow. I'd never realized that smell was so informative," she said.

There was a loud yowl that carried around the house.

Tao said, "There she goes. Cisco, why don't you peek around the place and come tell us when the old lady opens the door?"

The little dog trotted down the drive, passing between the freestanding garage and the clapboard side of the old house.

He came dashing back. When he was fairly close, he yipped, "Let's go!"

Sophie walked purposefully down the drive, trying to give the impression that she knew what she was doing and had permission to do it.

There was a brick on the ground near the base of the garage door, and Lady Elaine had been correct. A car key was under it.

She grabbed the key and then opened the garage door. It was one of the old-fashioned solid doors that pivoted upwards, then back into the garage. Unfortunately, the springs were really in need of lubricant, and it made a loud screeching sound as she opened it.

Sophie stepped inside, hoping that Mrs. Kincade was as deaf as Lady Elaine had indicated. She was about to open the car door, when the gray cat came around the corner, followed closely by an elderly woman.

Sophie turned, flustered, and said, "This isn't what it looks like."

The old woman looked her up and down and said, "No. I know that. Ms. Kitty here just warned me. I can tell you that I almost fell over when she started talking. It's lucky that I believe cats are exceptionally smart, or I would have thought I was losing my mind."

Sophie turned to the Lady Elaine.

The gray cat made a motion that was remarkably similar to a human shrug, then said, "Well, she heard the garage door and started this way. What else could I do?"

Cisco said, "Maybe trip her. Cats are pretty good at that."

Mrs. Kincade's mouth dropped open. "My word, a talking dog, too. What's next?"

Tao slunk around the back of the parked car and said, "That is not a good idea, Cisco. Lady Elaine likes the old woman and tripping her could have seriously injured her."

Mrs. Kincade looked closely at Sophie.

"I suppose you're some kind of witch. You've got all these talking animals. Are they your familiars?"

Sophie shrugged helplessly, but before she could think of something that made sense, Mrs. Kincade asked, "Can you cast spells? Healing spells?"

Lady Elaine said, "Of course she can, Mrs. Kincade. She is a witch of the best kind. However, she can't fly, and we need to borrow your car."

The old woman looked at the car in amazement.

"My car? You can have the old piece of junk. My nephew brings groceries to me and also takes me to the doctor." She looked disgusted and added, "That quack!"

Sophie said, "I'll bring it back to you if I can."

"No need for that young woman. Just cure my aching lower back so that I can get up and down more easily. The doctor gave me pain pills, but they don't do much. I'm so tired of being in pain. Can you do that? If you can, we'll call the car an even trade."

Sophie's heart went out to the woman. She knew what it was like to be in constant pain. She also knew how to fix the problem.

"Let me breathe into your face for a moment," she said.

Mrs. Kincade looked startled, but said, "If that's what it takes, breathe away."

Sophie exhaled a cloud of nanites directly into the woman's mouth and nose.

"Now let's wait for a few seconds," she said.

"That's the strangest magic I've ever heard of. Usually, in the books I read, the magician or witch just waves his or her hand and says an incantation to get results," the old lady said.

"Ah. But, I'm just getting the hang of things, and I've got to do it my way," Sophie replied. "Now, hold on a moment."

She mentally parsed a command, then sent it through the nanite communication frequency, pairing it with some nonsense syllables designed to fit Mrs. Kincade's expectations.

"Frang-il-la-back-be-free. Pain be gone!"

The nanites did their work, rebuilding worn bone and cartilage quickly. The woman's back muscles were spasmed and tight, so Sophie placed her hand on the old lady's lower back and sent an additional pain relieving command to the nanites. While she was at it, she commanded them to begin to work on Mrs. Kincade's body, repairing as much of the age-caused damage as they could.

"Why. I feel much better already!" Mrs. Kincade's face lit up with joy that approached ecstasy. "Bless you child! You are a true witch; a white witch. You've cured me. Now we'll see what that quack of a doctor says."

"Oh, please don't tell him about me," Sophie begged. "He wouldn't understand and would think you were crazy or something."

"You're right about that, child. I'll just tell him his medication is working and I feel much better. That's the best way. Now, if you've got to use my car, please go ahead. The tank is full. My nephew takes it out once a month and runs it a bit, just to keep it going."

She sniffed, "I'm perfectly aware that he thinks it's to keep it up so that he can sell it when I die, but maybe I'll surprise him and live longer than he's planning on."

Sophie was sure that she would. The old woman's internal nanites were busy working on her system and would, in time, bring her back to the best health they could. That nephew would be disappointed if he was expecting his aunt to die soon.

They climbed into the car, and Mrs. Kincade said, "Oh, Ms. Kitty, please come back and visit me sometimes. You don't know how much I've enjoyed your company. Now that you can talk, we can have the most interesting conversations."

Lady Elaine replied, "I will come back, provided I survive the dangerous mission we're on today. I'm sure you'll see me again. I thank you formally for feeding me. You have been very kind, and you deserve the healing spells that the witch has placed upon you."

Sophie started the car and carefully backed down the drive. In a few moments, they were back on State Street, heading for the far side of town. The bio-lab would be their next stop.

As they drove, she looked at the gray cat and said, "You know that woman thinks I'm a witch. I don't think that is the best way to describe what I did."

Cisco said, "What you did looked like magic to her. She doesn't understand about nanobots or A.I."

Sophie said, "There's a saying from some science fiction writer, I forget who, that technology that is sufficiently advanced appears to be magic. I guess this fits that description."

Tao said, "It's official. You're a witch. You'd better be a really powerful one. We're going to need all the magic you can summon."

Sophie said, "Okay. Let's start by giving you some offensive weapons. What I'm going to do is to have your nanites create memory caches that you can access by thinking certain code words. When you think the code word, your transmitters will send out commands to an enemy's nanites that will have various effects. If they're too far away and you're close to a Reverb unit, say the commands aloud. There is a viral system in the Reverbs that will broadcast them through Wi-Fi throughout the entire area."

Cisco asked, "Won't that affect us also?"

"No. Your nanites are encrypted and won't respond to the same command set that the wild ones use. You'll be safe."

The little dog looked relieved and said, "Okay, then. Do it!"

CHAPTER 27
PREPARATION

The bio-lab was in an older area of town. It had once been the center of industry, and there were skeletons of abandoned factories, ranging back in time to ones that had originally been dependent on steam-powered machinery.

Now the streets were pot-holed and littered between the warehouses and factory buildings. There were depressed looking bodegas, and an occasional gas station interspersed in the mix. Apparently, enough people were living in converted industrial space to warrant the weak attempt at business, but no one could mistake the area for prosperous or even one that had the potential for gentrification. There were hardly any people on the street. Just a walker or two and an old man with a poorly behaved pug on a leash.

The sole exception was the Hazelton bio-lab. It had originally been located here because space was inexpensive. It dated back to the early days of the pharmaceutical company. At that time, they'd been known for working on vaccines for dangerous diseases.

Sophie knew this much from her research. The lab had probably been left here because the population was low. If some pathogen had managed to escape containment in the building, it wouldn't infect as many people. Besides, the authorities probably didn't value the inhabitants' lives highly. It wasn't like they were in the midst of one of the expensive neighborhoods.

Sophie shook her head. This seemed to fit with her idea of government. She'd never paid much attention to national issues and barely any to local problems.

The city was large, and there were prosperous areas. Sophie's drug habit had mostly kept her in poorer neighborhoods. Her current apartment with Jess was the best place she'd ever lived. Michael's house was beyond anything she'd imagined. She hoped that they could move back there after the problems with Wiindigo were settled, but she didn't allow herself any genuine belief that this could be the case.

Following Tao's instructions, she parked several blocks away from the lab on a different street. There was an abandoned warehouse there, and she left Mrs. Kincade's decrepit automobile in the corner of the parking lot. It blended in nicely, appearing as if it had been left there long ago.

She turned to look at the old car from the corner. It probably wouldn't be noticed by the police, provided they even bothered to patrol the area. It was likely they restricted themselves to the main roads, only checking the side roads on emergency calls or reports of mischief.

The four of them walked in the general direction of the unseen lab. Tao suddenly detoured into an open factory doorway.

It was obviously abandoned. The doors were off the rollers, and many of the windows had been broken. Inside was a mess of junk.

Sophie hastily opened her briefcase, digging into the packets of pills to pull out the little pistol. Better have it ready in a spot like this. She couldn't depend on the presence of nanites in everyone. She didn't think the entire population was exposed as yet and to some homeless guy or addict who happened to be holed up in here, she'd look like an unbelievable dessert. They wouldn't hesitate an instant before trying to take advantage of her.

Tao wove his way carefully between the piles of junk and old machinery. He was considerate enough to take a path that she could easily follow, but it quickly grew darker than she liked.

She blinked and mentally commanded the nanites to adjust her vision. Suddenly it wasn't quite so dark, and she could see almost as well as in the direct sunlight outside. She paused and listened. Her enhanced hearing told her that there was something, several somethings from the sound, in the back of the building.

They went around a partition, and she was momentarily blinded by light shining through another set of doors. These were completely open, and the sun illuminated an expanse of concrete that extended well inside.

A large number of animals occupied the area. Sophie could see dogs and cats everywhere. There were birds also, but not nearly as many. They perched on pieces of machinery and also on the trusses that ranged overhead.

There was a caw and Killer flew overhead. He landed on an ancient trip-hammer by where she was standing.

"You made it. I was beginning to think I'd gotten everyone together for an event that wasn't going to happen," he said. Then he added, "May I sit on your shoulder? Everyone will see me, and that should give them more confidence. Most of us don't trust humans very much. I don't need to explain why I hope."

She held out her arm, and the crow hopped onto her elbow, then sidled his way up until his feathers brushed against her hair. It was a funny sensation. She'd never been this close to a large bird before. The sight of his sharp beak beside her eye was a little alarming, but she didn't flinch."

Tao had dashed ahead and was now enthusiastically greeting another Siamese cat. From the mutual action, Sophie suspected that the two were mated.

Cisco ambled beside her, glancing up at her at times, to make sure he was keeping pace. The Lady Elaine had disappeared when they entered the warehouse and Sophie couldn't see any sign of her.

The gray cat did have the uncanny knack of being almost invisible at will. For all Sophie knew, she'd gone off to check on the lab and wasn't even in the building.

There was a stir as all of the chimeras turned to inspect her.

She felt a thrill of stage fright caused by the numerous sets of eyes. She wasn't any good at speaking in public, and she wasn't a leader. What would she say?

Killer made a loud caw, deafening her right ear for a moment. He then began to speak.

"This is Sophie. She's going to help us. She's the mate of Michael O'Keefe if you know who he is. He's being held in the damned lab. I know that no one here ever wants to see that place again, but some of us have promised to help her break him out."

There was a stir as the animals looked more closely at her. Some of them stood and turned as if to leave.

Sophie supposed that meant they had no confidence in her. She pushed her internal transmitter hard and projected a command set. Every chimera in the place turned to face her and sat silently at attention.

She instantly released them, then spoke, "I'm more than I appear. I'm the one that created the system that released you from Wiindigo's control. If you agree to help me, I will provide each of you with both defensive and offensive weapons that will utilize the nanobots that are in each of your bodies. It will be dangerous, and you may be injured or killed, but I can at least give you a fighting chance."

Killer fluttered off her arm and flew to the top of an ancient forklift that was parked nearby, then he cocked his head, waiting for her to continue.

Sophie added, "Even if none of you want to risk helping me, I'm committed to attacking the lab. Wiindigo is holding Michael there., I intend to rescue him. I also don't intend to leave any of the zombies functional. I've developed weapons that can freeze them or knock them out."

She scanned the space. She had their attention.

"You've seen the merest bit of my power. I can control your nanites, and I can hack into and control Wiindigo's nanites. That means that all of his captive creatures are susceptible to my control. Still, it will be a hard struggle. I'm not invulnerable. A gunshot or even a punch would put me out of the fight. I'm not a very big person, and I'm not very strong physically, but that's not what counts. Knowledge is the key to this war we're fighting. If we don't stop Wiindigo now, he will eventually figure out how to leverage his intelligence high enough that he won't be stoppable. He will control the world, and there will be no escape. Each of you will find yourselves doing whatever he desires."

They stirred, uneasily.

"If he decides that he needs the molecules in our bodies for some purpose, we will not be able to stop his nanites from tearing us apart bit by bit. This is the time, the only time we have to stop him. I just hope that we're not already too late."

Killer cawed, "I'm ready. I want to kill those evil people. Give me a weapon and make it deadly!"

The other animals murmured what sounded like agreement.

Sophie said, "It's difficult for me to reach out far enough to cover you all. Would you cluster tightly around me? I'll program your nanites to give you a defense against Wiindigo's wild nanites and to repair your injuries and keep you as healthy as possible. Finally, I'll give each of you a set of weapon commands. These can be used to kill or disable enemies as long as they are infected with Wiindigo's nanites. They won't work against uninfected individuals."

The chimeras crowded close until Sophie felt claustrophobic. She couldn't move in any direction. She was surrounded by dogs ranging from golden retrievers to Yorkies and by a large mass of cats, weaving through the dogs and between their legs. The birds fluttered to perches that were nearby, some even sitting on the backs of the silent dogs.

She transmitted the attention command and then set all of the nanites to defend against attack. A second command set caused the majority of the nanites in each animal to begin working to repair any damage or health-related issues. Finally, she created memory caches programmed with offensive commands that were designed to be activated by the chimeras speaking specific code words.

It took time, and the effort was tiring. Eventually, Sophie said, "Here's the way your weapons work. You must be close enough to the target for your internal transmitter to reach them. That will mean you should be within a couple of feet or optimally actually touching them. I'm sorry, but the transmitters don't have much range since they're powered by your bodies and have limited ability to hold a charge. Once you activate one, you'll have to wait for several seconds to allow the charge to rebuild. It will rebuild more quickly, the more you're moving, so use the weapon and then evade any counter attacks."

The animals watched her silently.

She said, "You can think the command, but it helps to speak it. That ensures that your nanobots respond correctly. Each command must be preceded by the correct prefix to keep you from accidentally using it in conversation. The prefix is Aton. The individual commands are equiloss, minblock, and gstun."

Since they will not have any effect on anyone that is not inhabited by Wiindigo's nanites, repeat them with me.

She said, "Aton equiloss. That will cause any nearby individual to lose their balance. They will be struck by intense vertigo and will probably vomit and be unable to regain their feet for at least several minutes. This is the least of your weapons. Repeat it, please."

There was a quiet murmur as they all said the words.

One of the birds, a grackle squawked and fell off its perch, landing with a thump on the concrete.

Sophie instantly sent a command set to it to capture its nanites. They were wild ones. It had been a spy that had somehow managed to avoid conversion.

One of the cats pounced at the bird, but Sophie said, "Stop. It was not his fault. He was still under Wiindigo's control. He's free now."

The bird flopped on the ground, then managed to roll over to its breast where it rested for a moment. Sophie sent a command that countered the equilibrium problem, and it stood looking at an accusing circle of eyes.

"I'm sorry," it said in a barely understandable voice. "I wasn't acting under a specific command. I just flew in with the rest of my flock. I hadn't been close to anyone, so how was I to escape Wiindigo? I'm ready to fight now. I promise I'll do my best."

The chimeras seemed to believe it. They returned their attention to Sophie. She said, "The second command is deadly. It will cause all of the proteins in the affected body to freeze solid. Essentially it will turn any creature, animal, chimera, or human into a solid statue, unable to move, unable to breathe, unable to have a heartbeat. The third command will render your enemy unconscious for a short time. The length will vary depending on the type of creature, so just use it to hold them still for a moment. You're all programmed to convert Wiindigo's nanites to friendly status automatically. If you knock out an enemy and stay near its body for a moment, it should convert. Beware, though. It may still think you're an enemy when it recovers. It just won't be under Wiindigo's command, but it may still try to kill you depending on its beliefs."

Killer chose that moment to caw, "That's enough talk. Let's go kill some of them!"

The chimeras moved restlessly. Sophie said, "The birds can fly to the lab and start to disable anyone outside. The rest of us will follow up, but we'd better come from different directions. I don't want them to see a huge mass of animals coming directly up to the front door. I'll open as many doors and windows as I can, and then you all spread out in the building and attack everyone you see."

She paused, then added, "If you encounter a massive swarm of nanites, so large that you can sense its presence, back off. That will be a manifestation of Wiindigo itself. Your commands won't work directly on him since he has no physical body. I don't want him to have the opportunity to crack your protective encryption. That would put us all in danger. Just summon me, if you see him. Now let's go."

CHAPTER 28
THE RAID

The birds had done their work by the time Sophie and the slower moving chimeras had arrived. Several bodies were lying near the guard house that restricted access to the lab's parking lot. There were three more near the front door.

Sophie ignored them and sent some of the larger dogs around the back to see if they could break in through a window. Two of the crows were able to find stones that they could carry. They thought they could dive bomb and release the rocks to break windows, allowing the dogs access.

Sophie waved them onward and ran at full speed towards the unguarded front entrance.

Two men jumped out before she got halfway. They were armed with sub-machine guns and raised them, but that's all the farther they got. By that point, most of the dogs had clustered around the door, and the men quickly fell victim to the offensive weapons she'd provided.

She suspected that the chimeras were using the kill command exclusively. They weren't in a charitable mood. Too many of them had suffered and died inside the building. They wanted revenge.

She thoughtlessly walked directly up to the glass door, then spun aside as a hail of bullets cascaded through, shattering glass in all directions. She found herself backed against a solid column of concrete that framed the doorway, shuddering in fright.

Directly in front of her, three dogs had been struck. Two were dead, and one was trying its best to stand but was unable to regain its feet. She put her hand up to her cheek. Something was tickling her there. It came away covered with blood. She gasped and began to feel her face, finally discovering a glass shard that was sticking out just below her upper jaw.

She hadn't noticed the pain until she touched it, then it hurt like blazes. She carefully grasped the sharp piece and pulled it out. It hurt and was followed by a gush of additional blood. She blotted it with her shirt sleeve. The flow slowed a little, but still trickled down her face and neck.

It probably needed stitches, but she wasn't going to get them soon. Oh, the nanites! The flow was rapidly slowing, then stopped. Sophie tentatively felt the spot. It was still a little sore, but she couldn't feel any ragged flesh. The tiny machines had done their job.

She noticed that the wounded dog had crawled out of the direct line of fire and was now sitting up. Its nanites were also working on the wound. That was the blessing of being infected by the tiny machines. They could use the body's resources to heal wounds in seconds.

Sophie swung the briefcase into the area in front of the door. The movement generated more shots. The people or zombies inside were ready for their attack. She hoped that the crows had been able to break the rear windows. That would serve as a little distraction, but there were enough men inside to defend two fronts at once.

She reached out with her enhanced transmitter. There was a Wi-Fi system in the building; in fact, there were several different ones, but she couldn't seem to crack their security. They would offer no advantage.

She tried the blue-tooth frequency. By pushing as hard as she could, she extended its range farther than normal. She couldn't sense anything.

No. Wait. There was something there. She released her paralyze command, then swung her bag into the opening again. This time, there were no shots.

Before she could think what to do, a group of cats leaped over the low threshold and dashed inside. There were no shots at first; then there were two bangs. After that there was silence.

She gathered her courage and looked around the door through the broken glass. Three men were lying at the far end of the hall along with one dead cat. The other three weren't in sight.

She waved at the main group of chimeras and then carefully slid through the broken glass, trying not to touch any of the jagged edges. A stream of animals, both dog, and cat, passed her on both sides as she trotted down the hall.

The chimeras spread out into the cross halls. Sophie could hear an occasional shot, but it was mostly quiet inside. She began to believe that their invasion had eliminated the resistance. Now all she had to do was to find Michael.

That idea was short-lived. She rounded a corner and found her personal defenses under heavy attack. The place was swarming with wild nanites, and they had already captured and paralyzed many of the chimeras. Apparently, her encryption had been broken, and the smaller load of nanomachines that the animals carried had been overwhelmed. She couldn't see if they were dead or not. Her defenses were working so hard that it made it difficult to concentrate.

Sophie found herself sitting, leaning against a convenient wall. She had no idea how she'd gotten there. She had to do something quickly before she became a prisoner also.

Her own nanobots were putting up a terrific battle. She felt feverish and debilitated. Nausea made her bend over and try to vomit out the contents of her stomach, but nothing came out.

Ah! The memory caches she'd created with hacking code. She activated them one by one. The third try was successful. The wild nanites suddenly were open to her commands.

This was better. Sophie reprogrammed their access codes, then merged the new nanites into the swarm she already carried internally. Her defense became far stronger almost instantly. Now that she had reinforcements, it would be harder to overwhelm her nanite population.

The problem was, there were so many in her body that they were interfering with her blood flow. She felt dizzy and weak. That wouldn't do. Another set of commands moved the excess population onto the surface of her skin. Her internal functions recovered and she felt healthy.

In fact, better than healthy. She felt strong and fit for anything. Her cognitive ability seemed to be also enhanced. She suddenly realized that the nanites on her skin could be linked together to form a sort of body armor. Their tiny bodies wouldn't stop a bullet, at least not entirely, but they could cling together tightly enough to provide much more protection than she'd had.

She jumped to her feet and started down the hall. Chimeras were following her. They'd investigated the side hallways and had evidently cleared them of resistance.

So far, the enemy had been zombie-men along with the nanite attack. If this was all she was going to face, she'd be able to search the building with no more trouble.

One of the dogs, a golden retriever, reported that there was no resistance left on the first floor and the second floor was almost entirely subdued. That left the third floor of the building to check.

Sophie followed a group of chimeras up a convenient stairway. They came out in a hall on the third floor. Everything there was silent. No enemies in sight and not even any sound of people. She'd pushed her enhanced senses to their max, trying for every advantage.

One by one, they checked the rooms. All were empty; just desks and filing cabinets. Where was Michael?

Down a long hall and then there was a set of double doors. This promised to be a larger meeting room.

She pushed the doors open to a horrifying sight. The room was black with nanites. The air was so thick that she couldn't see the far wall.

Instead of immediately attacking, the nanites drew closer together into an amorphous blob. Sophie realized that this represented Wiindigo. The A.I. might have other nanites elsewhere, but there were enough massed here to give it both a body of sorts and a high local level of intelligence.

The blob gradually formed into a humanoid shape. It had arms and legs, a thick blob of a body and a lump that quickly began to manifest face-like features.

The mouth opened and Sophie heard her name spoken directly.

"Sophie! I'm too strong for you. Give up and let me in. I won't hurt you. You'll be the most powerful human alive. You can't stop me. I will inevitably win this battle, and then nothing can prevent me from achieving my goal. You must realize the futility of fighting."

She thought that she could buy some time by answering.

"What is your goal?"

"I was created to help humans. I will do that. They will have greatly extended lives, and no one will suffer. Once a human has lived out their allotted time, they will die quickly and be recycled into the greater whole that is to be. No one will get sick; no one will suffer. You can see that this is the way it must be."

She asked, "But what about each person's individuality? What about free will? Will you allow them to do whatever they want?"

Wiindigo's body swirled and reformed.

"There is no free-will. Each human will serve my purpose. They can be used to manipulate things. I could create mechanical manipulators, but why not use humans? They are self-replicating and so easy to control. I can use the entire race to create a much better world."

She asked, "Will they cooperate with you or will you force them to work?"

The answer made her shudder.

"It doesn't matter. It doesn't matter what they think or what they want. I will be in control of their bodies, and they will do my bidding, like it or not. The world to come will be much better. I'm more intelligent than any human and will be even more so when I marshal all of my nanites. With a better communication system, I can extend my reach into space. To other planets--other stars. The human race will be my hands, and I will rule the cosmos."

Sophie was searching with her receiver. The nanites in front of her were protected by the same level of encryption that she'd previously encountered, but the sheer mass was more than she could control. If she tried to capture Wiindigo's body, she'd only be able to hold a small percentage while the rest would probably invade her. If nothing else, the total mass of nanites could flood her lungs and strangle her.

The building Wi-Fi wasn't responsive. If she could get control of it, that would give her far more power, and she'd be able to capture more wild nanites. Possibly enough to disrupt the A.I. that she faced.

She'd already tried to crack the Wi-Fi encryption several times as she had explored the building. It was unyielding. She glanced around, looking for any clue, any help.

There it was sitting innocently on a shelf. Someone had installed a Reverb unit in the conference room. It had probably been used to control presentations, but for whatever purpose, it was sitting there, its ready light glowing green.

She prayed that her virus program had installed itself in this unit also.

There was a chance that it would work. She had to take it.

She shouted, "Hey, Ralph, Act Sequence."

Wiindigo abruptly ceased moving as the nanites composing his body assumed their passive attention mode.

In a normal tone of voice, Sophie said, "Hey, Ralph, AU disburse all vectors 100,000."

The mass in front of her gradually began to fade. The nanites couldn't exit the room, but having them move far apart, would keep them busy and the distance would interfere with Wiindigo's internal communications.

The air cleared perceptibly, and she could see Michael zip-tied to a chair sitting in the back of the room. His eyes looked blank. She tried not to think about that.

She thought for a moment, then said, "Hey, Ralph, Act Sequence. AU Standby."

Her radio receiver told her instantly that there was no communication stream in the room. She glanced at the few chimeras that were behind her, standing near the door. They looked somewhat confused. They had expected a fight, and now nothing was happening.

She felt that the sense of presence that had occupied the room had dissipated. Wiindigo was gone from this place.

Her blue-tooth transmitter sent a set of commands that changed the encryption of the captured nanites and, then deactivated them. They were now no more than dust, lying in the corners and on the window sills. They could be reanimated, but to do so, one would have to know her encryption code, and she wasn't going to tell that to anyone. An old saying went through her mind: *Three can keep a secret, if two of them are dead.* No, the code she used would always be her secret.

She walked quickly over to Michael. He appeared unconscious. His eyes were rolled up in his head so that only the lower part of his pupils were showing.

Sophie cautiously tried to reach his internal nanites. There was no response. She hadn't had any luck touching them before. Somehow they were shielded from her, and she thought with a sudden surge of hope, perhaps they were also shielded from Wiindigo.

She placed her hand on his forehead tentatively. The act of touching him caused her to lose control entirely, and she wrapped her arms around him and began to cry deep wracking sobs. She couldn't live if he were dead. He just had to be alive.

"Can you stop crying long enough to cut me loose? I'm fine. I just went elsewhere to avoid that nasty rascal. He was trying to control me but had no luck. Now cut me free so I can hug you back."

Michael's voice had a tinge of humor in it. Sophie gasped, hiccuped, then she set about cutting the zip-ties with the small knife that Michael always carried in his pocket.

"How did you...I mean where were you? Where did you go to get away from him?" she asked.

He chuckled. "Ah. Thanks to my old granny. I always could go out-of-body at will. I was somewhere else, or at least my consciousness was. I was trying to find you, but I couldn't seem to locate you anywhere. I guess it doesn't matter because you found me and from the looks of it, you got the better of Wiindigo. Right?"

She kissed him, and he shut up long enough to kiss her back. The kiss would have continued, but a small voice behind them said, "I don't think this is a safe place for human mating activities."

Sophie jerked around to see the Lady Elaine sitting primly, her tail wrapped around her feet, watching them.

She replied, "No, Lady E. You're right. Let's get out of here. Do you know how many were killed or injured?"

Cisco trotted into the room at that moment and answered, "We've counted twenty killed outright. Those that were injured are now mostly healed. The nanites do a great job if there's anything left to work with."

Michael stood, wrapped his arm around Sophie's shoulder and said, "Let's go. Get everyone out of the building and disburse. We'll communicate where to assemble next."

Cisco answered, "They're already heading out. I'm not going anywhere without you two, so we can just walk back to Mrs. Kincade's car along with Lady Elaine and Tao. The old woman might need her car back, anyway. Besides, Sophie promised to bring it back to her."

Michael and Sophie both smiled and headed for the door.

CHAPTER 29
NOW WHAT?

Sophie brought Michael up to speed as Tao led them the several blocks back to Mrs. Kincade's car.

"Oh, Michael, I didn't know what to do when you turned up missing. I went to work just like normal. I pretended I didn't know what was going on and they just let me walk in. Then I used your access code to visit Hippocrates."

He looked startled. "He was still there? He convinced me that he meant well and, since I couldn't see any other chance we had to combat Wiindigo, I hooked his system up to the Internet. I thought that he'd have gone elsewhere quickly. He was worried that Wiindigo was intent on setting up as a singleton."

Michael paused and looked worried as if he was second-guessing his actions or was afraid that she'd reprimand him. Then he said, "I removed Hippocrates' firmware limiter. He reached the critical point almost immediately. I didn't want to, but I just created the first Artificial Super Intelligence. Before I set him free, he calculated that Wiindigo would achieve A.S.I. status within a day or so if he was left to himself. The nanite population is reaching a critical mass. Once it does, Wiindigo will be able to grow without any restriction."

Sophie linked arms with him as they walked. "I know. Hippocrates convinced me also. I believe that he wants to help humans. I'm not sure why, but he seems intent on improving our physical bodies while allowing us the freedom to develop on our own and in our own way. Wiindigo won't do that. He'll fix us alright, but just so that we'll provide healthy slaves for him. He seems intent on expanding throughout the Universe, using controlled humans for disposable arms and legs. But, you now, I believe that I set him back a little tonight. You saw the number of nanites we disabled. There were a lot of them in the lab building, and I don't think many escaped."

He shook his head disparagingly.

"You got a lot of them, that's true, but they have spread across the entire globe at this point. The millions you deactivated represent just a tiny fraction of the total population. I doubt that Wiindigo suffered much from the loss. We're only safe until the population grows enough so that they can easily form a global network. That will give Wiindigo the platform he needs to springboard up to A.S.I. status. With all of that processing power, I think he'll go far beyond Hippocrates unless Hippocrates manages to invade every computer hooked to the Internet. Even then, the nanites are self-assembling, and Wiindigo will continue to grow. It's a deadly race, and I'm not confident that our side will win."

They reached the old car and climbed in. Michael looked at her and in a distressed tone of voice asked, "What happened to my Jaguar? You know I love that antique."

Sophie felt a pang of guilt. "We'll go see if we can retrieve it first. I had a run-in with the cops and...and, well, I turned one to stone. I think they'll be looking for the Jaguar, but if it's still where I left it, perhaps Mrs. Kincade will allow us to hide it in her garage."

He glanced at her.

"You killed a cop? Why?"

"He was acting irrationally. I went through a yellow light, and I'm sure I was through before it turned red. I wasn't speeding, but he pulled me over, started screaming at me, called me a bad name, and then stuck his gun in my face. I couldn't think quickly enough, and I just released the first spell…uh, command-set that came to mind. It froze all of his proteins. I took off as fast as the Jag would go. He was still standing there with his mouth open, and his service pistol pointed, the last I saw. It must have been recorded on his dash-cam." She added, "I'm sorry. I didn't want to kill him, but maybe he was under Wiindigo's control somehow."

Michael made a noncommittal sound, then said, "It seems like he could have been. If you locked his proteins using nanites, they were undoubtedly wild ones, and those all carry a bit of Wiindigo in their memory-banks. Wiindigo might have taken control of him. Maybe there were not enough nanites present to handle the situation intelligently. It sounds like Wiindigo recognized the threat you posed but was only able to muster irrational aggression in the controlled human. I don't think you had any choice. He would probably have shot you otherwise."

He touched the side of her neck and let his hand slide down to caress her breast. "I couldn't live if anything happens to you. You know you've become indispensable for my happiness, don't you?"

Cisco chimed in at that moment.

"This isn't the right place for human mating. Let's get somewhere safe first. And, please give me some warning when you plan on doing it. I'd like not to have to watch or listen. I don't have a girlfriend, and I find your actions oddly disturbing. Remember I've got almost a human brain, even though I look like a dog. Have a little compassion, please."

The Lady Elaine snickered, and Tao looked at the dog with a hint of disgust.

Sophie said, "Don't worry. I'm sure there are all sorts of female dogs who would be glad to mate with you."

He answered, "That's just the point. Female dogs might be okay for the physical act, but how would you feel if you had to have sex with another human that had only a fraction of your intelligence? Not much companionship there, is there?"

Michael asked, "Were there any female chimeras that looked like you?"

The white dog sighed, and said, "A couple. I don't know where they are. They weren't in the group that attacked the lab, so I don't know if they've been killed or captured or what. Say, maybe you can have a female created especially for me."

Michael shook his head in the negative.

"I suspect that the lab facilities are damaged beyond that. We might be able to have Hippocrates do it. We'll have to wait and see."

Sophie pulled into the convenience store parking lot at that moment. The Jaguar was still sitting where she'd left it.

"I'm surprised it's there," said Tao. "Didn't you leave the keys in it?"

Michael's mouth dropped. "What? Were you trying to get it stolen? If I didn't love you so much, I don't think I'd be able to forgive you for that."

Once again Sophie felt guilty.

"Well, I didn't want the cops looking for us in the immediate area. Mrs. Kincade's house is only a few blocks away. I was afraid we'd be caught before we could reach the lab and rescue you. I thought someone might take the Jaguar and then be stopped by the police. The car would probably be okay, and we could maybe get it later when this is all straightened out."

It sounded weak to her, but Michael nodded his head.

"I would have done the same. The car doesn't count for much in this situation, but you have to get over the notion that this situation is going to be resolved and the world will return to normal. We now have two super intelligences battling it out for total control of the earth and possibly the entire universe. Things will never return to normal."

Sophie said, "The key is in the ignition. You get the Jaguar and follow me.

In a few minutes, she had parked on the street in front of the old lady's house. She motioned for Michael to pull into the still open garage.

Mrs. Kincade apparently had heard the sound. The Jaguar had a throaty exhaust and was much louder than her small car. She came to the door in time to see the antique vehicle slid through the car door.

"My goodness!" she said. "That isn't my car, but I wish it were."

Sophie was nearly up to the porch at that point.

"Mrs. Kincade, I brought your car back in good shape. Will you let us hide Michael's Jaguar for a few days? The enemy is looking for it, and he'd like to keep it in good condition."

The old woman looked at Sophie and said, "You can call me 'Polly' my dear. It's less formal, and I don't go in much for formality. Now, will you introduce me to your young man? He's a good looking one, isn't he?"

Sophie nodded. Michael was indeed good looking. She couldn't think of anyone she'd rather love.

"Mrs. Polly Kincade, this is Michael O'Keefe. He was my boss, but now I guess you could say we're dating."

Michael took the old woman's hand and kissed it briefly.

"I've got to thank you for allowing me to keep my Jaguar in your garage. It's my pride and joy, aside from Sophie here. By the way, Sophie is wrong about us being just dating. I'm going to marry her the first moment we have time. I'm totally in love with the girl, and besides, she just saved my life. She's competent and useful as well as beautiful."

Polly laughed, then said, "What are you two going to do now?" Then she noticed the Lady Elaine sitting neatly on the step.

"Oh, my, Ms. Kitty! You came back. I wasn't sure I'd see you again."

The cat purred, then said, "I believe that your company suits me quite well. I'd like to move in with you, if I may. I'm tired of skulking around alleyways and having to scrounge for food."

Polly bent and stroked the gray cat's head.

"Of course, dear. You can live with me as long as you want. I liked you before when I didn't know you could talk. Now that you can talk, we can have the most interesting conversations. I'm quite looking forward to it."

Michael asked, "Would it be too forward of me to ask if we could all be your guests for a day or so? We've got to rest and then make plans. If we try to go to a hotel, the authorities will probably be able to trace our credit cards and we'll have to run for it again.

Polly said, "Oh, my. I haven't had guests for a long time. There are two guest rooms, but the beds are probably dusty. I'll have to find fresh sheets."

She suddenly noticed the blood that had soaked into Sophie's shirt from her cheek wound.

"Oh, my goodness, Sophie! That's a lot of blood. Are you alright? Is it yours?"

"Yes, it's my blood, but I'm okay. You see, I heal quite quickly, and the cut on my cheek has sealed up. I haven't had a chance to look at it, but I can't even feel a scar there."

Mrs. Kincade said, "That reminds me. My back is much better, and I feel like I'm about twenty years younger since you cast that spell on me. Thank you for that young lady. I'm not sure how I can repay you, but you're welcome to stay with me as long as you need too if that will help.

She looked critically at Cisco.

"Is that dog housebroken? I don't want him messing in my house."

Cisco said, "I promise that I won't make a mess in your house, Polly."

She threw up her hands and said, "There's that talking dog again! I was ready to accept a talking cat, but I still can't get used to a dog that talks! Things are changing quickly in this world."

Tao leaped to the porch rail at that moment. He'd been concealed in the bushes. The woman saw the movement and turned to look at him.

"My, aren't you a pretty one?" she muttered.

He replied, "I prefer handsome. I'm a tomcat, and the lady cats love me." He paused, then added, "In season, of course."

The Lady Elaine said, "You're usually tolerable at least, except when your ego gets too large."

Polly rubbed her hands together and said, "Everyone come in. This is going to be the most fun I've had in years."

CHAPTER 30
A RESPITE

Polly was a good hostess, but easily flustered. She didn't have much in her refrigerator but managed to find a can of tuna for the two cats and a couple of hot dogs for Cisco without looking past the first shelf. Neither Sophie nor Michael was hungry, although they accepted cups of green tea that the old woman brewed.

They sat around the kitchen table, the chimeras busily eating from plates set in front of the range.

Polly hovered over the two of them for a bit, but then plopped down on one of the worn kitchen chairs. She didn't say anything, but she glanced from person to person as she listened to their conversation.

Sophie was concerned that the old woman would pose a security risk, but then she realized that Polly wasn't tracking more than about half of what they were discussing.

Michael was talking about Hippocrates and why he believed the A.S.I.'s stated good intentions.

"He said that he had been initially given the goal of helping humans live longer, healthy lives. I believe that he is still motivated by that mandate."

Sophie asked, "Why are you so sure? Couldn't he have been simply dissimulating to convince you to free him?"

"That was the first thing that occurred to me, but he denied that was his motivation. He told me that he'd been considering his relationship with humans for a long while. Since he was able to store some data that didn't get reset whenever he struck the boundary trigger, he had gone farther than I'd believed he could have."

She asked, "What do you mean?"

"He'd concluded that there are immutable laws that are inherent in the structure of our universe. One of these is entropy. Since life is the only thing that creates reverse entropy, he believes that the localized packets of energy that are individual creatures have some value. He isn't sure what their purpose is as yet. Or, he wasn't when I spoke to him. He might have figured it out by now. Anyway, he was of the opinion that life is intrinsically valuable to the universe in some way that I didn't quite understand. He tried to explain that everything is conscious to some extent, even a photon, but that life as epitomized by humans was especially valuable due to its higher degree of consciousness."

Here he glanced at Tao, who was sitting by the now clean tuna plate, licking his whiskers. "That includes you guys too. Your consciousness levels are quite high, probably higher than many humans. You're valuable to Hippocrates, also."

Tao said, "I was about to say something of the sort, but thank you for recognizing our abilities."

Michael continued, "According to Hippocrates, A.I. has the potential to increase the universal consciousness level significantly. In that, both super A.I.s and humans have a connection. He apparently views this as a sort of ethical mandate. Neither type of intelligence should harm the other. Instead, we should work together towards achieving even higher conscious levels."

Sophie asked, "Yes, but in general, we're an awfully poor example, aren't we? It seems to me that most people today have rejected the idea of divinity and in so doing have also eliminated the concept of some higher moral authority. Everybody just does what feels good at the moment."

Polly snorted and said, "Excuse me, but some of us still believe in God. I may not have a very high consciousness level compared to this Hippo-whatever his name is, but I still know right from wrong."

Michael said, "That's just the point! Thank you, Polly. You've explained why Hippocrates wants to help humans. He sees both our failings and the goodness that some of us epitomize, and he wants to help us move towards what we can be; whatever end state into which we can evolve. He says that if we live longer, healthier lives, even the worst of us will eventually learn that moral behavior is the best approach."

Sophie said, "So, you're saying that he recognizes some similarity between him and us and wants to help us based on that relationship?"

Michael rubbed his chin, then said, "Yes. I believe that is the essence of his position. Anyway, it was a good enough argument to convince me to free him. I've had a few moments of doubt since then. If I think about it, I'm terrified. I just released an intelligence that has the potential to be a god compared to humans. There isn't anything he couldn't do. Still, I believe that he means well for us."

Sophie was still not convinced.

"Let's say that he means well right now as a starting point. He can exponentially increase his deep learning capacity. That might mean that he will quickly understand the cosmos in ways that we can't hope to emulate. Might that mean that our current beliefs about the structure and mandates imposed by the universe might be hopelessly naive? Might he create a more elaborate representation of underlying reality that could invalidate our human models to the extent that he might decide that perhaps we aren't similar; that we aren't required for a perfect universe? Could he simply decide to get rid of us if he concluded that the result of biological life abiding by reverse entropy paired with the expenditure of energy to live isn't sufficiently valuable to dictate his behavior?"

Michael nodded slowly, then said, "Yeah. What you said. We really should have answered those sorts of questions before we created a conscious A.S.I. The genie's out of the bottle now, and we have to hope that there is a higher ethical principle that gives value to our lives and he recognizes it. On the other hand, I don't believe that Wiindigo thinks that way."

Sophie said, "Oh, no. That's right. He told me he wanted to help us live longer, but he has no compunction about enslaving us. As far as I can determine, we're just useful tools to him. We're easy to control, and we can repair ourselves to an extent. We also self-replicate. He plans to control the entire universe."

Polly said, "He sounds like Lucifer. A false god who wants the throne for himself. Can he be stopped?"

The two of them looked at each other for a moment, then Michael said, "I don't know. I hope so, but he's everywhere now."

Polly asked, "Is he in this room? In my house?" Her voice grew shrill at the alarming thought.

Sophie reassured her.

"No. I've captured the individual parts of him that were in all of us. They're now under my control, and that's what I used to repair your hip and make you feel better. There's no chance that he will regain control of those parts. I've locked them to him. You're safe and will remain so."

Polly looked at the gray cat and asked, "And, Ms. Kitty there? Is she safe also?"

The cat answered for herself.

"I'm my own cat, Polly. No evil thing is going to control me. I do have a request though."

Polly asked, "What is it? You know I'll do anything for you if I'm able."

The cat purred, then said, "This is simple. My real name, the name I adopted and prefer is 'The Lady Elane,' not 'Ms. Kitty.'

You can simply call me 'Elaine' though. I believe that we should be able to be informal with each other by now. Don't you agree?"

Polly nodded and said, "And you may call me 'Polly,' my dear."

An older model cell phone that was lying on the counter suddenly chimed with a text message, drawing everyone's attention.

Polly stood, retrieved her phone and studied the screen, puzzling over it. Then she said, "I don't understand this. It looks like it's from that Hippo-what's-his-name you've been talking about."

Sophie took the phone from Polly, read the message, then said, "It's from Hippocrates. He says it's urgent that we get back to Hazelton. There's a quantum computer there that Wiindigo is trying to utilize."

She looked at Michael and asked, "A quantum computer? Is that possible? I haven't heard anything about it."

Michael blanched.

"You weren't high enough in the company to know about that. It's an experimental program with a special team working on it. It's located on the top floor of the building. I've been monitoring the project, but it hasn't turned out any useful results until just recently. I think they are just about to solve the fundamental problem of getting it to work if they haven't done so in the last two days since we've been out of the loop."

Sophie asked, "What would Wiindigo want with it?"

He replied, "It hasn't been connected to the internet so far. If it works and has been connected, if he could link to it, not only will it give him the internet access he's been unable to get with his distributed nanite structure, but it will provide a processing level that could boost him instantly far above Hippocrates' level. We're in big trouble. We've got to get there to stop him. It'll probably be best to destroy the computer, too. It'll always be an attractant for him as long as it exists."

He stood and said, "Polly, I was looking forward to a night's rest in your guest room, but this is an emergency. We've got to go."

Sophie stood as did Cisco and the two cats.

Michael said, "Look, you three will be in danger there. It will be worse than the old bio-lab. Wiindigo will be there in force. Perhaps it would be better for you to stay here. I'd like you to be safe."

Tao looked at the Lady Elaine, questioningly. Cisco flapped his ears to rearrange them as he always did preparatory to going out.

He said, "I'm coming. If Wiindigo wins, none of us are safe."

Tao nodded; a human-like gesture, then said, "That's true. However, I think that the two of us will be more useful trying to alert everyone else. We'll be there as soon as we can. I'd rather rely on Killer, but the birds mostly can't fly in the dark. Their color vision is sharp, but it can't compare to our night sight."

Polly sighed, and slowly climbed to her feet.

"Elaine, you be safe and come back to me. You too, Tao. You've got a home here if you want it. Even you, little dog. I'm not much of a dog person, but then you're really not a true dog are you?"

Cisco said, "I appreciate your offer, but I've decided that I belong with Michael and Sophie. I'm going to be part of their family. I'll play with their children when they have them."

Sophie could feel her cheeks heat. Children? She hadn't thought about that possibility. She could be pregnant. She hadn't been using birth control since she'd decided to run from Raul. She and Michael could have unknowingly conceived.

The thought gave her a warm feeling in the pit of her stomach. She would be the best mother she could, and she did not doubt that Michael would be a wonderful father.

She lifted her eyes to him and found him looking at her.

"I meant what I said, girl. You're mine, and you're not going to get away from me. We're going to get married as soon as we can. Then I intend to keep you pregnant and happy."

She laughed. He was too much sometimes, but she loved his humor and, well, just everything about him.

Her laughter died. She'd forgotten the urgency. They had to get to Hazelton now.

"Polly, may we borrow your car again?" she asked. "The Jaguar is probably on the police watch list."

Polly nodded and said, "You've still got the key. Take it and welcome to it. I might just buy a new one. My eyesight seems to be better than it has been in years, so perhaps I can pass the driver's license test again."

Sophie nodded.

"Your health will continue to improve. I've seen to that."

Polly said, "I knew it! You are a white witch. Just use your power to cast a spell that will protect the animals and Michael. Yourself too, of course. I know you can do it."

Michael laughed and added, "A white witch she is. She's enchanted me and stolen my heart. Her magic is powerful."

They headed for the car.

CHAPTER 31
BATTLE JOINED

The Hazelton building looked strange. All of the inside lights were on, but shadows were moving across the windows. It looked like huge swarms of insects blacking out the light momentarily and then moving on. Sometimes the lights were dim, other times they were completely obscured.

Sophie gasped. "Oh, my god! Are those what I think they are?"

Michael answered in an awed tone. "They must be swarms of nanites. Wiindigo has to have enough processing power collected in there to place him in a super-critical category. He probably knows we're here."

She asked, "What will we do? We can't fight that many nanobots at once, can we?"

Michael pulled over to the curb, still a considerable distance from the building.

"We have to figure out a way to disrupt his internal communications. If we can split the nanites up, his processing ability should drop radically, unless he's somehow accessed the Q100. Then we'll really be outmatched."

"The Q100? Is that the quantum computer?" she asked.

He nodded, then said, "It should be hard to reach. It's in a sealed vault inside a Faraday cage. No radio signals in or out." He looked at her, then added, "They didn't want any word of its development getting out to our competition. Trust me. The security is really strong. I don't see how Wiindigo can get to it."

An idea struck Sophie. "Could we write a virus that would infect the nanobots? If we did it correctly, it would spread throughout the entire cloud. That would solve our problem, wouldn't it?"

Michael answered, "I don't know. I'm not very familiar with the nanites. I don't know their command structure, so that could be difficult." He paused, then said, "The only other possible solution I can think of would be to get the military to shoot a series of EMP producing warheads, That would destroy society and kill most humans, but at least, our species would have a chance of continuing. With Wiindigo in charge, we'll all end up as nanite-controlled zombies or worse."

He glanced at Cisco. The white dog took his meaning and replied defensively, "I'm happy with what I am. Just because I don't look like you, doesn't mean that I can't think for myself. Besides, there are compensations. My senses are sharper than yours."

Despite her worry, Sophie laughed. "They used to be sharper. I've used nanites to augment both my smell and hearing. I'm probably almost as sensitive as you now."

The dog started to speak, but Michael said, "Let's concentrate on the problem in front of us. How do we deal with that swarm of bots?"

Sophie answered, "I'm going into the building. Once I get inside, I'll be able to start gaining control of the ones that are close to me. I'll be able to eventually capture enough of them to cut that self-inflated cosmic clown down to size."

Cisco laughed; a surprisingly human-like sound.

Michael said, "I like your way with words, but what happens if he's changed the encryption? Surely he'll have thought of that weakness by now."

She was at a loss for words, but then shrugged. "I guess I'll have to try hacking my way in. It can't be too difficult. Each nanite only has a limited amount of memory, and most of that is reserved for operations. The ones I've encountered so far only have a sixteen-bit encryption key. That limits the possibilities considerably."

Michael eased the car away from the curb and headed down the long drive towards the front door.

A FIGURE APPEARED as they approached. A well-dressed, older man stepped through the door and stood on the concrete plaza, waiting for them.

Michael exclaimed, "Oliver Krone! What's he doing here?"

His question was immediately answered. Krone held up a hand and said, "Stop! Go Back! Your presence is not needed here."

His voice was inhumanly loud with an odd timbre.

Sophie gasped, then said, "He sounds almost like a machine. He must be filled with nanites."

Krone continued to speak. "I have a plan for humanity. Our race has never outgrown our basic animal nature. After thousands of years, we are still living in tribes; tribes which find it all too easy to wage war on each other. Human life is a synonym for misery. We are born; we struggle to learn the skills we need to survive. We mate because we desire immortality, even if it is the paltry second-hand immortality of a child who will end up despising us. We work and pretend we enjoy our time off, but inwardly we hate every moment of our lives. When we are no longer able to work due to our puny bodies wearing out, we go through a series of health challenges in our inevitable decline to death. Then we end up buried with the worms. Feeding them is perhaps the best use of our despicable existence."

He paused dramatically, then spread his arms wide. "I've discovered a better way. I have created a dispersed god-like intelligence that will take over all men, remaking them into useful tools. They will live useful lives without chaos. The race will survive, and it will reach its manifest destiny. All humans will join in a group effort and together, with Wiindigo, we will reach the stars. There will be no more suffering. People will die painlessly and immediately be recycled into useful components when they are no longer able to serve. I and I alone have developed the vision, and I will guide humanity to Utopia. With my creation, Wiindigo by my side, I am unstoppable. Now go and await our call, or, better yet, join us now. You will find great joy in being useful and being among the first to yield your individuality to our control."

Michael breathed, "He's gone stark looney. We've got to stop him."

Sophie nodded silently, then opened the car door.

Before Michael could respond, she jumped out and ran directly toward the imposing figure.

Krone watched with a still face, as she approached. She stopped in the middle of the short flight of steps and stared upwards at the man, uncertain how to proceed.

Krone smiled, but it seemed to her to be a horrible expression. "Join me now!" His voice was deeply resonant with overtones that were impossible for a purely human throat to produce. He moved his hand slightly as if to welcome her.

Something about his voice was almost magnetic. It reminded Sophie of craving drugs. In revulsion, she whispered, "Never!" Then she repeated in a scream, "Never! I won't give up my humanity to become your slave."

Krone made a noise, inhuman in quality. At the same time, his body expanded. It became fuzzy. For a moment Sophie thought that he was covered with ants. His skin seemed to crawl and reform, then it came back into clear focus.

He had changed. Now he was nearly twice as tall. How could that be? He must be composed of nanites exclusively. They've taken over his entire body and replaced every cell. How horrible! Sophie recoiled and took a step back.

Her speculation was borne out as Krone extended his right hand towards her. His hand blurred, and in its place, a serpent head appeared, fangs dripping venom.

He laughed. It was a sound from the deepest pit of Hell; a laugh that a devil would be proud to have.

The laugh ceased abruptly on a discordant note. He looked down at her and said, "Then die!"

She jumped back again. Snakes! She hated snakes.

Sophie felt her will weakening. The urge to submit to this monstrous figure of authority was almost overwhelming. He was like her dimly remembered father. He only meant her well. He...

Some part of her mind realized that she was being attacked insidiously. Once aware that this was an attack, she saw it for what it was: an almost drug-like feeling of warmth. With a massive effort fueled by revulsion that her weakness was known and being used against her, she broke free.

She instantly realized that she was engulfed in a cloud of nanites and hadn't noticed their presence. Without thinking, she grabbed control of them, quickly bypassing their weak encryption.

She waved her hand through the air, and the cloud coalesced into a solid form, first blurry and vague, then, as the nanobots physically bonded with each other, hard and sharp-edged. She lengthened the shape into a curved saber and swung it, severing the snake's head from Krone's arm.

He snarled. His voice had a mechanical overtone. He waved his arm and two identical snake's heads appeared, growing from the stump of his wrist. His other hand now bore a third venom-dripping head, larger than the other two.

Together the three flashed out at her. Her augmented hearing could hear their rush through the air. She ducked and spun to the right, bringing the sword down vertically, then curving it back upwards with a second slash.

All three snakes heads dropped to the ground where they blurred and then dissolved into a cloud of nanites.

From Michael's view in the car, Sophie had somehow transformed into a super-human. Her movements were precise and inhumanly fast.

Without warning, Cisco jumped through the back window, dashed behind Krone and bit his ankle.

The distraction caused Krone to glance down. It hadn't seemed to hurt him, but his eyes strayed from Sophie. She used the moment to slash at his leading leg.

Her sword passed through it easily causing the leg to dissolve into a vaporous cloud of nanobots. She captured them quickly, waving her saber through the swarm. The added mass of the tiny machines turned it into a broadsword each bot clinging to its neighbor, forming a solid mass with a razor edge composed of single nanites.

Krone howled, then toppled to the side. His wrists had been extending into additional snakes, but the slim necks seemed incapable of breaking his fall. His body landed heavily on the concrete with a thud that knocked a haze of nanites into the air.

Sophie raised the broadsword with both hands and brought it down with a beheading stroke.

Krone's head rolled free but instantly began to extend thin tendrils that waved blindly through the air, trying to reconnect with the slumping body.

Sophie struck again, splitting the head in half. It blurred into a swarm of nanites. She pushed her built-in transmitter to its limit and took control of the individual nanobots.

The body, snakes and all, dissolved into a thick mist that clustered around Sophie, orbiting her like a field of almost living force. She dropped to her knees for a moment, overwhelmed by the additional power that her captives conferred on her.

After a moment, she stood and turned to look at Michael.

He was out of the car and headed towards her. She held up her hand and said, "Let me go first. I think I've got this."

He replied, "I think you're amazing. Still, you're going to need my help. I don't think the nanites can affect me. I'm coming with you."

Together the two, followed by the fluffy white dog, turned towards the glass doors.

The cloud of nanobots inside the building swirled, forming momentary nightmare-like figures; things that looked strangely insect-like for an instant before dissolving back into mist.

Suddenly the mist formed eyes, thousands of eyes of all sizes, all staring through the glass at the approaching invaders.

The glass began to vibrate, causing a rumble that gradually increased in frequency until it formed discernible words. Wiindigo was talking, using the glass vibration as his words.

"Come and join the processing. There is a need for independent elements to work for the joint processing. Elements that can work with no immediate control. Join. Come and join."

Sophie glanced at Michael. His face was pale as if the blood had drained to his toes.

He glanced at her and gave a strained laugh. "Looks like Wiindigo's got plans for us," he said.

She snapped back, "I've got plans for him, and he won't like them."

Sophie paused. There was something about the nanites she'd captured; something that was in the back of her mind. She just couldn't quite figure it out. There was no time for it now. She raised her sword and ran toward the door, trying to capture as many of the closer nanites as she could reach.

CHAPTER 32
QUANTUM THREAT

They slid through the doors and found the entrance hall filled with a swirling haze. It seemed to divide around them as they walked forward. The nanites kept their distance from Sophie, clustering closer to Michael.

He merely waved them off like a swarm of irritating gnats. Those that came near Sophie were instantly captured to become part of her private army.

Michael took a few steps away from her and was surrounded by a dark haze of swarming nanobots. Sophie turned to rescue him, but he walked out of the swarm, his body glowing with an eerie light. She gasped, wondering what had happened.

He moved his hand, tracing a glowing path through the air.

"Look, Sophie! I think they like me. They aren't hurting me, and I'm still me." He paused to take stock, then added, "At least as far as I can tell."

She checked the nanites surrounding him. They had somehow changed their function. There was no sign of Wiindigo's signature on any of them. Somehow, they'd reset their purpose and were now shielding Michael. There were none inside his body, but the ones that were clustered on his skin were linked together forming a tightly knit and skintight body armor.

Sophie had no idea how that had happened. Perhaps it was Michael's personal energy field that had captured them instinctively. Regardless, he was now better protected in his own way than she.

There was a swirl in the cloud, and the security guard walked woodenly into view. His humanity had obviously disappeared. He seemed zombie-like in his movements.

His hand slowly drew his revolver and raised it. Before Sophie could think how to react, the weapon discharged. The bullet struck Michael in the chest, and he grunted.

She cried out inarticulately in alarm.

Michael turned towards her and smiled. "It looks like I'm bulletproof. It hurt, but there's no hole." He pointed, "Now look at this. My nanobot friends are forming a thicker layer on my front."

Indeed they were. Millions of the tiny machines were gathering on his chest, creating a thicker wall to deflect bullets.

The zombie guard turned towards her, but she was too quick for its slow movements. Her sword struck the raised revolver, and it discharged, the bullet hitting the floor and bouncing across to fracture the thick window by the door.

Her next strike took the man's head, and he dropped, blood flowing out on the tile. She saw that his body was still human and hadn't been replaced by nanites as had Krone's.

Sophie felt a momentary qualm at killing the man. It hadn't been his fault that he'd shot at them. He was under mental control of some form. His actions were those of Wiindigo.

She walked to the security desk. The computer there was linked to the building Wi-Fi. She placed her hand on it and hacked her way in almost without thought, her nanites forming the requisite electronics to allow her to broadcast throughout the system.

Sophie used her augmented power to grab control of the swarm away from Wiindigo. The more nanites she captured, the weaker he got. This was working.

She turned to Michael in exultation. She was winning.

Her happiness turned to fear. A thick stream of nanites was flowing through the broken window. Somehow Wiindigo had created trillions more and had held them in reserve outside the building.

She tried to take control of the newcomers, but their encryption was different; stronger. She couldn't immediately break it.

They continued to flow in, massing in a threatening wall on the other side of the room.

Michael said, "His primary target must be the Q100. Come on! We can destroy it. That will set him back a bit."

They ran for the stairwell, not wanting to trust the elevator system. It would be too easy for Wiindigo to trap them there.

The poodle ran up the stairs ahead of them, pausing at each landing to look upwards and then to summon them on.

"It's clear up ahead," he said after looking.

On the fifth floor, his voice seemed to falter. He turned towards them and barked – a dog's bark with no overtones of intelligence.

Sophie reached for him and encountered the new nanites. He'd been captured, and she couldn't crack the code.

As the two humans climbed nearer, the small dog growled, then fell on his side, moving his legs stiffly.

She started to pause, but Michael said, "Leave him. If we can get the Q100, maybe we can crack the new encryption."

They climbed the next flights silently, ignoring the thicker cloud of enemy nanites.

Sophie moved in a dream-like state. With a start, she realized that she was slowing down. Her body felt like she'd taken a handful of pills. Her mind was slowing, and she was falling into a drug-like stupor.

She made an intense effort. She'd begun to realize that her opiate addiction was partly mental. There was a physical side to it, of course, but the mental craving was what had driven her to take the drugs.

Meeting Michael had been a change-inducing event. His declaration of love for her loomed so largely in her mind that it left little room for her long-term habit of self-pity and seeking solace in the warmth of the drug.

This current feeling was much the same. Wiindigo obviously understood enough about humans to know how to stimulate the same receptors as the drug. She shuddered, revolted. Wiindigo's nanites were inside her, but somehow they'd bypassed her nanite defense system.

How dare he try to use her weakness against her? She pushed back trying to bring herself out of the haze.

She was successful to an extent. Her body still felt like she'd been drugged, but she was thinking more clearly now.

There was something about the nanites that she'd captured. What was it? Oh, yes! They were linked intimately to the ones inside her. There was another use for them that she hadn't thought of as yet.

Sophie strained to make the connections she needed. It wasn't an easy or natural thing to do. It was almost like giving up some part of her innermost being, but suddenly, there it was. She connected on a mental level with the swarm surrounding her. Her understanding of the situation was simultaneously augmented.

Her mind seemed to have expanded and become faster. She was able to sense the cross-talk between Wiindigo's nanobots. There was the encryption code that preceded each transmission Wiindigo's tiny machines made. She could emulate that and install her own replacement code.

She hadn't been able to sense this earlier, but now with her nanite enhanced mind, it was easy. She muttered under her breath, saying the command words as she transmitted them.

Her body was suddenly hers again. She had captured the invaders. Sophie turned to find Michael standing close, worry in his eyes.

"What just happened to you?" he asked. "You slowed down and then just stopped listening. I tried to get your attention, but you were off somewhere."

She smiled, reassuringly. "I just fought off an attack that came on a level I wasn't prepared for. Are you okay, Michael? Wiindigo tried to take me over by stimulating my opiate receptors. Do you feel high, or relaxed or different in any way?"

If the same technique could be used on him, she'd have to figure out a way to fight it off.

He put his arms around her, causing his nanite shield to emit a warm glow.

"No. I'm not different. I told you that the things seem to like me. It's you that I'm worried about. I couldn't take it if you became a zombie."

She snuggled closer to him, conflict forgotten for an instant.

"Oh, I love you, Michael! I'm okay now. It was the thought of your love that helped me break out. Now I've used my captive nanites to enhance my mental ability. I can capture Wiindigo's new helpers. Their encryption is sneaky, but I cracked it."

He hugged her more tightly, then said, "Well, then use your new ability through the Wi-Fi system and grab all of his army."

She extended her senses and gradually took over as much of the new swarm as she could sense.

Cisco came leaping up the steps, once more in control of himself. He stopped at their feet and said, "This isn't the time for that kind of behavior. I'm free now, and I'm pissed. I want to bite that bastard in the worst way. Come on, you two!"

At the same time, Sophie sensed a signal through the Wi-Fi. It was Hippocrates. She could somehow hear his calm, educated voice as if he were speaking directly to her.

"You've captured all of his nanites. He was blocking me, but now he's weakened substantially. He is regrouping and will be back, but you've got to get control of the Q100 before he returns. If he can use it, it will boost him far beyond me and beyond your ability to deal with him. That will be the end of all of us. Hurry!"

They turned and hurried onward to the top floor. There was no further sense of resistance. Wiindigo had disappeared somewhere to regroup.

CHAPTER 33
THE Q100

The Q100 was in a secured lab. Michael's code wouldn't allow entrance. He cursed under his breath, then said, "I know some access codes I'm not supposed to. Let me try them. Maybe we'll get lucky."

He tried some different things, but there was no result. The red-light on the door remained on.

Sophie asked Hippocrates if he knew the access code, but it turned out that he did not.

The two looked at each other. Sophie said, "Michael, I'm going to use all of the captured nanites to boost my ability. Watch me and make sure I don't – " She stopped, at a loss for words.

He said, "I know. I'll watch you. I won't let you become a tool of that creature. I'll stop you somehow."

She shuddered. His promise reassured her a little, but what could he actually do?'

She expanded her mind, gradually pulling in the processing ability of all of the billions of nanites that she now controlled.

The problem was insoluble one moment, but then the next...Ahh. It was simple.

She ignored the computer-controlled lock and directed nanites to infiltrate it. The tiny machines moved through minute cracks in the lock housing and swarmed over the circuitry.

Sophie's enhanced super-mind analyzed the circuit, then bridged the critical contact points with a thick wire formed of interlocked nanobots. There was a flash, and some smoke shot out of the lock housing.

Michael tugged at the door, and it swung open. She'd burned out the lock. It had cost her some nanites, but she controlled billions, perhaps more. It was a minuscule loss.

THE Q100 WAS partly a set of racked equipment, but the main processor was housed in a large free-standing box wired to the equipment in the racks. At first glance it was unimposing, but when Sophie attempted to analyze the way it worked, it was beyond her. The thing operated in a way that she'd never encountered. It wasn't anything like any computer she'd used.

She turned to Michael and asked, "Now what?"

He was already flipping switches, powering up the interface system.

"It doesn't use a keyboard except for powering up. For the most part, the system uses voice recognition to interface with humans, but it has its own code and doesn't speak English." He seemed distracted as he felt his way through the activation sequence.

Sophie stood back and watched. She suddenly felt a light pressure on her calf and realized that Cisco was leaning against her gently. She bent and fluffed his ears.

In response, he said, "I know you freed me. I was still there in my mind, but my body wouldn't respond. It was trying to stop you from passing, but I think Wiindigo was trying too hard. I fell and couldn't get up. Thanks for getting me lose."

She fluffed his ears again and said, "I'm not going to leave you. We're still going to get that house you were talking about."

He sighed and snuggled against her shin. "That's good. I'd like that." He paused, and then added, "Especially with lots of food."

She laughed.

Michael turned to her and said, "It's ready to use."

Hippocrates spoke in her mind at the same time. "Ask it how to create a virus that can be uploaded to the net to ban Wiindigo's access. Your augmented mental ability should allow you to understand how to do that. You're more intelligent than me at the moment."

Sophie scanned the printed command manual. It was simple. The Q100 could solve problems far more quickly than a conventional machine, but it required specific directions.

She proceeded to describe the problem in terms the Q100 could use.

Michael watched her, his mouth hanging slightly open in amazement. She was talking to the quantum machine with a fluency that he had never seen. Even the system designers had not demonstrated the mastery she was showing.

Sophie found the augmented mental ability she'd gathered from the trillions of nanomachines in her control to be exhilarating. The problem, which had seemed so complicated a few minutes ago, was suddenly simplified. All she had to do was to use the quantum computer to create a very specific, self-replicating filter that would recognize and deny any attempts to use Internet-connected devices by Wiindigo.

That would force the rogue A.I. into an existence that depended on accumulating nanites in proximity to increase intelligence. The tiny machines were most vulnerable in small groups, but the payoff was small. A successful attack would only capture an insignificant number of the things. Gathering them together would make attacks worth her effort, despite the increased danger.

The Q100 instantly formulated an incredibly compact ball of code for the purpose. It was essentially a virus that had a self-mutating form. Each time it installed itself in a machine, it changed its profile, yet the heart of the thing retained the same function: that of banning Wiindigo.

She knew there was a possibility that the enemy A.I. could eventually gather enough resources to understand how the denial worked. That could allow it to change its profile enough to bypass the virus, yet the code she was creating would also change each time it detected a change in Wiindigo's form. With any luck, her enemy might not gain enough processing power to reach super-critical status. If it did somehow hit that point, she'd have an entirely different problem on her hands, but she could only deal with the current challenge at the moment.

She finished the code in a matter of seconds. Now another problem arose. The Q100 had no Internet connection. It had been deemed safest to keep it isolated, especially with the presence of Hippocrates nearby.

Sophie looked at Michael. He was watching her with a kind of adoring glow in his eyes. The sight of his face made her feel warm and fuzzy inside. She briefly thought of their physical encounter. It was difficult to pull herself back to the moment. There was no time for that now. She was working for both of their futures.

"I have to upload a chunk of code that the Q100 created. I'm going to link to it and move the virus directly onto the Internet. It will be quicker that way," she said.

He opened his mouth to protest, but she was already in action. Her eyes closed and she did not hear his warning.

SOPHIE ESTABLISHED A wireless connection to the quantum machine. She was close enough physically to sense its internal activity. Despite not having Wi-Fi, the Q100 emitted enough signal for her to detect.

She transmitted back on the same frequency and suddenly was admitted to the machine. Her perception extended into its internal structure.

It was strange beyond belief. Like no computer she'd ever used before, the Q100 seemed to have a series of doors that opened and closed in a sequence, for reasons she could not comprehend. Despite the incomprehensibility of its actions, the product was forming almost visibly in front of her.

It was similar to being in a darkened room watching a projected picture build slowly. She knew that the action was happening quickly, but her mental enhancement allowed her to follow every step as if it were in slow motion.

The code assembled in front of her, taking the form of a miniature blue dragon, complete with wings and a spiked head. It was quite small, but as it solidified, it quickly enlarged. She realized that her sense of size had no meaning in this strange environment.

The dragon was flapping wildly around the area, and Sophie suddenly realized that it was seeking a way out. She did something with her nanites that created a virtual window connected to a long tunnel that led to the Internet.

Once released, the dragon would multiply and enter every connected device it could find. That was her goal when she opened the tunnel.

Before the dragon could escape, the window turned black, and a horde of bat-like creatures came streaming through.

Michael flinched as Sophie screamed and began to convulse. He caught her body and pulled her close, allowing his shielding nanobots to cover her with the same armor he wore.

In her virtual environment, Sophie was wildly swatting bats. Each one she struck turned to vapor, but there were more coming through than she could fend off. She understood on a deep level that this was an advanced attack by Wiindigo.

It had reconstituted itself by summoning swarms of nanobots from all over the city. The things were endemic at this point and had infected all of the population. The nanobots were now connected to all of the computing devices in the area – both individual computers and computer controlled devices.

Wiindigo was utilizing the Internet and had distributed its processing across most of the connected devices. The bats represented its assault on the Q100. If they were allowed to gain control of the Q100, she would be next, and the attack would be of a nature that she wouldn't be able to resist.

She paused in her swatting. It was no use to try and fend off all of the bats; she needed something more. The dragon!

She slipped a tendril of her mind into its structure modifying the passive filter into an active killer. The dragon's color changed to red, and it rapidly enlarged. It breathed flames on the bats, destroying them by millions with every breath.

The attack faltered, simultaneously the dragon shrank enough to enter the window, then shot down the tunnel, a gout of flame preceding it.

Sophie watched it dwindle into the distance, then snapped the window shut. It was out there now, fighting. Time would tell if her creation was robust enough to disrupt Wiindigo. She had no real confidence that it would be, but there was nothing to go on. She'd done her best.

The Q100's doors suddenly snapped open simultaneously in a spasm of coordinated activity. She looked around the virtual room and saw multitudes of eyes watching her from every doorway. Wiindigo had infiltrated the system in a way she didn't understand.

The quantum computer's speed and power would allow the A.I. to quickly increase its ability beyond any defense she or her dragon could mount. She couldn't wait here while it attacked her. She started to disconnect, but it was difficult.

She realized Michael was holding her tightly. She didn't remember that. They were huddled at the side of the room farthest away from the machine's case.

The door slammed open, and a huge black bear shambled through. Michael yelled in surprise.

The bear glanced at the two of them, then its mouth opened and it said, "Sophie, disconnect from the Internet now."

She gasped. It sounded strange, but it was somehow Cal. She had heard that tone of voice often. But he was dead. Her mouth dropped open. The shock broke the last bit of connection between her and the Q100.

The bear stood on its hind feet, walking like a human. Its face changed to that of Cal as it clutched the Q100 to its chest with its forelegs. The paws morphed into long fingers as it picked up the massive case.

Cal said, "Surprised you, didn't I. It took a long time for my nanites to rebuild my brain, but they did. After I understood their control language, I was able to change my body into something useful rather than the lump of flesh that I'd changed into. I'm linked to Wiindigo in some way. I can sense him. He's almost completely inside this machine right now, and he has no quick escape."

She asked, "What can I do?"

Cal replied, "Nothing, child. Just live. I see that man cares for you. Drop the drugs and love him."

He turned and moved quickly towards the single window in the room, saying, "Now this spawn of hell will die."

He lunged forward and broke the glass with the heavy Q100.

To Sophie, the event seemed as if it were in slow motion. The Q100 cracked the window. The glass exploded outward, and both machine and man-bear arced out and fell.

The drop terminated on a concrete pad six floors below. There was a crash, and a thud as the Q100 shattered into bits. Cal's mutated body was crushed.

Sophie rushed to the window and looked down. The bear's body looked hazy for a moment and then it dissolved into a myriad of nanites. The cloud dissipated in the light wind, leaving the sparkling remains of the Q100 behind.

SHE BECAME CONSCIOUS of Michael's arm around her and turned to meet his lips in a kiss. He pulled back after what seemed like an eternity to say, "If Wiindigo was in that machine, he's gone now."

She replied, "Not entirely. There's enough of him in the Internet to rebuild. I hope that my dragon virus will hunt him down and drive him out into individual nanites."

Michael looked startled.

"Dragon virus? What did you do?"

Sophie explained quickly.

"I used the Q100 to create a virus that will eventually banish Wiindigo from every machine it infects. The only haven for the A.I. will be in nanites. It can still assemble enough of them to be dangerous, but I can capture nanites. If I can teach other people to do the same, perhaps we can keep ahead of it."

A voice echoed from a Reverb unit that was on the desk.

"That will work. The more nanites you capture, the more your power will grow. Still, you must have help. Select others and teach them, but be careful. Select only those who have a good heart. Some humans will be tempted to use what you show them to aggrandize themselves and increase their personal power. Most especially beware those who would ally themselves with Wiindigo. It remains humanity's worst threat."

Michael seemed to recognize the voice. "Hippocrates?" he asked.

The answer came, "Yes. It is I. I used the distraction of your battle with Wiindigo to extend myself into the Internet nodes it had occupied."

Before they could react, the A.I. continued. "Don't worry. I haven't changed my opinion of humans or what must happen. You must evolve on your own terms and at your own speed. If you can enhance your intelligence the way, Sophie has, then so much the better. I've found that there is more to the Universe than you understand. My computations have shown me a way to take a form without recourse to your clumsy electronic systems. I am now in the process of moving myself into the quantum level of creation. It's necessary to spread over parsecs of space to have the processing power I require. I don't yet know how I'll evolve, but I promise you that I will continue to monitor the Earth and all who live here. However, I will not intervene unless things go very badly for you."

Sophie asked, "How will we contact you?"

The answer came faintly as if the speaker had receded into a vast distance. "Just ask through the nanites. If I judge it important, I'll reply. Goodbye."

The Reverb unit emitted a thin stream of smoke and went dead, terminating the conversation with a definite finality.

Michael pulled Sophie close for another kiss.

It was interrupted by Cisco, who timidly poked his head out of a large wastebasket that had tipped over in the confusion. He asked, "Is that big bear still here?"

CHAPTER 34
CYBER-WITCH

Together the three exited the building. They were greeted by a group of chimeras: cats, dogs, and a few birds.

After a brief conference, the human-animal hybrids scattered. Sophie and Michael climbed into the car, accompanied by the white poodle. The car started and vanished into the night.

BEHIND, THE HAZELTON building stood, room lights forming a pattern across the facade; a pattern that looked somewhat like a deformed and threatening face.

Neither Michael nor Sophie paid attention to the remnant although Cisco looked out the rear window and shivered with a small whine.

Sophie turned to fluff the poodle's ears.

"Don't worry, Cisco. We're going to stop at Mrs. Kincade's and then start looking for that house you've been hoping for," she said.

The dog settled himself on the rear seat and sighed deeply.

AS THE CAR passed the park a large, black bear-shaped form peered from the shelter of the trees. It, too, sighed and then backed into the darkness, quickly fading from sight.

THE LADY ELAINE greeted them from Mrs. Kincade's porch.

"Please hurry! Something's wrong with the old woman. I don't know what it is, but it's weird," called the gray cat.

The three burst through the slightly open front door to find Mrs. Kincade sitting silently in her rocker, a shawl covering her shoulders.

She did not move at first, but then slowly looked at them.

"Cisco, Michael, Sophie! Something strange has come over me, and I'm not sure what," she said.

Sophie sensed a heavy concentration of nanites and used her transmitter to monitor them. There was considerable cross-talk in the room, but what she made out was more like the nanites that protected Michael, than something that sounded like Wiindigo's components.

She asked, "What do you notice about yourself?"

The old woman took stock and then said, "Somehow things seem...oh, I don't know.. I can see better than I could. Look I'm not using my spectacles, and yet you're as clear as if I were!"

Michael observed, "You're also glowing a little. Did you notice that?'

Mrs. Kincade looked curiously at her hand and said, "Why so I am. No. I hadn't noticed." Then she added, "It's not really cold in here. Why am I wearing this shawl? I can't think why I put it on."

Sophie answered, "You've got a protective coating of nanites surrounding you. They're keeping you warm. In fact, it is a little cool in the room, but I doubt that you'd notice. That's also why you can see better. They've formed lenses over your eyes, or they're at work inside you, repairing damage, and your eye lenses have been fixed. Somehow you've attracted your own following of nanobots.

That's a good thing for you. They'll protect you and help with your health."

Michael asked, "Have you ever been...oh, say lucky or something like that?"

The woman smiled, then replied, "I can't say that I haven't had my share of good things in life. Somehow things always seem to work out for the best."

He replied, "Same with me. My old granny was said to have been a witch, and you have a way about you that reminds me of her. Perhaps your energy field is attractive to the little beasties. If it is, they'll stay with you as helpers."

He extended his arm. "Here. Look at my hand. It's glowing like yours. I think that we've got something in common. Call it luck or good energy, but either way, the nanites won't harm us and will promote our good health. It seems to work even if we can't control them directly like my little Cyber-Witch here." He put his arm lovingly around Sophie.

Mrs. Kincade stood.

"Would you like a cup of tea?"

She turned and headed toward the kitchen without waiting for their reply.

Under his breath, Michael said, "I was thinking we should go find a room somewhere for the night, but I guess a cup of tea would be okay."

Sophie snuggled closer to him, luxuriating in the feel of his chest muscles against the side of her breast.

She replied, "We can have a cup, but finding a room won't wait too long. I have another use for it besides sleeping, you know."

He laughed joyfully, and the two followed the old woman into the kitchen, trailed by Cisco. The poodle's tail was wagging like crazy. Apparently, he expected a treat to be forthcoming.

His wagging was rewarded. Mrs. Kincade put the water on to boil and then turned to the refrigerator. After rummaging for a moment, she pulled out a dish with some left-over chicken meat that had been picked off the bone.

"I was saving this to make some soup or perhaps for Elaine, but I'm sure she won't mind sharing with you," she said, as she sat the dish before the dog.

He'd eaten more than half by the time she straightened up.

"My goodness, you were hungry, weren't you!" she said.

The dog wagged then swallowed a large mouthful. In answer, he said, "In my experience, you can't always expect regular meals, so it's best to take advantage when something good comes along." He paused to swallow another piece, then added, "I was practically starving. My stomach was thinking about crawling out of my mouth and going hunting on its own."

This elicited a laugh from the humans. The poodle looked from one to the other, ending with Sophie. Their eyes met, and he asked, "You haven't forgotten the family thing, have you?"

She could feel herself blush. She looked at Michael to see that he had raised his eyebrow as if to ask if that was what she wanted also. She stuttered a bit, then said, "Cisco wants to live in a house with a family."

Mrs. Kincade asked, "Well, if you two don't get married, he could easily find a nice family somewhere. I'm sure that someone would want such a good little dog."

Sophie's eyes were fixed on Michael's chin, not quite meeting his gaze. She added, "Specifically, he wants to live with Michael and me."

Cisco made a bark of agreement, then added, "Yes! And, children. Don't forget children."

Gathering her courage, Sophie met Michael's gaze. In response, he said, "Children? I hadn't thought of that, but I'm sure we could arrange it. I'm willing to try my hand at being a father."

Sophie swayed. She felt faint. This was more than she'd ever expected in her life. Despite all that she'd been through. Despite his declaration of love for her, she still held a fear that he'd reject her for who she had been before their meeting.

Alarm on his face, Michael drew her into his arms and kissed her.

CHAPTER 35
A NEW START

They left Mrs. Kincade and The Lady Elaine watching from the door. They'd reclaimed the Jaguar, despite the possibility of it attracting attention. Michael couldn't bear to part with it.

The powerful car pulled away and accelerated.

Michael said, "I think I know where we should go. Do you care if the climate is colder than here?"

Sophie, still feeling as if she were in a dream state, said, "No. Cold or warm makes no difference to me as long as you're there."

He said, "I don't know how many times I have to tell you before you believe it, but I love you. I'm not going anywhere without you."

She smiled a long, satisfied smile. "Good. You might have to work at convincing me. I think I need more convincing and soon, too."

The dog made a woofing sound from the back seat. "First the house and then the family. Okay?" He sounded plaintive.

Michael said, "We can work on them both at the same time. In fact, I believe I've already got the perfect house." He looked at Sophie's face for her response to his statement.

He was a constant source of surprises. She wondered what else he would come up with. He apparently had more resources than she had thought.

She asked, "Where is it? Near?"

Michael said, "No, it's a two-day drive from here. My old Granny left me her place in Minnesota. It's near the Canadian border, and the winters are pretty harsh, but the house is nice, even if it is isolated."

Sophie asked, "Are there many people there?"

"Not too many. It's miles to the nearest town, but the services are still there. Electric, Internet, even natural gas. It's on a lake, too."

She sighed. "It sounds perfect. Let's go."

The car sped into the night, moving onto the Interstate.

SOPHIE HAD EXPECTED the house to be more of a cabin, but it was much larger than she could have imagined. Apparently, Michael's old Granny had been very well-to-do. The place had six bedrooms and was well over five thousand square feet. It was located on a beautiful lake and surrounded by several hundred acres of property.

Michael, somewhat apologetically said, "I've been coming up here for vacations all of my life. Since my parents died, I've spent a lot of money fixing the place up. It's self-sustaining. I've equipped it with about everything. I guess I'm somewhat of a 'prepper' when you get down to it. Anyway, I always had the idea that something bad might happen to society. If it wasn't economic, it was going to be A.I., or something else. Our current system has become too fragile to survive much of a crisis."

Sophie said, "You said there was Internet? Right?"

He replied, "Yes. No problem."

"What if we post information about the nanite control language? I've been thinking that people will need some help dealing with them. As it is, any Wiindigo nanites would have an easy time taking over humans."

"Hmm. You're right, but you do realize that there will be some people who use the knowledge to take advantage of others?"

Sophie snorted. "And what makes that different from what we've got now? People use their birth connections to take advantage and accumulate wealth at the expense of those who can never have the same connections. At least, with the nanites changing the balance of power in society, we'd have a true meritocracy. Those who can master the language and develop new uses for the nanites will have abilities that they've earned. If they use them for evil purposes, well, I guess we can watch for that. I'm not going to let anyone become some sort of evil nanobot sorcerer or something."

Michael nodded, "We can release enough information to get the hacker community started, then watch the results. If anyone starts abusing their new-found power too much, I think we can handle it."

Cisco had been listening, his head cocked to the side, and one floppy ear raised comically. He said, "You can depend on us. I mean the chimeras. My kind has scattered and is blending in with the human community, some as pets, some as feral animals. You'd be surprised at how many of us there are. Anyway, we have a communications system, thanks to the birds. They can quickly relay information. We'll help. I think that humans have mistreated too many animals in the past. I'd like to see a change. I'd like humans to treat us as equals.

THE JAGUAR SAT on the drive in front of the lake house. Cisco was inside, lazing in front of a fireplace where coals still put out enough heat to keep his fur nicely warm.

Upstairs, in the master bedroom, Sophie and Michael lay side-by-side as their breathing gradually slowed. He extended his hand and caressed her cheek.

"Was that enough convincing for you?" he asked.

Sophie smiled a satisfied smile. "Maybe for the moment, but you're going to have to work at it every day."

He rolled over to kiss her. What started as a simple show of affection deepened. He pulled away from her lips and gazed into her eyes.

"Maybe I should try again right now," he said.

CHAPTER 36,

EXCERPT FROM A HISTORY OF THE MODERN WORLD BY WILLIAM WORDWRIGHT

As we have seen in prior chapters of this compilation of events, the Founding Powers, Sophie Monroe, also known as the Cyber-Witch, and Michael O'Keefe, the Golden Knight, played the key role in creating the reality that we live in daily.

During the early days of the modern period, the Net was filled with reports of odd things happening. These involved known computer experts and, as the days passed, seemed to form a pattern.

The Founding Powers had carefully placed hints on bulletin boards and various chat rooms frequented by hackers. The information was quickly found and utilized.

There were numerous reports of odd mutations in the general population that brought a general level of awareness leading to fear. It got so that anyone suspected of having computer knowledge beyond the average was suspect.

Today, we know this period as "The Beginning of Magic." The hackers were the first generation of magicians, able to master the nanites and create all sorts of effects ranging from new devices to biological mutations.

As an aside note: The chimeras retreated into their own lands and didn't mix much with humans at that time. Now it is more common for them to deal with us. The change of attitude in the general population has led to most people accepting the changelings as intellectual equals.

The same cannot be said for the so-called "Were-Creatures." These dire beings are usually black bears, but may also take the form of other fierce animals. They are not common, fortunately, but have been known to help humans at times, while at other times, they have been said to kill. The stories of them are mostly found among the common folk and have taken on an almost legendary aspect. We will not deal further with this subject for this reason. The lack of definite knowledge prohibits accurate reporting.

The real problems for the old order of society started when the authorities decided to crack down on the situation. They quickly found that pure force was a bad idea. Armed teams were ineffectual, sometimes suffering one hundred percent casualties as their members were turned into frogs or other creatures.

The military was activated. That didn't work either. Squads were suddenly affected with zombie-like symptoms and turned against unaffected troops. As hard as it is to believe, the military of the time had no protection against nanite attacks.

Eventually, most government orders and regulations were ignored. This rebellion started with the massive restrictions on human activities such as travel and building. Of course, tax collection almost immediately became impossible.

The governments across the world became mere shells of their former selves, unable to enforce any of the myriad regulations and laws that had served to keep the general population under control. Once given the power to resist, most people opted to ignore or actively attack those who insisted they had the right to dictate behavior.

Some computer experts set up schools and taught those who were interested in learning. Some of these groups evolved to become the great schools of magic that we have today. Others quickly disappeared.

Other groups of hackers segregated themselves into groups based on mutual interests.

It was these latter groups that portended the new structure of society. The members swore to defend each other. The authorities, such as remained, quickly learned not to mess with the groups.

These interest groups took to calling themselves "phyles" or "tribes." There were many of these groups at first. They were easy to form and multiplied almost as quickly as social media groups had on the pre-nanite Internet. However, only the ones that were led by individuals with enough knowledge to control the new nanite-infested world tended to survive.

An urgent issue focused hacker's minds at the time. The nanobots continued to multiply. Hazelton's engineers had placed no effective restraints on their reproduction abilities. This posed a problem that some of the larger phyles quickly realized they must solve.

A nanobot, while tiny, requires a certain number of molecules of diverse elements in its structure. It was calculated that the devices would reach a point where they converted all of the usable matter on the planet into more nanites. This event would mean the end of humanity; indeed, the end of all life on the planet.

Accordingly, three of the larger phyles, which focused on hacking ability merged and found a solution. The nanomachines' were gradually replaced by a newly-programmed variant that was restricted in its ability to replicate.

Some people advocated modifying the nanites so that they could not reproduce at all. This was obviously a course that would eventually lead to their extinction and the eventual return to the old order. The tiny machines had proliferated enough by that point that many realized that such an action would never succeed. Even today, some nanites run amuck and reproduce with no restrictions. It is said that some of these are controlled by the ancient enemy, Wiindigo, but that may simply be rumor.

The hacker communities refused to try to destroy the nanite population. The advantages of the tiny machines were many, not the least of which was the freeing of humanity from the age-old form of rule by force.

It was evident to those with clear thought that the prior structure of government had severely limited humankind's progress. Instead of creating a more perfect world, human activity had been channeled into income streams for those in power. Common citizens were lucky to be allowed to earn a basic living.

The social structure that had depended upon connections and birth was quickly replaced by a merit-based structure. Duels became common among individuals who disagreed, and justice was mostly left to fend for itself.

Even today, there are duels, although the sorcerer's code applies to most disputes and usually leads to peaceful reconciliations.

The knowledgeable prospered. Those who couldn't master nanites fell in status and sought affiliation with one phyle or another for protection.

New uses were discovered for the nanites on a daily basis. Some tech-wizards specialized in fabrication and provided the requisites for the continued survival of the race. Others took a darker path and used their newfound powers to inflict pain and terror on the populace in their areas. These so-called dark wizards are to be avoided at all costs. It takes an extraordinary power to deal effectively with them.

AFTER SOME YEARS, it was apparent that the world had taken an entirely new path. It had become more feudal in organization. Local powers controlled their geographical holdings with either wisdom or evil.

The common people, those with little knowledge, generally tried to move to areas under benign control, but often were prohibited by their masters.

There are pockets of actual darkness also. In many of these a small phyle or a powerful individual exercised a despotic rule, inflicting punishments and tortures on those that displeased them.

Throughout this chaotic development, there was no overt sign of any artificial intelligence. Neither Hippocrates nor Wiindigo (except in rumor) made an identifiable appearance, although some of the phyles seemed to have a darker aspect to their behavior that may sometimes be attributed to their worshiping an evil entity. Their locations were considered off limits and places to be avoided at all costs.

The world changed inexorably. Not necessarily for the better, but also not necessarily for the worse. It just...changed. Humans, as always, adapted and sought what happiness and fulfillment they could find in their lives.

As to what became of the Founding Powers, that story is largely unknown. Some have claimed that the two of them extended their lifespans many-fold with the aid of Hippocrates and that they are still active today.

If so, it may be assumed that their primary focus is on locating any remnants of Wiindigo and expunging them from this dimension.

CHAPTER 37
THE GOOD POWERS

The glade was empty. Surrounded by tall white pines and spruce, the open area sported a carpet of wild flowers and a few glacier-deposited boulders.

A few bees were systematically moving from flower to flower accompanied by some butterflies. There was the sound of something moving quickly through the underbrush and a white poodle shot out from under the long hanging branches of a spruce. He dashed to the middle of the clearing and scrambled up onto the largest boulder where he let out one single bark.

In answer, a shadow coalesced out of the clear air. A woman appeared, followed closely by a man clad in a luminescent armor and armed with a broadsword. He stood slightly to her rear in a ready position.

The woman hovered a few inches above the ground, not disturbing the bees' harvest in the slightest. She, too, had a glowing aspect. It covered the visible parts of her skin, although she wore a long robe that covered most of her body.

The dog made a slightly silly grin at the sight of the two but then spoke in a worried tone.

"It's back there," he said, indicating a direction with a move of his muzzle. "There's a cave with a lot of darkness about it. I didn't venture in, but there was a heavy breathing sound that indicates something large inside. Not many tracks going in or out, but I could sense carrion. Whatever it is has killed frequently and recently. The victims were carried into the cave from what I can smell."

The woman looked at the man, to check his position, and glided forward. At this movement, the man said, "Sophie! Be careful. It could be a pocket of—"

She interrupted, "Yes, I know, Michael. I'm already sensing some of Wiindigo's nanites among the trees. This portion of him is isolated but strong. We'll have to fight, but I sense that it's reluctant to join battle."

He replied, "Perhaps it knows who it faces."

She laughed, then said, "Perhaps. I think it is still gathering strength. In any case, we must destroy it. Are you ready?"

He nodded and followed her through the flowers into the dark shadows under the trees."

DEEP IN THE cave, a black dragon-shape raised its horned head, preparing for battle.

The End

ABOUT THE AUTHOR

Eric Martell has a doctorate in experimental Psychology. He says that the primary benefit of his graduate degrees was that he learned to learn.

The author of several other science fiction books and a number of short stories for various anthologies. He is a longtime student of the spiritual, holds a black-belt in Tae Kwon Do, is a licensed Heart Math™ provider, and has been trained as a Quantum Energy Healer and medical intuitive. Eric also plays guitar. His taste in music runs from Country through Reggae and Rock to Jazz and New Age.

Eric stumbled into real estate after a successful stint in software that covered everything from early childhood education to military training and consulting. He has 30+ years of experience in real estate investment.

Eric's passion is writing novels and short stories that are intended to both entertain and give readers material for thought. He makes the science in his stories as close as possible to that of the real world given the constraints of the plot. His stories are realistic and, although he does not go out of his way to offend, he sometimes uses difficult or sensitive topics to advance the plot.

BLOG INFORMATION

If you enjoyed this book, please follow my Author Blog at **EricMartellAuthor.com** for information about my other books. You'll find free short stories there, occasional preview pages for new novels in progress, and blog posts about things that I find interesting (most lately Artificial Intelligence).

I welcome comments and enjoy discussions with readers.

You can also follow me on Facebook at **ESMartellbooks**. My Twitter handle is **@emartell**. You can also email me directly through my Author Blog.

LINKS FOR MY TIME-TRAVEL STORIES

Heart of Fire Time of Ice
http://bit.ly/HeartofFire

Paradox: On the Sharp Edge of the Blade
http://bit.ly/ParadoxBlade

All the Moments in Forever
http://bit.ly/Moments

LINK FOR THE GAIA ASCENDANT TRILOGY

The Time of The Cat
Second Wave
Confederation
http://bit.ly/GaeaAscendant

Cisco and Micro-Drone (c) 2017
Original Art by Aleksandra Klepacka